This is a work of fiction. Names, characters, places, and incidents either are the product of the author's imagination or are used fictitiously, and any resemblance to actual persons, living or dead, business establishments, events, or locales are entirely coincidental.

Wahida Clark Presents Publishing
60 Evergreen Place
Suite 904A
East Orange, New Jersey 07018
973-678-9982
www.wclarkpublishing.com

Library of Congress Cataloging-In-Publication Data:
HEAT/ by MECCAGLOBAL
ISBN 13-digit   978-1-936649-13-6 (paper)
ISBN 10-digit   1936649136 (paper)
ISBN 978-1-936399-42-0 (e-book)
LCCN 2014916391

1.   Fiction- 2. Newark, NJ- 3. Drug Trafficking- 4.
     African American-Fiction- 5. Urban Fiction   6.thug life

Cover design and layout by Nuance Art, LLC
Book design by Nuance Art, LLC –
NuanceArt@aCreativeNuance.com
Edited by Linda Wilson
Proofreader Rosalind Hamilton

Printed in USA

OCT - - 2018

D0912562

WAHIDA CLARK PRESENTS

HEAT

A NOVEL BY

MECCAGLOBAL

HEAT

CHAPTER 1
Order to Kill

~Flashback~
January 1, 2000

"We gon' show motherfuckers what happens when they steal from us!" Will shouted into the phone.

"Yo, what's up, Mike?" Samad asked curiously, with the cell phone pressed to his ear. He sat at a stop light in a red BMW with the top down. "What's goin' on?"

"This Will, boss man. It's done. We kidnapped some of them niggas that stole from us. We got 'em here at the warehouse."

"Good. Everything is going according to plan. Did y'all follow every detail down to a tee?"

"Yeah. We set up a fake drop-off and pick-up to get them niggas here. They thought they were meeting somebody else. Then they lookin' all surprised when we show up."

"Don't let none of 'em get away," Samad said.

"They won't make it out of this warehouse alive. Especially ya man, Eli."

"Good. Keep that thieving ass nigga breathin'. I want my face to be the last one he sees before he goes to hell. I'm gon' make him an example for other crews. It'll teach people what happens when they steal from me, or try to take over my territory. We need to send a message to all these brave niggas out here. I'm on my way."

3

Samad ended his call, tossed the phone in the passenger seat, then sped to the location with murder on his mind.

Ten minutes later, he walked in the warehouse door with both guns drawn. A dead body lying on the ground with no head attached snatched his attention. *What the . . .*

Loud voices came from the far end of the hallway. He tipped through the hall listening for intruders and braced himself against the wall when he heard footsteps approaching.

A tall, dark-skinned guy turned the corner and ran right into the barrels of both guns. Startled, he cursed before putting his hands up in surrender mode and slowly backing away. The frightened young man continued backing up, even around the corner in the direction he ran from. Samad followed.

"Please don't shoot," the helpless young man begged. "I got a daughter and a son at home."

Samad put his guns down slowly, sensing the man's instant relief. But Mike's .40 caliber was drawn and ready to shoot his head off. Samad leaned on the wall and watched the guy turn, coming face to face with Mike.

"Nooooo! Please don't shoot!" the guy yelled.

"Happy New Year, motherfucker!" Mike fired the pistol twice. The young man's body made a loud thump as it hit the floor.

"Where's Eli?" Samad asked.

Mike gestured with his head to indicate he was

down the hall. "I left him with Will."

"Ay yo! Stop him! He's tryna escape!" Will suddenly yelled, his voice echoing throughout the warehouse.

A dark figure cut around the corner and collided with Samad and Mike. All three men stumbled, but quickly gained their balance. Eli stopped in his tracks when he saw Samad. They stared at one another for a split second. Will rushed toward them with his 9-millimeter cocked.

"Don't shoot him!" Samad ordered.

A bullet exploded from the chamber. The blast ripped through Eli's back, causing him to fall flat on his face.

Eli's blood splattered on Samad's jeans. Samad looked down at himself then took a step back.

"Why the fuck you shoot him before we get the info from him!" Samad shouted.

"He was trying to get away!" Will replied.

"I needed to know where he hid the money he took from my other stash house." Samad glared at Will. "Before he took his last breath, I wanted that snake to watch the video footage of him sneaking out my spot. So he could know why he was about to die! He didn't know I had cameras, and I saw him with my own eyes. He also got some important papers I need."

"Damn, I ain't know all that, Samad," Will said.

"I know you didn't because this was before me, you, and Mike linked up and started gettin' money. He was fuckin' around with my ex, and she trusted him, not knowin' Eli was one of my enemies. But *he* knew who *she* was. So one day he set up a break-in at the house and got away with a lot of money and paperwork out the safe. Lucky we wasn't home."

"My bad, boss," Will added.

"A lot of valuable stuff was stolen," Samad said, looking directly at Will. "He got a lot of shit that belong to my ex girl Keisha. Her brother's comin' home from jail next year too. I know he would want her personal things. I mean, he still got the safe deposit keys to the lock boxes."

"Like the lock boxes they have in a bank?" Mike asked.

"Yeah. Insurance papers are in there naming me as her beneficiary too."

"Straight up?"

"Yeah. We were gonna get married, so we was tryna get shit in order. Around that time she inherited some serious money from her father. But that's why I need to get my hands on that stuff."

"I understand," Will said. "My bad for real."

Samad stared at the blood leaking out of Eli. "He just got a lot of important paperwork from my old lady, and I need it.

"Damn, Samad . . . I ain't know."

"I'm just gonna have to go a different route to get it now. Maybe his girl knows something. But from now on, wait until I give you the order to kill!"

Will clicked the safety on his gun. Samad shook his head and turned his attention to Mike.

Mike glimpsed movement from Eli. "Yo, he still alive!"

Eli put his hand in his pocket, as if reaching for a gun. Mike aimed his gun at his head. Eli grabbed his phone and tried speaking, but he coughed up blood and gurgled.

Samad moved closer to the blood pooling near Eli's side. "He's done, Mike."

Finally, Eli took a deep breath before dying with his phone in his now limp hand.

Samad, Mike, and Will stood over his lifeless body. "Whoever he was tryna call must've been important," Mike joked.

"Or he was tryna warn a nigga," Will said.

"It is what it is, but that'll teach 'im about stealin' from me!" Samad said.

"And anybody else who even thinks about crossin' us!" Mike added. Will nodded in agreement.

Samad kneeled and went through Eli's pockets. He took the phone from his hand and looked at the display. "Born?" he said, glancing at Mike and Will.

"Born?" Samad said the name again. "I know this nigga Eli not workin' with my so-called homie, Born!"

Mike, Will, and Samad stared at each other, letting Born's name sink in.

"It's clean up time, boss man," Mike finally said.

"C'mon Will. We got work to do." The two soldiers dragged the other two bodies to the center of the room.

Samad grabbed a metal can from the warehouse floor and poured gasoline on the bodies, then lit a match. The 'whoosh' of the fire backed all three men up as the fiery flames spread, burning the bodies.

Mike, Will, and Samad picked up the duffel bags full of coke and the briefcases filled with money and exited the side door.

"Y'all know his peoples gone be looking for him, right? The streets gon' be talkin' up a shit storm," Will said.

"Let 'em talk. I don't know shit. Ain't heard shit, aint see shit," Mike responded.

"Dead men tell no tales. I'll meet y'all at the trap spot," Samad said, heading to his car.

An hour later, Samad sat inside the trap house watching the money counter as it came to a halt. His eyes widened as he read the numbers. "Three hundred thousand!"

"Betcha Eli won't be touchin' nobody else skrilla!" Mike said, sitting across from Samad.

"I hope that dirty nigga burn in hell!" Samad said evenly.

Mike stood and stretched, letting out a loud sigh. "Whoo wee! Three hundred g's sound lovely. Man, listen, it's about to be on! Competition is dead! Nobody gettin' it like we gettin' it! They gotta come to us!"

"Word!" Will agreed.

"Ten kilos of pure, uncut Columbian coke!" Mike and Will both said as they tossed a few kilos to Samad.

"Now it's time to take over every spot. Drop the price, and get richer than we are. Making sure everybody on this team eat. Fuck the competition!"

He caught the coke and smiled with greed in his eyes. "It's on!"

CHAPTER 2
Crushin'

Six months later . . .
July 4, 2000

"Forty-second Street! Times Square is the next stop!" the voice announced to the passengers.

"Come on, this is our stop!" Heat barely heard her girl Ebony yelling. She'd fallen asleep during the short train ride.

"Wake up, Unique! Wake up, Heat!" Ebony shouted as she shook and nudged her girls. Unique and Heat jumped up and rushed behind Ebony to exit the train.

"I love this spot. It has all the classic video games in there."

Every Saturday, the three best friends had the same routine: go to Play Land arcade on Broadway and later on sneak into the movies.

Hanging out allowed them to have fun and chill, but it also got Heat out of the house and away from her misery.

As soon as they entered Play Land, Unique spotted Heat's crush and his boys.

"Oh shit, Heat! Ain't that the handsome guy that you like?" Unique asked, tapping her shoulder and pointing.

"There go your man, Heat!" Ebony teased.

Heat turned toward the video games lined up against the wall and spotted the same guy she always noticed staring at her at every local ghetto celebrity spot. The same guy she could not stop thinking about from the first time she laid eyes on him. She liked everything about him; he wasn't one of those persistent pests who couldn't take a hint. He never chased Heat, and vice versa. For the past six months they both were subtle with their flirtation. The mere fact that he turned her on in every way infatuated her. That, and the brother had style and the "It's All About Me" attitude to match hers. In a nice, quiet, and confident way, his actions spoke for him. He complemented Heat's style and she, his. She knew they would be perfect together. He just didn't know it yet.

"How does my hair look?" Heat asked, running her fingers through her long curls.

"Like it did five minutes ago!" Ebony barked.

"Forget you! Unique, how does my hair look?"

"Like you paid Classy too damn much," Unique answered. "I could have done that shit for free! You know I can do hair too!"

"Girl, you got lint in your hair!" Ebony laughed.

"Forget both of y'all!" Heat waved them off. "That nigga look good as hell. He got good taste in footwear, too. I like a man that keeps his footwear on point."

"Them shits ugly!" said Ebony

"Hater!" Heat retorted.

"That nigga tall as hell!" said Unique, stealing another glance at him.

"He just right for me!" Heat answered, slyly licking her lips and popping a piece of gum in her mouth. She pulled strawberry lotion from her bag and rubbed it on her hands, dabbing some behind her ears and around her neck.

"His friends cute too," said Ebony.

"All of 'em cute!" Unique chimed in.

"Damn! Did you take a bath in that lotion? It's scorchin' hot out here today. That lotion is gon' make you sweat strawberries. I can smell you a mile away!" said Unique.

"Good! Then I know he'll smell me too," Heat answered.

"That was an easy $500! Pay up, niggas!" Heat's crush shouted to his mans. "Fuck outta here . . . ain't nobody fuckin' with me in this!" He gripped the joystick tight as he dodged left and right. "Yeah!" he said as Ms Pac-Man ate the blue ghosts. "I'm the best!" He'd just beat five people for $100 a game.

"Who else wanna lose they money?" he boasted.

"I got next," Heat spoke softly.

"Shorty, what you know about this? You not beatin' my high score! What's the highest board you ever got to?" he asked, looking her over.

"The junior boards," she replied,

Mike, the loudest of the bunch, snapped. "Ha! Stop frontin', shorty."

Heat's crush shot him an icy stare. "Mike. Chill," he demanded.

"A'ight, Samad. Damn, my nigga." Mike laughed it off.

"Do one of y'all have change for a hundred?" Heat waved a hundred dollar bill directly at Mike.

Samad jerked his head left, signaling Mike to leave. "Mike, can you get me some change?"

Catching the hint, Mike then gestured to the other four guys. "Come on, my niggas. Let's bounce!"

"So, do you wanna play or not?" Samad asked, giving Heat his full attention.

"No, not really. I'm not really into playin' games," she said in a low, seductive voice.

He chuckled a little, noticing the hidden message behind her remark. *Hmmm, I like that.* Without missing a beat, he retorted, "Me either, ma! I'm not into playin' games either, other than these." He pointed at the video games lined up against the walls. "Straight like that. I'm the realest nigga you gon' ever meet!"

"Oh? Is that right?" she asked, raising an eyebrow.

"Yeah, that's right!" He puffed his chest out, nodding as if it put the stamp of approval on what he just said. He gave her the sexiest smile.

"What's up with you, love?" Samad asked, licking his lips and looking her up and down.

She leaned back on the game. "I'm good, sexy. Maintainin'. "

13

"So where ya man at?"

"Wit' ya girl," she answered. "I don't got no man!"Samad laughed again. "Where your girl at?" she asked.

"Wit' ya man! I don't got no girl."

"Hmph!" Heat mumbled. "Why is that? Why don't you have a girl?"

A brief silence fell between them. Never once did he look at Heat when he answered. "I'm tired of these women acting like little girls. I need a real woman. I had one real woman when I lived in Brooklyn, but she died in a car accident." He paused. "She knew how to satisfy a man and even keep my attention for that matter, because I get bored easily."

"You do, huh?"

Samad ended the game and walked a few inches closer, close enough for her to smell his breath.

Tic Tacs score one point for you, handsome! Breath smelling right. Heat smiled and said, "Well, this is your lucky year, 'cause I'm the realest woman of the year! The chick, chicks love to hate!" she bragged, feeling herself. "You need some *Heat* in your life!"

"A'ight, shorty." Samad enjoyed watching her go through the motions. Spitting her little whatever-she-wanted-to-call-it.

"You smell good," he said.

"Thank you.

Samad smiled as he looked her body up and down, noticing her big butt fitting nice in her jeans.

14

"You know who you look like."

"Who?"

"The girl from that movie *Boyz in the Hood*. Nia Long."

"Oh? I know you gon' look at me like I'm an alien, but I didn't see the movie."

"What! That's a hood classic. She played in *Friday* too, pretty girl. You got her same brown complexion. You sexy just like her."

"Oh! I know who you talking about." Heat blushed. "Thank you."

"Why a sexy girl like you don't got no man?" Samad flashed his pearly whites. *Here we go with the bullshit! I caught him cheating on me with one of my girlfriends. When in reality, it was probably her ass creepin'. Probably fucked one of his boys! Or, he must've run out of money and couldn't supply her shopping habit, 'cause shorty look like she high maintenance like a mutha! Shorty got a phat ass too!*

"Well, I had one special boyfriend. He got killed." Heat lowered her gaze, still missing Eli like crazy.

"I'm sorry to hear that about your dude. How'd he get killed?"

"Ummm, I don't really wanna talk about that." She looked away, trying to avoid her eyes welling up. "Some things are real sensitive like classified information."

"Oh, it's like that?" he asked.

"Yeah, it is. I'll see you around though," she said,

abruptly turning to leave.

Samad caught up with her. "Why you leavin'? I was just trying to find out who you are."

"I know. I'll see you around though," she said, not offering up an answer for her quick change in attitude.

"A'ight. My bad, shorty." *Damn! Didn't mean to do all that . . .* He let her leave, aware he'd hit a sensitive spot. Whatever she didn't want to talk about, he'd find it out eventually. He had ways of getting information.

CHAPTER 3
Man of the Year

"I'm glad you met that guy on the Fourth of July. Now maybe he can take your mind off Eli," Unique said as the three girls walked to Play Land the following week.

"I'll never forget my boo and y'all know that. Do you know how devastating it was when my brother Aaron told me Eli had to be identified by dental records? That just wasn't right. How you do somebody like that?"

Unique regretted bringing up Eli. She knew it could turn into a full-fledge Eli session. "Dang, I'm sorry, Heat. Everybody knew how much you and Eli loved each other. No doubt. It's just cool as hell to be back to hanging out on summer days like this, laughing and having fun again."

"Yeah, Heat. You were low key for six months."

Ebony interrupted Unique. "Chick, you let your grades slip. And that's when I knew for sure that you were depressed. You ain't never messed around and got a D out of a class. Look, I know how much you miss him, but I'm sure he'd want you to fall in love again," Ebony said. "He'd want you to be happy."

"Eli spoiled your butt rotten, girl. Money, clothes, and bling. A real baller gettin' it," Unique said.

"You mean a real hustla . . ." Ebony added.

"And don't forget the most important thing—a real love. He was my King. Thought he was gone be the man I married. But these damn streets . . . ain't nothin' good in 'em," Heat said.

"Well, I'm sure you'll find another fine, rich ass nigga to love," Unique joked, changing the flow of the conversation.

Heat's slanted brown eyes filled with tears, but she wiped them away as she laughed at Unique. And so did Ebony.

"You stupid, Unique," Heat and Ebony said simultaneously.

"I know it." Unique shrugged.

Heat was hoping the guy would be there at the arcade again. After all, he really was fine as hell.

Although her heart still ached for Eli, Heat wanted to see the guy again, but she was frontin' like they were only hanging out there before they went to the movies. And just as she wished, they found him on the Ms. Pac-Man game. His crew stood around the pool tables. Inside, Heat grinned.

"What's up, ma? I forgot to get ya name?" he asked, catching sight of her from his peripheral. Samad grinned, and then left off playing the game.

She giggled. "One week later, *now* you asking for my name? I gave it to you already. Heat. Well, it's Heather. My friends call me Heat for short."

"Heat?" he questioned with a puzzled look. "What kind of name is Heat?"

"It's just a nickname. My family and close friends call me Heat," she said as she blushed.

Samad laughed.

"Something funny?" she asked.

"Naw, baby. I'm not laughing at ya name. It's cute. I just thought ya name was something else." Samad checked her out with no shame. "Nah. You just don't look like a Heather. So, Heather is your real name, huh?" he asked, still not believing her. "For real?"

"Damn. You work for the Feds, nosey?"

"Damn. You hiding from the Feds, fugitive? You on the run or something?" he shot back.

They both laughed, noticing each other's sharp tongue and quick wit.

"I don't like the name Heather. So call me Heat, or do not call me at all."

It was something cute, corny, yet innocent about this moment that made the two enjoy their little conversation about nothing. Butterflies fluttered in Heat's stomach when Samad smiled. The uncomfortable silence that followed left them both to conclude: *This might be the one.*

"Where you from?" she asked.

"LG! The Stuy. Crooklyn! BK, Land of the Gods! Land of the coffins! Do or Die Bedstuy! County of Kings."

"Ummm. What?"

"I'm from Lafayette Gardens. Brooklyn, New York!" he said proudly. "You, mamí. Where you from?" he asked.

"Newark, New Jersey."

"Okay, okay. So, tell me about yourself, Miss Heat."

She looked off to the left, thinking of how much she wanted to reveal. "I just graduated from high school last month in June."

"Oh, congratulations."

"Thank you. And if there's one thing you definitely should know about me from jump, it's that family is everything to me."

He nodded, feeling the same way. That's a beautiful thing." Samad looked directly in her eyes. "So you said you from Dirty Jersey? New Jeruz? Brick City, huh?"

"Born and raised."

"I fuck with Newark. I got mad family out there, and I do business out there too! I got love for Jersey."

He do business in Newark. Mmm hmmm, she thought as her antenna went up. *What kind of business?*

"Ma, how old are you?"

"Eighteen. Why you ask? How old are you?"

Samad smiled. "No reason. Just askin'. I'm older than you, that's all you need to know."

What's up with him not telling me his age? "What kind of business you do in my hometown?" she asked, instead of pursuing the age question.

"I do a few things in the music business. I wear a few hats. People call on me for certain things."

"Oh really?" *What kind of answer is that?*

"Yeah."

Heat was caught up in their conversation, but then she remembered something important. *Damn, I still don't know his name.* "So, what's ya name?" she asked.

Lost in his lust, Samad admired how sexy Heat looked as the sunlight bounced off her beautiful, caramel-brown skin tone. He noticed every detail about her, including her pearly white teeth and brown cat eyes. *Sexy ass.*

"Oh, my name?" he asked, still mesmerized.

"Ummm yeah!" She tilted her head. "Your name. You do have one of those, don't you?" she asked with sarcasm in her tone.

"Oh, my bad. I'm buggin'. You can call me S, or Samad. I answer to either one." He paused. "Just don't call me out my name," he said. "What you doin' all the way over here in the Big Apple by ya'self?"

"New York is only fifteen minutes over the water. Please! It's not all the way over here, and I'm not all the way over here by myself!" she answered. "I'm wit' my girls."

"What girls?" he asked.

She pointed to Ebony and Unique.

"Oh, a'ight!" He glanced over at Ebony and Unique shooting pool with his crew. "So, what's on y'all agenda for today? Meetin' niggas? Gettin' numbers? 'Ho-hoppin' in the city?" he asked with a straight face.

She frowned. "Eeew. No, nigga! Do I look like a 'ho?"

"My bad. Calm down, shorty. I ain't mean nothin' by that! I'm just playin'. Damn! All sensitive and shit!" He laughed.

She folded her arms and took a deep breath. "We just hangin' out. Probably catch a movie, do a little shopping, eat—you know, girl things. What y'all fellas doin' tonight?" she asked. "Pickin' up tricks? Gettin' numbers? 'Ho-hoppin'?"

He smirked. "Nah. We about to go cop some gear. See what new butter leathers they got out for the summer. Pick up some sneakers, jeans, shirts, you know . . . We might go out tonight. I'm not even sure yet," he stated.

Heat looked at her nails, ignoring him. After the 'ho-hopping comment, she was ready to leave. She checked her lips in her compact mirror.

Samad pulled her arm as he began walking to the door, trying to get her into the sunlight to see those brown eyes again. She followed.

As they walked outside, a hustle man strolled in their direction. "Hey, I'm out here trying to make some honest money. I do photography. Can I capture this moment and take you and your lady's picture?" he said, holding a Sony camera. "This is the new Sony digital cyber shots. It prints out right on the spot like the old Polaroid camera. The pictures come out nice and clear."

"Nice camera. How much?" asked Samad.

"Thanks. I got a Fourth of July special going on."

"Fourth of July was last week." Samad laughed.

"Come on, man. I'm out here hustlin'. I got a summer special going on. You get four 5x7 pictures for fifteen dollars."

"I respect your hustle. Fifteen not bad," Samad replied.

"I respect his hustle too, but you don't need no pictures, fam'," Mike intervened from out of nowhere.

"What's up?" Samad asked Mike. "What you trippin' on?"

"Naw nigga, *you* the one that's trippin'. Fuck outta here . . . takin' pictures and shit. We businessmen." Mike looked at Samad funny.

"What's your problem?" Heat asked, clearly irritated. Face set in a frown. "It's just a picture."

"That's a nice Gucci jacket, my man!" Hustle Man complimented Samad, trying to ease the rising tension. He also wanted to make a few dollars today.

"Thanks," Samad replied, grimacing at Mike. "My guy hooks me up. A lot of stuff I wear is custom made by him."

"That jacket is kinda fly," Heat agreed, rolling her eyes at Mike. "Does he make dresses?"

"I'll take you to him one day. He makes everything for everybody!" Samad said.

"Man, fuck what y'all talkin' about! Samad, let me holla at you for a few seconds," Mike ice-grilled him, tilting his head.

"Hold up, man. Damn!" Samad grew agitated. He leaned against the wall. "Stand right here, ma." He pointed in front of him. Heat assumed the position.

As he squeezed his arms tighter around her waist, Samad grinned, pulling her closer as he inhaled her strawberry fragrance.

Hustle Man held the camera up, taking aim. "Y'all look nice together."

Mike shouted, "Stop lying, nigga! You just wanna make a buck."

"Ready?" Hustle Man ignored Mike. He counted to three and began snapping pictures. Twice Mike ran in front of Heat and Samad, causing them both to yell, "Move out the way!"

Finally Mike gave up and pushed Samad in his chest hard, hoping to wake up his common sense. "Yo, you realize what you doin', fam'! Do you really know what you doin'?" His eyes darted toward Heat.

Samad's hard gaze never wavered. "If you ever put your fuckin' hands on me again, it'll be the last time you use them."

"Nigga, I'm tryna to stop you from—"

"I know what I'm doing!" Samad snapped. "Now chill the fuck out and let us finish takin' these pictures. You got people starin' at us, drawin' more attention than we need."

"That's not a smart move though," Mike warned, backing away.

Heat waited in the same spot, right hand on right hip, lips tight, and brows narrowed. *Hater!*

"Fuck it! I tried." Mike waved them off and turned and walked toward the arcade.

Samad exhaled and again stood behind Heat.

"That sure is one dedicated third wheel you got there, man," Hustle Man said, making them smile for the first time since Mike appeared. He took advantage of their grins by pressing the camera button several times.

"What's up with ya boy?" Heat asked, once they were done. "Why he hatin' so hard?"

"He on some crazy shit. Don't pay him no mind. So uhh, I wanna keep one of the pictures, so I can have something to remember you by. I couldn't stop thinking about you since last week," Samad said.

She watched him flip through a wad of money looking for a small bill. Samad handed the money to Hustle Man who handed him the pictures and his change.

After quickly scanning all four of them, Samad said, "I'll keep these two." He pulled a pen from his jacket pocket and began writing something on them.

While they stood there, the glare from the jewelry store window caught Heat's attention. She slid off from Hustle Man and Samad and walked to the big glass window to see the display. In awe, she admired the diamond stud pear-shaped earrings. They were beautiful. The different earrings, bangles, and diamond necklaces were all neatly arranged in the window.

Samad walked up behind her, putting his hands around her waist. "You like those?"

Heat smiled and shook her head yes. "They cute, but I can't afford 'em."

"They would look nice on you."

"You think so?"

"Yeah, I think so." Samad released his grip from around her waist.

By that time, Mike and the others were approaching. Heat noticed Samad writing something else on the pictures, and then he handed them to her.

Mike came up behind him and yelled, "Oooh, this nigga went Hollywood on us! Takin' pictures, signin' autographs!" He laughed, but it wasn't genuine. The others laughed also. "While you at it, can you sign my sneaker?" Mike raised his foot. "Autograph my T-shirt too!" he teased in a girl groupy's voice.

Samad's laugh mimicked Mike's. "You a crazy ass nigga!"

"This cute." Heat showed Samad the pictures, ignoring Mike.

"This cute," Mike aped. "We gotta go, Samad."

"*All* the pictures look nice," Samad said. "Chill, man!" he barked.

Heat made quick introduction since Ebony and Unique were already behind Mike and the other goons.

"Yo, I'll see you again, shorty," Samad said, ready to make his exit. "Sorry about my man."

"I'll see *you* again," she said, smiling from ear to ear. Then a line replaced the sweet smile. "But next time leave your bitch at home," Heat spat, glaring at Mike.

Mike smirked, seeing himself draw on her and shove his gun down her throat like he would his dick. *Smart-mouth bitch gon' be the death of Samad.* He knew not to act on his thoughts, nor spew the words sitting on his tongue. Mike didn't want to piss Samad off. "That's Mr. Bitch to you, Miss Lady. Nice meetin' y'all."

Chapter 4
Anything Can Happen

One hour later . . .
The trap spot

"Shorty Smart-Mouth got some cute dimples, a phat ass, and a set of pretty eyes! I knew, I knew her from somewhere," Mike said to Samad and the guys as they all gathered in the warehouse to package up the coke and stash their guns.

"She got some pretty hair too," Will chimed in.

"It's probably a weave. You know how some girls do," Face said.

Bizz laughed and gave Face dap.

Mike looked across the table at Samad. "You know she's that nigga Eli's old chick, right?"

Samad shrugged. "Oh well, his loss."

"Nigga, I tried to warn you," Mike said.

"Eli knew the rules of the streets and he violated," Samad said, taking the pictures of him and Heat out of his pocket.

"Look at this nigga, falling in love already! This nigga fell in love in fifteen minutes, just from rubbing up against her ass!" Mike joked, snatching the pictures out of Samad's hand. "Look!" He showed the other guys the pictures. "If I'm not mistaken . . . Hold up!" Mike examined the picture.

"Yo! I think this nigga dick got hard from rubbing up against shorty's ass for real!"

"Get the fuck outta here!" Samad laughed as he snatched the pictures out of Mike's hand, embarrassed because his dick was as hard as a roll of quarters.

Mike chuckled. "Damn, nigga. I can't leave you alone for fifteen minutes."

"Shut the fuck up, nigga!" Samad responded as they all laughed.

Mike put his hand on Samad's shoulder. "S, you better be careful with this one. If she find out we—"

"I already told you I got this." Samad watched Face and Bizz place bricks in a duffel bag across the room. "Trust me."

"A'ight, nigga. I ain't scared to kill no bitch. I'll put that .40 cal' right to her head and pull the trigger," Mike said, thinking of Heat.

"You ain't gone do nothin'. She a'ight," Samad said. "And she ain't gone find out nothing."

"I don't know why you sound so sure. Anything can happen. Remember I said that." Mike gazed at Samad for a long time, hoping his words penetrated into his head.

"Anything can happen. Remember you said that," Samad mocked.

When he met Heat in New York City, he asked questions to see if she was going to lie. Her honest answers told Samad where he would truly place her in his life. Yeah, he needed her to see if Eli left her the letter, keys, and insurance papers but something about her sent out positive energy, and he liked that. But that alone wasn't enough. He knew people crossed each other for money, power, or simple revenge, and more than likely, the betrayer always turned out to be somebody close. Someone you let in who grew to learn your every move. Knew all of your spots, your likes and dislikes, knew your weaknesses. Just as he already knew hers.

Samad knew things about Heat that she wouldn't even think he knew. Like, after her father died, she was afraid of the dark, too scared to sleep with the lights off until age fourteen, and she had nightmares. Her brother, Aaron told Samad her secret, because Heat's screams made him believe a stick-up kid entered their home to rob it of the drugs he kept there. That was the first and last time Aaron ever hid work in his parent's home. He called Samad right away to let him know he wasn't on bullshit, but that he was being jacked. Aaron burst in Heat's room expecting to find some fool holding her hostage, but what he found was his sister still asleep, sweat pouring down her face, and tears falling from her closed eyes as she fought off some invisible creature. Aaron called Samad back, relieved his stash was safe but worried about Heat and poured his heart out to Samad.

Well-respected in the game, Aaron's name rang bells in the streets. Samad figured since her brother was in the same line of business—Heat had to know a little something about the code of the streets. Samad had the utmost respect for Aaron, who was never about bullshit, always real. He liked doing business with him, and they made a lot of money together.

With their guns and coke stashed away and all money counted, Samad and his men all began leaving. Samad slapped Mike on his arm. "Mike, if it'll make you feel better, you can get rid of her if we ever find out she on some revenge shit."

"A'ight. Now that's what I'm talkin' 'bout." Mike smiled. Samad's words satisfied him because he knew that, that day would come.

Chapter 5
More Drama

I'm really feeling this thugged out dude already!
Infatuated with Samad, Heat reached in her Gucci bag, taking out the two pictures and staring at them. She smiled, feeling warm and fuzzy inside every time she thought about him. As her girls walked over to her, she put the pictures back in her bag.

"Damn! That's like the hundredth time you looked at the picture!" barked Ebony.

"So what!" Heat turned the photo over. Samad had written his number on the picture along with a note.

(718) 555-5555

Let this be the first and last number you get, ma! Don't be fucking with these wack ass niggas! You need a real nigga in ya life.

Samad, The Man of Every Year. $$$.

Although she'd looked at the picture more than a dozen times, she hadn't called him. That 'ho-hoppin' comment put the brakes on a phone call from her, real fast. Three weeks had come and gone.

"Hey, Classy, do you think you could make my hair look like Toni Braxton's? I want the short, short haircut," Unique asked.

Classy waved an imaginary wand and responded, "I'm a beautician, not a magician!" Heat and Ebony chuckled. Unique twisted her lips.

"Y'all remember the comedian's joke from BET?" Classy asked. Heat and Ebony nodded yes, still giggling.

"I'm just kiddin', Unique," she said. "No problem. You look just like you could be Toni Braxton's sister or something. You look like her."

"I know. I sure wish I could sing like her." Unique laughed.

"Go let the shampoo girl wash your hair first." Classy pointed to the girl at the last sink.

"Heat, you got some more candy or gum in that big ass bag?" asked Ebony.

"No, but the store across the street got a lot in stock!" They both laughed.

"Very funny. You got jokes? You know I keep money. Forever ballin' out of control!" Ebony flashed a bank roll of cash, then put it back in her jeans pocket.

"Does anybody want anything from the store?" Ebony shouted, making sure everybody heard her. "I'm going next door to the beauty supply store, then stopping at the bodega on the corner.

"Yeah!" everybody said in unison.

Requests for gum, lottery tickets, and a Nestle's Strawberry Quick drink came one after the other.

"Can you bring me back a Pepsi and some Newports?" Classy asked.

"Hold up, hold up!" Ebony snapped. "I was just saying that to be courteous. I am not carrying all that shit back from the store. What y'all think this is?" She walked out the door.

A few women shook their head. "That girl is a trip! A hot mess!" said the receptionist, Dawn.

Classy laughed. "Ebony is a mess. You know who she look like—she look like the girl from *Two Can Play that Game*. Gabrielle something."

"Union. Gabrielle Union," the shampoo girl said as she walked by.

"Yeah that's it! Gabrielle Union," Classy repeated. She glanced around, and then whispered in Heat's ear, "I Heard Sean, and your girl Unique had another fight."

Heat shook her head. "What?"

"Yeah girl you know they talk around here non-stop."

"He needs to be dealt with, any man that put their hands on a woman is a pussy!".

Gossip was an everyday thing at World's Finest Hair Salon. Usually, by the time Heat got home, the information was twisted five times over, until the truth wasn't even in the story anymore

Classy walked toward the front door.

Taking a break from the gossip, Heat looked out the window and gasped as her heart paused. *This lying nigga!*

Samad had just pulled up out front and got out of his BMW. A female passenger exited the vehicle at the same time. *Who's that?* Heat narrowed her eyes trying to see the girl's face. *He droppin' bitches off here where all the*

34

dope boys bring their baby mamas or their girlfriends. So she must be somebody special to him.

"Heat! Heat! That guy Samad told me to give you this!" Classy approached her chair and held out a brand new Motorola two-way SkyPager and a piece of paper, along with four small black velvet boxes.

"Give me what? What guy? This is not mine!" She laid the items on the hair station by the mirror.

"Girl, open the boxes!" Classy screamed.

"Nah, I didn't see any guy," she said, looking in the mirror and putting her lip gloss on. She watched Samad stand at the door and let her smile translate that she admired his swagger.

"The guy I was just talking to at the door . . . Samad . . . The one buying the T-shirts from hustle man."

A few girls whispered in passing. "What she grinnin' at that nigga for? Ain't that the snake-nigga they say killed Eli?" the brown pretty girl with the long ponytail asked.

The other girl turned and looked. "Yeah, I think that is him. Ol' girl right there" —She pointed at Heat with no shame—"used to kick it with Eli strong. She's the reason we never hooked up." They walked by Heat shaking their heads, giving her the side eye.

"You supposed to always know your enemy," one of the chicks said directly to Heat.

"What!" Heat looked at the two girls. *Why they shaking their heads and whispering like they know something that I don't know?*

"Whatever!" She waved off their cryptic talk and turned her attention back to Classy.

"Girl, you buggin'. I ain't paying him no mind. I don't know that nigga from nowhere! Besides, didn't he just drop that trick off?" Heat asked, saying it loud enough for the girl she saw get out of Samad's car to hear.

The girl turned and stared at Heat for a minute. Heat remembered his comment when they met in New York. *No games, no nothing, huh? What was all that bullshit he was kickin' to me on Forty-second Street? About he don't have no girl.*

Unique put the battery in Heat's back, hyping it up more. "He don't be just bringing gifts up to the shop while dropping bitches off at the same place! Tell him to give it to his girl," she yelled.

The female turned Heat's way and responded, "Who you talkin' about?"

"What!" Ebony walked in the door, hearing Heat's conversation. She walked toward the girl, shooting her a long, heated gaze. The words, "Bitch, I wish you would leap" were written all over her face. Ebony was always on point, ready to whoop somebody's ass.

"Who, what?" Unique said as she moved closer to the girl. As soon as Ebony popped off, she would follow.

Who the fuck is this girl? Heat thought.

Before she had another thought, Ebony swung on

the girl, hitting the side of her face. Unique followed with a punch on the other side of her face, knocking the girl on the floor. Ebony kicked and stomped her several times. The girl tried to swing with one arm and kick while covering her face with her right arm.

"Hey! Stop that fighting!" The security guard at the door rushed in to break up the commotion. He pulled Ebony off the girl, all the while Heat laughed and loosened her hair out of the ponytail, letting it flow down her back as she looked in the mirror. The other guards came over to make sure the fight was broken up.

One of the security guards yelled at Ebony and Unique, "Keep that drama out of here! Don't be bringin' no drama to this place of business! Do it again and you won't ever be allowed to come back in here!"

The girl had taken a quick ass whooping, and she didn't even know why. She looked dazed and confused. The other stylists were whispering. They did not dare jump in it, or try to break it up.

Chest heaving forcefully, the girl stormed off toward the sink, glaring at Ebony and Unique as if to say 'I will see y'all bitches again.' She put her hands under the cold water, stared at Heat, and splashed water on her face.

The girl's phone went off. She walked to the stylist's chair, ready to get her hair done. She, shot Heat, Ebony, and Unique a cold-blooded stare.

Classy finally came to start on Heat's hair. "Calm your lions down, girl!" she said, popping Heat on her arm with her comb.

"Ouch, Classy! I didn't even do anything!"

"Oh, yes you did. Slick ass. First of all, don't be bringing that drama up in this salon. Second, all three of you are ladies, so act like it. That fighting shit is for the hood rats, and not worth it over a guy at that." Classy gave the three girls a quick glance. "That's his sister y'all just stomped out."

"Whose sister!" Heat asked.

"Samad's, dummy!" Classy replied.

Heat glanced at Ebony and Unique, who also wore surprised expressions.

"Damn!" Ebony mouthed, bumping Unique.

"I could have told y'all Iyana's his little sister, if you had just asked first! You know I know everybody coming in and out of here! Y'all are crazy! All three of y'all! She probably gone kick all y'all asses though." Classy shrugged. "I suggest y'all stick together. Better hope she don't tell her brother."

"My stomach just dropped," Heat said.

"It should have. But anyway . . ." Classy looked over her shoulder. "Girl, he got skrilla!" she whispered as soon as Iyana was out of earshot.

"I don't care about his money. That's his money. I got my own stacks!" Heat snapped.

"I know you don't care about his money, honey. Don't kill the messenger! I'm just sayin'!" She playfully held her hands up, palms facing out as if being robbed.

"I just wanna know one thing: Does he have a

girlfriend?" asked Heat.

"I don't think they're together anymore. He used to kick it with this older woman, Keisha. Very flashy, boss kinda chick. He used to bring her in here every week. She got killed in a car accident though. Then he started messin' with this girl named Mercedes. I don't really know if they are together anymore."

"Hmmm," Heat mumbled.

"I probably shouldn't even say nothin', 'cause it's really not worth repeatin'. But I also heard that Samad had somethin' to do with Eli's death. Rumor has it, he was the one who either ordered the hit on Eli, or he had somethin' to do with it some kind of way. But I don't believe it, because I know Samad real well, and he's more about gettin' his paper than killin' people."

"What! My Eli?" Heat placed her hand over her pounding heart. "I feel sick."

"Yeah, but like I said, he's more about his skrilla, girl. It's too far out of his character to me."

"For sure Aaron would've told me if Samad had somethin' to do with Eli being killed. Aaron still keeps his ears to the street waitin' to hear anything about Eli. They were real close. So that's just not possible." Heat nodded no.

"But what I do know is, Samad is the man in these streets! He is filthy. You hear me? Filthy rich! He does business with my brother."

Heat knew Classy's brother was kind of shady. "This nigga better not have nothin' to do with Eli gettin'

39

killed! Who did you hear this from, Classy?"

"You know how girls come and go in here, and they talk in this shop. I was ear hustlin' and overheard some girls talkin'—sayin' Eli had been missing for a few days, then they found out that one of those burned bodies was his in that warehouse."

"Let me call my brother." Heat stood up, her belly swirling with emotions.

Classy swept the hair up around the chair, while Heat called Aaron.

Heat waited for his phone to ring before walking to the back, toward the small sitting area where the stylists and customers ate.

"Hello?" he answered.

"Aaron, quick question. Please don't lie."

"Hurry up, sis. I'm in the middle of handlin' something."

"Did you hear that a guy named Samad had somethin' to do with Eli's death?"

"What! Hell naw! Don't believe the rumors, sis. I heard something about that a long time ago, but it was just a rumor. That's my man. I gotta go." Aaron hung up before Heat could say another word.

Heat looked at the phone then hung up. Her brother's word was bond. She returned to her seat. "My brother said it was just a rumor. I knew that couldn't be right. Eli ain't never even dealt with anybody named Samad. I knew most of his business. But not all. Some things Eli just wouldn't tell me about because he said I probably wouldn't be able to sleep at night. Anyway, so what about this Mercedes chick?"

"I'll have to find out for you if he's still fucking around with her."

"That's what I'm talking 'bout," Heat said, slapping her five. "I wanna know about every girl that he *used* to mess with. Every chick that look like they wanna fuck him, or even thinking about fucking him! I need names!" Heat said with a dead serious look.

"Damn, I'm good, but I'm not that damn good!" Classy said, looking at Heat with both hands on her hips. She finished styling Heat's hair and pulled the smock from around her neck.

They hugged. "Bye, girl. You too funny," Classy said.

"Make sure you call me as soon as you get some news for me," Heat said.

"Quick, fast, and in a hurry. Let me make a call now. And by the way, you better watch ya back. Iyana owe you for that one. Ya girls too."

"Yeah, thanks for the reminder, Classy. But please . . . don't remind me," Heat said, trying to figure out a way to smooth things over with Samad's sister.

A guy pulled up in front of the shop blowing the horn.

"That's my ride. Bye y'all!" Ebony yelled, heading for the exit.

Classy waved good-bye as Unique, Ebony, and Heat parted ways, and they promised to hook up the following day.

"Watch ya back," they told one another, ashamed of beating up Iyana. Yet they stayed on alert, in case Iyana had called her girls for some getback.

CHAPTER 6
Black Velvet Box

Worry filled Heat's mind as she stood waiting for a cab. She felt her heart racing and decided to just let it go and see if Samad even brought up his sister Iyana. She'd deal with it at that time. Excitement about the note and the four boxes Samad had given her quickly replaced her fear. Heat flopped down in the backseat of the cab, placing them in her lap. She picked up the silver two-way Motorola Pager and the ripped piece of paper Classy had given her and looked closely at all four black velvet boxes. *Why didn't he say anything? Yet, he wanna give me gifts! That nigga on some other shit! I ain't into no mind games! What type of game he playing?* Heat looked at the neatly wrapped gifts once again, smiled, then put the items in her bag.

She heard the voice of reason in her head. *He's playing the same games you playing for no reason.*

Many times in the past, Heat had seen Samad talking to Classy when she came to get her hair done. Back then, Eli used to drop her off, and she assumed Samad was Classy's man. Heat didn't wanna play herself, so she played her position until she figured out Samad's situation and history. It all made sense now. Thanks to Classy, she'd just filled in the missing pieces. The piece of paper read:

Since you didn't give me your number when we met and you didn't call me, I got this for you so I can call you. The

43

number is 1-800-999-9999. The pin number is 7400.

I used the date we met: the Fourth of July holiday. So it would be easy for you to remember the pin number. Get it? The seventh month. The fourth day. The year two thousand. 7400. You better not give this number out to no other niggas!

I hope you like your other gifts. I know they will look right on you. I got good taste! My sister told me you get your hair done where she get hers done every Friday, so I made it my business to drop her off today so I could see you.

Heat's stomach sank after reading that line. She continued reading.

Oh, so it's like that, ma? Why you didn't call? You gon' have a nigga waiting around for your phone call? Sick. It's cool though. I'll be a'ight. I'll live. Just keep it real with me.

One.

Samad 7400

Heat smiled, remembering the day they met, knowing she had gotten to him like he got to her. Her cell phone rang. She immediately picked up. "What's up, Classy? That was quick investigating, girl."

"Well, I really didn't want to say this while your friends were around either, but there's talk about ya girl, Ebony AKA Regular Coke Mule. She movin' weight for a few niggas in the street."

Skeptical, Heat's pressed her lips together tight. "Are you sure, or that's just gossip?"

"Well, you know how they talk up in this shop. I saw that big bankroll Ebony pulled out, so you be the judge."

Heat didn't want to believe that. She couldn't see Ebony moving drugs for anybody and risking her freedom. She hoped it wasn't true, but the thought of all that money she flashed, created a reasonable doubt.

"Maybe you should talk to her. She gone do some serious time if she get caught up."

"Yeah, I know. And I am gonna have to have a conversation with her. No matter how awkward. I don't wanna see my girl—my sister—get locked up and sent someplace in southwest hell."

"Exactly! Also, I heard something else that's just as bad."

"What else?"

"Your girl Unique got beat up right outside the shop by her boyfriend Sean."

"What!" Heat frowned.

"I wasn't here, but the new shampoo girl—Destiny—told me it happened around the time the shop was closing. Nobody was here but them two. She called the big security guards to come back and they had just clocked out. The ones that's normally there, but they left a few minutes before the guards came. Destiny said she wasn't trying to jump in and fight no man, so she did what she thought was right."

"Classy, you have a phone call on line one. It's urgent!" someone yelled in the background.

"Let me go take this, but I'll see you next week, girl. I hope your gifts from Samad are nice."

Heat didn't respond. She thought of her girls,

45

Unique and Ebony and the only words that came to mind were 'dead' and 'jail.' *I gotta talk to them first thing tomorrow. Both of them trippin'!*

She dropped her cell phone inside her purse. The soft velvet brushing across her fingertips reminded her that she had gifts inside. She pulled out the first box.

"Oh my god!" Heat screamed after opening the smaller black velvet box. It was the pear-shaped diamond earrings she saw in the jewelry store when she first met Samad. "Awwww, he got the earrings!" Heat was ecstatic.

"Whoa!" she said when she opened the second box that contained a beautiful friendship ring and diamond bracelet to match. "Wait until my girls see this shit! Oh, I'm wearing this tonight!" She opened the third box to find a Cartier bangle bracelet. "Damn!" she whispered. "This is off the chain!"

The last box she opened was the largest of the four. "Save the best for last!" she exclaimed in a sneaky voice and hurried to see what was in the last box. *Awwww, this is cute.* To her, Samad was the nicest guy in the world.

Inside was the prettiest, most beautiful necklace she had ever seen. It had Samad's and her name—with a heart in between. Diamonds flooded the charm.

"He's so sweet," she said aloud.

Samad was more than sweet. He was smart, marking his territory and making it known that she belonged to him. He knew Heat was always out and about. This way, any guy she met would see Samad's name on her, which meant she was off limits.

Heat couldn't wait to put it on. Lost in her thoughts, she gazed at her gifts in admiration and thought of Eli buying her gifts for no reason . . . She missed Eli in the worse way.

Her mind wandered back to the earlier gossip Classy shared with her about Samad and Eli.. Heat had heard something totally different. She was told that some out of town guys were beefing with Eli about drugs. That sounded more genuine than the Samad killing Eli story. But this news about Ebony didn't make things any better. She didn't want to lose her too. *This shit better not be true about Ebony transporting coke. She, of all people should know that only leads to death or jail. Her entire family is mixed up in the drug game, and she always tells me she hate the fact that that's what her family was known for back in the day, and she didn't want to follow in none of their footsteps. So what the hell happened?*

Heat dismissed both stories, she glanced out the window. Gossip always got twisted, so she knew not to give it much thought. *Now Unique's situation, I can believe. I've seen a bruise or two that she tried to hide, but didn't do such a good job at it. How could Sean beat her up at the hair salon? That's a bitch ass move and it's embarrassing.*

I know her dad used to beat her mom; she saw that growing up. I hope she don't think that's normal behavior—the way a man is supposed to treat a woman. Heat let out a loud sigh. "Whewwww! Drama drama drama."

47

"Seven dollars," the driver said, interrupting her thoughts. She gave the thin man a ten dollar bill. "Keep the change!" Heat said, stepping out of the cab. The cabby honked as he pulled off.

Heat walked a few feet and stepped up on the curb. She stopped in her tracks to take heed to a warning from her conscience. *Dag! My mother's not gon' let me keep all this stuff. I need to hide this before she gets home from work! That lady would flip out. But it's all so beautiful though. Damn, this nigga got money buying shit like this. How many other girls did he do this for? I need to be careful messing with Samad's fine ass. There's always drama when dealing with a street dude. I must be crazy for even thinking about hooking up with him. Maybe I love bad boys. Losing Eli should've been a lesson learned. What if this time, I'm the one who gets shot?*

CHAPTER 7
A Misunderstanding

"Hey, brown eyes!" Samad said from behind, startling Heat as she inserted her key in the lock. Classy's comment about Iyana had her on high alert. She should've apologized to Iyana to squash any beef, but she let the opportunity pass since the incident was still fresh.

"You wanna go to the Apollo Wednesday, or catch a game at Madison Square Garden?" he said.

"What the—" she squealed.

"Did I scare you?" he asked, without waiting on an answer. "So, do you like your gifts?"

"Yes, I love my gifts."

"I got you another gift." Samad extended his hand to give her a black garment bag.

"Really? What is it?"

"I got you the custom made Gucci dress from my guy. You look like you about a size fourteen. If it's too small, or too big, let me know. He'll make the alterations."

Heat reached out to take the bag. "Awww. Thanks." She leaned against the door, happy to see Samad's handsome face.

She gave him an up and down glance, checking out his Pelle Pelle leather jacket that showed his Polo rugby shirt beneath,crisp jeans. She looked down at his brand new fresh white sneakers. She smiled. *He always looks fly! I like his style.* In a low, sexy voice she asked, "You stalking me now?"

"Nah, ma. I don't have to stalk nobody. Stalking is such a strong word. Do I have a reason to?" he asked with a devilish grin, inching toward her as she backed up against the door.

"Stalking?" he asked again and laughed.

"Well, uh, you at my house," she said. "I never told you where I live."

"I know everything," he answered. "I made it my business to come to your house. I'm really feelin' you."

"I see. And just how do you know where I live?" she asked, trying not to let her lips break out into a smile.

"I told you, I know everything, mamí."

"If you say so."

"I'm also saying I'm gon' make sure I make time for you. I wanna see where this could lead."

Heat didn't reply but thought, *Me too.*

Samad moved closer. "Let me ask you something."

"Yes?"

"The other day my sister told me you and your friends stepped to her at the hair salon."

Oh shit! I knew it! "No, that's not accurate. I didn't do noth—"

"So I asked a few questions to my peoples over there, and my home girl Classy let me know it was a misunderstanding, and everything is okay now. But my sister said you must've thought she was my girl or something."

Heat was embarrassed. "Oh! Well, yeah, it was a misunderstanding. We thought she was this girl who was talking shit to Unique about her baby daddy Sean," Heat lied, quickly gazing down in the garment bag, fumbling with the dress. Whenever she lied she could not hold a straight face.

"Yeah, okay. Well, I don't get involved in girl shit like that. My sister can hold her own, and from what I heard, you can hold your own too. Do you keep your girls on standby to fight for you?"

"On standby?" she asked, playing dumb.

"Yeah, on standby. Let me just say this one time." Samad spoke with ice in his voice. "Don't *ever* put your hands on my family again and don't let nobody you know do it for you either." The threatening look in Samad's eyes shook Heat to the core. "You told me you had a strong belief in family and so do I, so I know you feel me."

"Yeah, I do." She swallowed the lump in her throat. "Well, I'll apologize to your sister when I see her."

"Yeah you do that. Make sure you do that."

"I will." *Should I be scared of him? That look was no joke, and for real, for real . . . How in the hell does he know where I live?*

A brief, but intense silence lingered. He moved closer, and she inhaled his Burberry cologne.

"Mmmm, you smell good," she said, getting a whiff of his scent and changing the direction of their conversation for both of their sakes.

He took his chances and made a bold and daring move by leaning in and gently kissing her soft lips. The world stopped moving. All the loud noises from the streets diminished. She didn't hear anything! No horns blowing, nothing! Dead silence. Only she and Samad existed in this world right now.

He wrapped his arms around her waist and pulled her close. Her heart melted from his soft touch. His kiss sent a warm chill oozing through her body, relaxing her, calming her. He parted her lips with his thick tongue, teasing her. Heat wanted to give him a head rush—wanted their first kiss to be as memorable to him as it was to her. She wanted to send signals throughout his body, the same way she was experiencing right now.

Biting his bottom lip, she then drew it into her mouth, gently sucking and teasing.

Damn! Samad thought, but he also spoke it aloud. "Mmm," he moaned. "Whoa!" His body reacted and his dick rose.

They stood in front of her door kissing passionately for all of sixty seconds, which felt like forever. Moisture pooled between Heat's thighs, but so did this warm, throbbing sensation. Heat knew her body was ready for Samad. The loud horn from a school bus jolted the two out of the moment.

"I been wantin' to do that since the day we met in the city. But I didn't wanna play myself, or overstep my welcome. When I see what I want, I go after it," he said with a sincere smile.

"And what is it you want?" Heat asked.

"You!" he replied, looking her directly in her pretty eyes.

She blushed and looked at the ground.

"May I use your bathroom?" he asked, breaking the nervous silence.

"Yes," she replied and turned to open the door.

Samad turned to Heat. "Yo, who's the woman across the street giving me the eye? I peeped her lookin' me up and down."

"Just my neighbor, Ms. Smith."

"Mm hmm. I see," he replied sarcastically.

"How you see her from all the way over here?"

"I'm aware of everything around me at all times, ma. I got eyes in the back of my head! I see what a lot of people don't see. I watch my back, my boys' back. I watch over everybody's back." Samad looked down at his text messages on his phone, then let out a long sigh as if exhausted.

"My paranoid ass be tired just from watching my back." He caught himself and corrected his last comment. "I mean, not that I do anything where I gotta watch my back. Not like that. I'm just sayin' . . ."

53

"Since you watching over everybody's back, *Mr. Gangster*, who's watching your back?" she asked.

"Mr. Gangster? Where you get that from?" He laughed off her comment but wondered what she knew about him.

"You know where I got it from. I meant exactly what I said. Since you watching everybody else's back, who's got your back?"

"I'm good . . . I'm good," he said, as if needing to convince himself. "I got people watching my back. My soldiers, Mike and Will—they're my main right hand men . . . Those are the two men I can count on out here in these streets.

"My best friend Pezo hold me down too; he's the smart one I call Einstein. He's always telling me to invest in businesses and stores. He's into real estate. My man be in and out of town handlin' his business, making moves for me for real." Samad gently stroked Heat's hair. "But there's no reason for anybody to wanna come and get me." He laughed, realizing how comfortable he felt opening up to her. "Damn, I ain't never told no girl any of my business. I must really like you, Miss Heat."

Heat carressed the side of Samad's face, then stroked his wavy hair.

"So, you're saying you don't have enemies?"

"Right. I don't have any enemies."

"Are you sure about that?" *How stupid does he think I am?*

"Well, it's a few niggas out here that are always gonna feel like I'm takin' over their spots 'cause my crew gettin' money. The only two I can think of who feel some type of way about me is this nigga named Bono. He's a grimy nigga. He rob dope boys and trap houses; he works under this nigga named Moe. Anybody that's not ridin' with me on this side is considered an *enemy*. You either ridin' with me, or against me. Street rules I don't need to explain in detail, but . . ."

"Here we go with the street code bullcrap," Heat responded. "That life always comes with enemies, whether visible or not. You always gotta be watching out."

"I wouldn't say I need to watch out for Moe, but he and his crew are the only other ones out here gettin' it. Not like me and my crew gettin' it, but they doin' their thing. And we all know money breeds envy and jealousy. So anything can pop off. So I don't put nothing pass nobody. If anything, they need to be watching out for us!"

I'm surprised he's telling me his business. "Money does breed envy," Heat said. "Actually, I know who Moe is. I don't know him, know him, but I heard he had a crush on me." Heat laughed and blushed.

Samad gave her the side eye gaze. "The only reason I'm telling you this is because you're easy to talk to. I can see myself with you when I look ahead. But yeah, Bono works for Moe, doin' his dirty work, and all them other crews out here was gettin' money until my crew took all their customers. They the only guys out here that should be mad that I'm gettin' money.

"I make sure everybody around me eat. My soldiers are disciplined."

Heat was uninterested in the conversation. It's not that she didn't want to hear about street stuff, but she'd heard enough about crews, enemies, drugs and guns, and getting money. She wanted to talk about just them two.

Samad turned to face Heat and lifted her chin, knowing he had her full attention. *Man, he's real aggressive. Like Eli.* She didn't dare move.

"Let me tell you something else about me, shorty. I don't play no games when it comes to my enemies. And I see you think it's funny that Moe had, or has a crush on you. Look, I know we're just getting to know each other, but let me be very clear right now, early. Don't fuck with none of my enemies."

"I was just saying he—"

Samad cut her off. "Like I said: Don't fuck with none of my enemies, and that's all I'm gonna say. Point blank period." The hard, long menacing stare he gave should have burned Heat to ashes.

She lowered her gaze, seeing the wrinkles in his forehead. *Damn, he didn't have to look at me like that.* She swallowed hard, then took a deep breath. *I feel like I just got punked.*

"Damn, Samad, you ain't have to say it like that. Someone once told me the same thing—in a much nicer way though. But let me ask you a question, Samad. Do you know a guy name Eli?" Heat wanted to get right down to the business. She needed to make sure she wasn't dating Eli's killer.

Samad didn't flinch or change his expression. Without missing a beat he replied, "No. Never heard the name before." He lied. Samad turned and looked away.

He repeated himself. "No, never heard the name before."

Heat exhaled a sigh of relief. *Good!*

He checked out her living quarters, admiring the Art Deco Paris pictures on the wall. He touched the thick, green leather couch as he walked through her house. "Nice. Real leather, not pleather. By the way, you got a really nice house."

"Thank you," she replied humbly.

"Nice looking family," he said, viewing the family pictures in the glass china cabinet.

"Thanks," she said.

"So tell me about your ex—Eli."

"Well, there's not really much to tell. He was a nice guy. He spoiled me all the time. I never really knew what he was into in the streets," she lied, knowing he was a dope boy. "We were just getting to know each other before he got killed." Heat stopped talking.

Samad detected the sadness in her voice. "Wow! That's too bad. So do you try to keep his memory alive or anything?"

"What do you mean?"

"Like . . . Do you have anything to remember him by? Did he leave you anything sentimental?" Samad asked, thinking only of the safe deposit box keys, a stolen letter, and insurance papers belonging to his ex-girl Keisha. He wondered if Heat knew anything about the items Eli stole.

Heat felt her eyes watering. "I don't want to talk about my ex."

Samad didn't want to press her. He wanted to leave her alone with her feelings for a moment, so he excused himself. "So where's the bathroom?"

She took his hand. "It's right here on the left!" She led him out of one room and into the long hallway. Once she stopped in front of the huge mirror on the wall, Heat dropped his hand and pointed left. "The light switch is right there as soon as you walk in."

Heat stared in the mirror, thinking of all three basketball jerseys, his jewelry, and wifebeater T-shirts she had of Eli's in her closet. *I need to go through Eli's things that he told me to hold in that black leather bag one day. All I know is, it must be important if he told me don't tell anybody about it, something about he made a copy of the contents but nobody knows. I don't think I'm ready to open them old wounds though. Don't need to see any reminders of him right now. I'm still not ready.*

Wiping the tears away, Heat then put on lip gloss. She watched Samad's reflection as he walked down the hall and into the bathroom.

He had the same bop in his step as Eli had. The sight made her grin. She just knew Samad was going to be her man. The random gifts he gave her reminded her of how Eli used to pop up with gifts for no reason. She couldn't place her finger on it yet, but at the same time, something about Samad nagged her. Maybe the rumors she'd heard about him created the new feeling. His aggressive nature threw her off a little too, but Eli had been that way, but not to Samad's degree. She felt like he was the one, but then again she wasn't 100% sure. And anything that was not one hundred percent wasn't real. This too worried her.

CHAPTER 8
The So-Called Ex-Girlfriend

October 2000
Three months later . . .

"Don't you get tired of your phone ringing every five minutes?"

Samad looked down at his phone and pushed the reject button, sending whoever it was to voice mail.

"Yeah sometimes. But that's how it is out here. Certain people need to get in touch with me, and I need to be in touch with certain people about business."

"Hmph. I hear you, I guess."

Heat and Samad had grown closer than close. He loved making love to her, and she loved how he hit it from every angle. She appreciated his honesty about everything. He told her many secrets and she did the same. She felt comfortable with him, yet, they weren't officially a couple.

They had just entered the hallway in her house, and Heat's brother Aaron walked out and bumped right into Samad.

"Oh shit! What's good, my dude!" Samad said to Aaron.

"Yo, what you doin' here at my crib, man? And how you know my sister?"

Heat took over the conversation. "This is my friend Samad. Samad, this is my brother Aaron."

"I already know who Samad is. This my man," Aaron replied and extended his hand. Samad gave Aaron some dap, then pulled Aaron in closer, showing him genuine brotherly love. They hugged.

Samad stepped back. "Damn you got tall. How tall are you now?"

"I'm catchin' up to you. I'm six feet three. Two-eighty solid . . . What!" Aaron laughed.

Samad laughed too. "You got about two more inches to catch up with me. I'm six-five. Damn, I can remember when you was a short, lil nigga." Samad hugged Aaron again.

"I remember when you had braids going to the back. Now look at you. Ha!" Samad laughed.

"Yeah, I grew out of that. I like 360's better. Ha!" Aaron laughed as he stroked his deep waves spinning in a circle. "I see your waves too, Samad." "This my man for real," Aaron said as he embraced Samad again.

"Yo, treat my sister right."

"Man, I'm a gentleman." Samad smiled.

"You better be."

Aaron turned to Heat. "You gonna be here by yourself. Mom won't be back for two days. Her flight comes in on Halloween morning. Tell her I bought candy just in case kids ring the bell." Aaron pointed to all the bags of candy on the table.

Instinctively Samad and Heat turned their heads and looked at all the bags of candy.

"Where she at? Where's Mommy?"

"At a legal conference for work."

"Oh, she forgot to tell me the conference was out of town."

"Well, now you know. Lil sis, I gotta go handle some business. Hit my phone if you need me."

"I'm here. So your sister is in good hands," Samad said, looking Aaron in his eyes.

Aaron nodded once. "You right. You a stand-up dude. So I know you'll keep her safe. All right then. I'm out." Aaron threw up the peace sign and made his exit.

From the window, Heat and Samad watched Aaron get into his black jeep and pull off.

"I'll be right back." Heat ran upstairs to see if her mother left her some spending money. A hundred dollar bill lay on her dresser. She smiled.

While Heat was upstairs Samad looked through the stack of mail sitting on the table. He flipped through a few stacks of papers then stopped when he heard Heat coming back downstairs.

As she walked back downstairs, Samad was looking around and checking out her house. This was the third time he'd visited within their three months of hanging out.

He picked up a DVD off the glass table. "I see you got the movie *Boyz in the Hood.*"

"Yeah that's my brother's DVD. I told him I wanted to watch the movie since I never saw it."

"Okay." Samad set the movie back down.

"I really like ya house. It's cozy." He pointed at all the original artwork. "That's nice too. Oh, y'all doing it like that? Ya parents got money like that? "I see y'all got money on these walls." He pointed to the Vincent Van Gogh picture on the facing wall. "Let me find out y'all rich on the low."

"Rich? I wouldn't say rich, but we're comfortable."

"What do your parents do?"

"My mother is a lawyer, and my pops was a basketball player—well, back in the day he played ball. He was a business owner when he passed away."

"I'm sorry to hear that about your pops. What's your father's name?"

"Bobby Jordan."

"Oh, I heard of him. That's your father? MVP Hall of Famer. I read about that. Sorry to hear that"

"Thanks," Heat replied and continued walking down the steps.

Once her foot touched the bottom step, he grabbed her hand, pulling her to him. He gently pushed her up against the front door and slid his right hand around the back of her neck, bringing her lips closer to his lips. He kissed Heat hungrily and more passionately this time. Her body responded to his touch. She relaxed, resting her head against the door. Samad planted soft kisses from her lips down to her neck, sucking her flesh. She let out a soft moan.

Slowly, he began unbuttoning her shirt, then he lifted her red bra and cupped her breasts, caressing them. Tracing her neck with his tongue, he eased down to her breasts, nibbling and biting on her now fully erect nipples. Samad massaged her supple breasts and sucked on them one at a time." *Nice and firm,* he thought.

Heat moaned, relishing the pleasure. She ran her fingers through his wavy hair and down the sides of his face. Samad lightly gripped her wrists, lifting them above her head. He teased her with his tongue, moving away from her mouth, making her beg for it. Her body ached and throbbed for him. Her pussy was wet and he knew it.

He brushed his dick up against her leg, letting her feel its hardness. Samad turned Heat until her back was facing him. Once he let her hands go, he reached for the clasp and unfastened her bra. Pulling her hair to one side, he planted light kisses on the nape of her neck. His dick now rested on her butt. Caught up in the moment, Heat laid her head on his shoulder. He grabbed a handful of her hair, gently pulling it.

Samad turned her to face him and kissed her lips. Then he moved his tongue down her neck and going even further, kissed both breasts again. He traced his tongue down her stomach, gently teasing her navel. Once he dropped to his knees, he lifted her skirt and caressed her hips. Palming her round butt, he turned her once more to get a good look. *Mmmm. Nice, phat ass!* He kissed Heat on the small of her back and on her butt cheek. Then he kissed the other one, lightly sucking on the fatty part, going back and forth and noticing the beauty mark on her back.

Samad wouldn't leave until he felt the inside of her pussy. He never wanted anybody the way he wanted her right now. He grabbed her hand and led her to the couch, where he lifted her skirt and slid her red thong down. Then gently he brushed against her moist entrance with the palm of his hand, eventually sliding one finger in and out, feeling her tight pussy grip his finger.

He pulled her in front of him as he sat on the green leather couch. Samad opened her legs and began kissing her inner thighs while teasing her clit with his index and middle fingers. Making her pussy even wetter. He stuck his tongue in her wet pussy and sucked her juices.

"Ssss . . . Samad . . . stop. Let's go to my bedroom."

Once inside the large bedroom, Heat sat on the edge of the king-sized bed. Samad pushed her backward. She looked up at him as she rested on her elbows.

He slid her Gucci sandals off her pretty, neatly manicured feet, and he kicked his tan Timberlands off and kneeled between her legs. He opened and lifted her legs and placed them on his shoulders, then lowered his head between her legs, teasing, sucking, and nibbling on her clit.

Heat purred softly. "You like that, mamí?" he asked.

Instead of answering, she bit her bottom lip.

My pussy throbbing. She felt the moisture between her legs as they undressed and she watched him put on the condom.

A smirk crept across his face. After he climbed on top of her, he grabbed her wrists and placed them on the soft white, goose down pillows above her head. He controlled his every stroke and teased her with just the tip of his dick. Her juices invited him in. Beneath him she squirmed and flinched.

"This pussy feels good. Damn, you real tight," he whispered in her ear as he pounded in and out, hitting her walls from every angle. "Mmm . . . Damn." Samad went deeper, hitting the back of her walls. After several minutes passed, he reared his head, looking up at the ceiling with his eyes closed tight. Like king of the jungle, he roared. He gritted his teeth when he felt himself cumming. He exploded inside the condom, inside of Heat. Slowly, he pulled out. Sweat dripped from his face as he collapsed next to her. "Damn, ma! That was a good nut!"

Heat smiled as she kissed Samad's chest.

"I know we've only been hanging out for three months, but I just want you with me. Heat, I want you to move in with me. I already put some money down on this new little brownstone. If we gonna be serious about each other, I want to live together."

Heat was caught off guard by his question. "I'll think about it, Samad. That's a big step."

"Get me something to drink, would you?" he asked while his text messages kept going off.

She smiled instead of frowned. Eli used to do her the same way and not because he wanted to order her around, but nobody had ever said please or thank you to him. She had to teach him that saying please got him what he wanted quicker and without an attitude. Samad and Eli shared a lot of similarities.

Heat grabbed her pink robe off the back of her door. She kissed his lips before leaving.

The minute the door closed, he jumped up and went through her drawers searching each drawer looking through her papers. "Nothing." He unfolded her papers scanned through them, then folded the papers back quickly. His alerts continued going off. "Shit." Samad stopped searching her room, he reached for her cordless phone and dialed his voice mail and retrieved the first message.

"Yo, Samad, it was a shootout earlier at the barbershop. One of the customers popped off over some nonsense, and the bullet hit a little kid. It was one of them niggas from Eli's crew. Come here as soon as you get this message."

"Damn!" Samad ended the call. Then he looked at the other number on his two way Motorola pager. He didn't recognize the number, but it had his code for emergencies at the end. Maybe one of his men needed him. He pressed the star key to block Heat's number before calling the number back. Patiently he waited while the phone rang. He was about to hang up after the third ring when a girl answered.

"Hello!" the female yelled in the phone with music blasting in the background.

"Hello?" Samad asked with his face twisted, trying to detect the voice. "Who's this?"

"This is Mercedes! Who is this?"

Samad shook his head in disgust when he recognized the voice and heard the name. "What you want, yo? Why the fuck you keep calling me!"

"This Samad? Where you calling me from? Why you block the number out?" she asked. "Why's the number private? Oh, you over one of your bitches house?"

"Why you asking me all these questions? What you want, yo? And why you put 007? I thought you was somebody else!" he barked.

"That's why you called me back? Oh, you wouldn't have called back if you thought it was me?"

"I told you stop putting that code in when you hit me! Stop hittin' me anyway. I told you a hundred times!" he yelled. "Don't call me no fuckin' more!" He didn't even wait for her response before he hung up.

Click!

He walked away from the phone then stopped in his tracks. An afterthought popped in his head, and he doubled back to the phone. Samad picked up the cordless phone and pressed ten numbers, just in case Heat wanted to press redial once he left. He had called his own cell phone number. As soon as his voice mail came on, he hung up and placed the phone on its base.

Heat walked back in with a glass of orange juice and handed Samad his drink. She leaned in and kissed him.

"I gotta go handle some business," he stated coldly. "What you doing later?"

"I . . . I don't know yet. Why?" She walked to her vanity and sat down in front of the mirror. She tilted her head, examining her neck closely, spotting a few red bite marks.

His sudden personality change from five minutes ago slightly annoyed her.

"You wanna catch a movie, or get something to eat later? Or we can check out the Apollo, or Madison Square Garden again?" he asked as he finished getting dressed. Not once did he look in her direction. She stared at him in the mirror, trying to detect his feelings.

"I'll let you know when I check my schedule."

Samad was distracted by his phone vibrating off the hook. His text message alerts was going off too. He ignored it.

"Yo! I'm out! Hit me later!" He walked over to Heat. She picked up her brush and pulled her hair down from the damp ponytail. She pulled her hair to the right. Her robe fell half off, exposing a left bare shoulder. He leaned down and kissed her there. Then he kissed her neck, turning her face toward him. He kissed her lips, sticking his tongue in her mouth.

"I gotta go, ma!"

Heat stood and then walked him down the stairs.

When they reached the door, Heat finally spoke, breaking the awkward silence. "Are you okay?"

"Yeah, I'm good. Why?" Now he was flashing his white teeth, seemingly in a better mood than a few moments ago.

Her brows knitted in confusion. She thought he was upset about something she did, or said. But quickly dismissed that thought when he filled her in on his sudden mood change.

"This fuckin' girl keep on callin' my phone. Yo, she get on my fuckin' nerves!"

"Oh?" Heat raised an eyebrow. "What girl?" Curiosity laced her words.

"Mercedes...My ex-girl! She ain't nobody! That ain't about nothin'! We broke up like three months ago."

Heat rolled her eyes. *Buzzkill!* Definitely fucked her natural high up! Now she was in a sour mood.

"To be honest, it wasn't really that serious anyway! She still callin' my phone. Be callin' me from all these different numbers. Playin' little kid games." He noticed the blank look on Heat's face. He didn't want her to feel insecure or threatened.

Samad walked closer to Heat "You don't have to worry about her. She's nobody. She just don't get it! I don't fuck with her no more!" Samad leaned in to kiss

Heat on her lips. She turned her head, allowing his kiss to land on her cheek.

He opened the door as if he lived there and stepped outside, inhaling fresh air into his lungs. While glancing up and down the quiet block, he squinted from the blazing sun. Indian summer.

"The sun still shinin' bright this afternoon." He pulled his Louis Vuitton frames out and placed them on his face. "Later, ma! Call my phone! Turn your two-way on. I'm gonna put code 7400 after the number. Same as your pin number. That's gonna always be my code for you. So whenever you see that code, you know it's me." He gave her a quick peck on her lips.

"Later!" she replied softly.

From the doorway she watched him walk over to his red BMW parked across the street.

Hot bubbling jealousy was getting the best of her. It's not like she and Samad were officially a couple. But just the slightest mention of his ex made her somewhat bitter.

"What she keep calling him for? The fuck! What she want? If she's his ex, that's all she is. Just that. His ex! It's all about Heat now!" she said, puffing out her chest. *But what if she wants him back? What if he wants her back?* She shook the conflicting emotions off and let out a long sigh. Samad blew the horn as he drove off.

Heat closed the door with her lips pouted and picked up the cordless phone and pressed redial. The call went straight to his voice mail. *Oh, he just checked his messages.*

Her mind was unsettled about his ex-girl, Mercedes. She needed to get to the bottom of this and find out who this so-called "ex" is. The last thing she wanted to go from was being treated well by Eli to getting played by Samad. Hell no!

CHAPTER 9
Same Drama

Friday . . .
Harlem

Samad pulled up to his barbershop in the midst of chaos. He saw police officers questioning the customers, so he drove around back to avoid them all. *They probably trying to find out who fired the first shot, or what the argument was about. That's what I would like to find out. I told them niggas to keep a low profile in here.*

He walked inside the barbershop from the back door, and he walked right into more police officers.

"Who are you?" the tall, blonde haired, blue-eyed officer yelled.

"I'm the owner." Samad picked up the overturned barber chair lying on its side. He grabbed the broom and started sweeping the broken glass in a pile. The picture had fallen from the wall and onto the floor. He looked at all the shattered glass everywhere.

"Excuse me. This is a crime scene. There is crucial evidence on the floor. You cannot do that. You're not supposed to be in here anyway."

"This is my place of business. I built this from nothing. I have every right to be in here," Samad said.

Samad turned his back on the police officer and continued sweeping the glass. *I can't stand the fucking police.*

The police officer walked up behind him and grabbed the broom out of his hand. Samad turned, standing face to face with the cop. "For the last time, you're not supposed to be in here."

Samad noticed his business partner, Pezo, talking to the other police officer. Pezo saw an angry look on Samad's face; he had seen it before. Samad always did something stupid without thinking . . .

Pezo walked up. "Samad, think about it. Be smart, man."

"Yeah, Samad, be smart. Think about it," the cop mocked.

Samad swung. The punch connected with the cop's jaw before Pezo had a chance to pull him back.

Another cop was walking in while Samad was taking a swing at his partner. He rushed Samad.

"Are you fucking crazy!" Pezo grabbed Samad's arm to restrain him. Do you know how long you can get in jail for assaulting a police officer? You on probation. You don't need this shit. Be smart!"

It was too late. The officer grabbed Samad and shoved him against the wall, pushing Pezo out the way.

The other officer grabbed Samad's arm, placing cuffs on him.

"You are fucking under arrest for assaulting a police officer! If I'm not mistaken, your homeboy just mentioned you're on probation. Not to mention tampering with evidence. Do you know you are in direct violation of your probation?"

Samad looked at Pezo. "Call Heat. Tell her to tell Aaron to have some bail money ready. I'll take care of him when I get out."

"Okay. Don't say another word, Samad. I'll call your lawyer. What the fuck were you thinking? You know they been wanting you from day one."

Samad did not answer.

The other officer took Samad out the front door and put him in the squad car. He was going to be in a lot of trouble.

Chapter 10
Unexpected Calls

Anxiety flooded her body rather than serenity from the lovemaking she and Samad just made. She hated the idea of entering a new relationship with competition already in place. This hadn't happened with Eli. She was always number one and sure of her position in his life. Now with Samad . . . this nigga was a slightly different animal. With his hot and cold moods.

Her phone rang, and she jumped to answer it, hoping Samad was calling to take her out.

"Hello!" Heat answered in a frantic tone that she didn't mean to reveal.

"Hey, Heat. Is Unique there?"

Her smile damn near evaporated. "Who is this?"

"This Sean. I called her house but she's not home, and since I know she's always there I thought I'd just call to check and see."

"How did you get my number?"

"I got it off Unique's notebook."

"Oh, okay. But anyway she's not here."

"Okay, that's cool. So umm . . . what you doing?"

"Nothing. Chillin'." She rolled her eyes.

"Cool, cool . . . So can I come over then? We can just chill together," Sean flirted.

Heat couldn't help but stare at the phone. "Chill together? As in you come over to my house?"

"Yeah, that's what's up. Nobody ain't gotta know."

"Nigga, you supposed to be liking my friend Unique! You *know* you and me not cool like that. And I don't even know nothin' about you—except for all the foul shit I heard you did to my friend—hittin' her and shit. Hell no, you can't come to my house—witcha' lame ass. Don't call my fuckin' house no more! If you do, I will let my big brother Aaron know about this." Heat slammed the phone down.

She dialed Aaron's number, but not for the reason she'd just told Sean.

"Hello?" Aaron answered on the first ring.

"Hey, I need to ask you a few things about Samad. He just left. Who is he dating? What does he do? He told me he's into music and stuff."

"Normally when somebody asks me about another man in these streets, that's none of my business, because I think that's real bitch shit discussing a person, especially another man behind his back."

"Well, I ain't just anybody. Certain shit I need to know, Aaron. Dang! But I know you won't lie to me about anything. Besides, he asked me to move in with him."

"Oh word! Samad asked you to move with him? Damn!"

"Why you say it like that?" Heat asked.

"'Cause it's kinda shocking."

"So what you think I should do?"

"Well, you are eighteen now, and you already graduated from high school. Just think long and hard about it. If that's what you want to do—then do it. Mommy is the one you need to convince, and make sure she's okay with you movin' out, but I already know she's gonna snap. So ummm, just make sure you finish college like your lil smart ass promised us."

"Boy, shut up! I am gonna stay in school. That's a must. Samad already put money down on a brownstone in Jersey. I told him I would think about it. But I don't want Mommy to know about it yet. So please don't say nothin' until I tell her."

"Well, first of all, he must really be falling for you to put money down on a brownstone already out of state, even though it's right over the water. By the way we live out here in these streets, I can understand why he's movin' fast like that. God forbid anything happened to him, at least his lady will be taken care of with a roof over her head. He must be in a space where he trusts you. Because I know Samad. He don't trust too many people. Not that fast. Especially a woman, unless he really loves you."

"I trust him too. Aaron . . . I really am falling for Samad. I love him already." *He reminds me so much of Eli.*

"Nope. I'm not getting' into all of that mushy stuff with you, Heat. Besides, I'm handlin' some business. But I will tell you this, because you are my sister. He's a stand up guy. Niggas respect and fear him out here in these streets. If anybody got a problem with anything, they call on Samad to come check niggas about anything goin' on in the streets."

Heat smiled.

"If I didn't trust him, I wouldn't have allowed him to stay at the house when I left. He's older than you though. He's twenty-seven. His old lady Keisha, the one he was real serious about, was the so-called Queen of Brooklyn in the streets. He even proposed to her and got her a ring. I think she cheated on him with some dude. Samad started hustlin' at an early age. It took him some time to reach a certain status, but he's there now. Back when he was sixteen years old, Samad was doin' way better than old head niggas twice his age because of Keisha. She was the one plugged him in. Niggas went to her to re-up and cop drugs and guns. She died though."

"Yeah, he told me. In a car accident. He was serious about her." *Queen of Brooklyn in the streets, huh?*

"A few months ago I heard he was fucking with this other chick named Mercedes. She went to school with me. If you look in my yearbook, her picture is in there. She a big, tall girl. Her last name is Best. She's pretty. But not prettier than you. That's real talk."

"Oh really?" Heat said, blushing.

"Yeah. She's in college now studying to be a police officer or a corrections officer or some shit dealing with the law. I haven't heard anything major about them being a couple anymore. Look, I gotta go. I'll fill you in whenever I get back home. Later."

"Later, Aaron. You gave me enough information." *Now I see why Samad lied, telling me some bullshit story about him being in the music business. Hmph. He's the muscle all right. Well, at least I know I will be safe with him. Let me see how this Mercedes Best chick looks.*

She ran to Aaron's room and located his yearbook in the closet, then she rushed downstairs to the kitchen, searching for Mercedes' photo.

Heat studied the picture as she plopped down in the chair nearest to the answering machine. *Oh, she ain't all that. Pssst.* "She looks just like the TV twins, Tia and Tamara. They're cute and all, but they can't get with me." Heat did, however, admire Mercedes' long, dark, wavy hair and thick eyebrows.

She listened to the messages. Unique and Ebony called trying to get into something the following weekend. She put them on her to-do list. Over a three month period, she had been kicking it with Samad so hard that she never addressed Unique or Ebony's issues, which should have been a priority. And now the idea of "the other girl" made her feel some kind of way, frantic to make sure she moved her out of the picture forever. Mercedes' history with Samad was a little shaky.

Nobody was real clear about what was going on between those two, although Samad said they were through. Either she was still in, or completely out of the picture. When exes still called phones, there was always a reason—lingering love, or bitterness. Heat didn't want to get it twisted. Her feelings were involved now. This was serious. She needed to know their true status.

After she showered and then got dressed, Heat cleaned up the house and stayed in her room thinking of how she was going to tell her mother that she would be moving out. She wanted to live with Samad, and she had several reasons to justify doing so.

Later that evening as she was dozing off, her phone rang four times. Heat answered, "Hello?"

"Heat, this is Pezo. Sorry to wake you, but I gotta let you know they locked Samad up today. He told me to call you so you can ask Aaron to set some bail money aside for him. He'll take care of him later."

"What!" Heat sat up on the bed and wiped her eyes and stretched. Samad had introduced Pezo to Heat three months ago when they first began hanging out. He wanted her to know how important Pezo was in his life, being another right hand man of his. She and Pezo got along right away. He was laid back and funny, but just as serious about business as Samad.

"Yeah, they locked him up earlier today." Pezo told her about the barbershop shooting and the fight Samad started with the cop.

Heat gasped. "Oh my god!"

"Crazy. I know, right?"

"What! He hit the cop?" *Is he freaking crazy!*

"Yeah. Samad knows better."

"Pezo, is the child all right?"

"I don't know yet. I will find out though."

"If it ain't one thing it's another." Heat walked to her closet to grab some clothes to throw on. "Where did they take him?"

"To the police station over on Green Street. I spoke to his lawyer, Mr. Weinstein. He said they might end up keeping him because he violated his probation."

Heat stopped digging through her clothes. "Oh my goodness! So what are you saying, Pezo?"

"I'm saying more than likely they will keep him over the weekend—number one because it's Friday. He won't see the judge until Monday. If they keep him, they can deny his bail and ship him off. He will eventually end up doing time for violating his probation. You know how these judges act when niggas violate probation."

"Oh boy. I'm so tired of this street life shit." *First Eli. And now Samad. Different nigga same drama.*

"Don't forget to hit Aaron up for the bail money, and Samad will take care of him when he get out."

Heat instinctively glanced over at her brother Aaron's safe that he trusted her to keep in her possession. She sat on the edge of the bed. "So now what?"

"Now, it's a waiting game. He might not hear what he wanna hear. It might be bad news."

Heat fell back on the bed and let out a loud sigh. "Well, at least I'll have some good news for him when I speak to him."

"He needs to hear some good news. What is it?"

"I took a home pregnancy test. I'm pregnant."

"Oh wow! Congratulations. Yeah, he definitely needs to hear that right now. Also, congratulations on your high school graduation. Samad told me you recently graduated."

"Thank you." She paused. "You know what, Pezo? If they end up sending him away, he's not going to think my pregnancy is good news at all . . . Shit! That was dumb to hit a cop. All they wanna do is put black men in jail. Anyway, I umm . . ." She coughed. "I gotta go. I feel like I gotta throw up."

"Hope you feel better, Heat."

"Thanks, Pezo. What we should be hoping is to hear some better news than what you just gave me. Thanks for letting me know about Samad. I appreciate it."

"No doubt."

Heat hung the phone up and ran to the bathroom. Not only was the fetus in her belly making her sick, but so was the thought of Samad going to jail. How he thought he could punch an officer while being on probation was a mystery to Heat. *Damn, people do stupid stuff sometimes. And he's the one that's always telling me to use my head, but he doesn't. Samad knows who the prison system is designed for and why. How can a minority of the US population be the majority of America's prison population? Bullshit!*

She released her truth into the commode and flushed it down. If Mr. Weinstein gets Samad off, it'll be a miracle, and those don't happen too often.

Chapter 11
Consequences

November 1, 2000
Monday . . .

Where is he? On Monday afternoon Heat raced into the court building passing all the reporters near the wall. She looked in each room hoping to see Samad, or his lawyer, or Pezo.

Mr. Weinstein, Samad's lawyer, stood in the hallway talking on the phone and yelling at someone. "My client, up until this point was complying with the terms of his probation. He's a mentor in the neighborhood. He donates tremendously to the National Boys & Girls Club. You mean to tell me you can't take his community involvement into consideration and grant my client a bail?" The lawyer walked away to the small room and closed the door for privacy.

Heat approached Pezo. "What's goin' on?

"I been tryna call you. The judge was here early. Samad went in front of Judge Coleman, the same judge that gave him probation. Last time he told Samad if he ever saw his face in his courtroom again he would give him the max. He won't grant him a bail."

"Are you serious!"

"Yeah. They found drugs in one of the barber's stations, and since no one is claiming responsibility, they put the drugs on Samad since it's his barbershop. They about to ship him. His lawyer is trying everything to prevent that from happening. He's about to do some time."

Heat's eyes watered. *I knew it!*

Pezo hugged her briefly. "Weinstein been on the phone calling everybody and their momma. It's not looking good. Damn! He might be gone for the holidays. Thanksgiving this month . . . Then Christmas next month . . . Damn, the New Year right around the corner. What a way to end this year! If they make him do his time, he won't be home until November 2005. If he's good, then Summer 2005. On good behavior."

"This is too much. I can't . . ." Heat rubbed her stomach thinking about her baby. *Oh, Samad!*

"I'll be right back. I'm going to find his lawyer and see what's going on," Pezo said.

"Okay. I need to use the ladies room and get some water. I feel dehydrated."

"A'ight. I'ma holla at Weinstein and see what's up." Pezo went looking for Samad's lawyer.

Heat asked a police officer where the nearest bathroom was. Once he pointed to the right, she walked down the hallway but stopped at the vending machine and bought a cranberry juice. Once her change dropped, she headed to the ladies room and pushed the door open. She walked smack dead into Samad's sister, Iyana, who bust her right in her mouth with no spoken words. Heat swung back, cranberry juice in hand, but missed as she stormed into the large space.

"Oh, so you by yourself now? You not with ya girls. You don't have nothin' to say now, huh? Let's go! Insecure ass bitch! Thought I forgot, didn't you?" Iyana bounced from side to side.

Heat placed the juice on the sink and got with her, punching Iyana on the nose and causing her to stumble.

"You wack just like your wack ass punches." Iyana socked Heat twice. "That's for your friend Ebony putting her hands on me." The first punch landed on Heat's right eye. "And this is for your friend Unique." The second blow landed on her nose. "You better be lucky you with my brother Samad, or your ass would have been dealt with."

Heat fell backward into the wall. The door opened, and an older woman wearing dark glasses walked into the bathroom holding a cane and the leash to a seeing-eye dog.

The golden retriever barked at Iyana. She jumped back and gathered her things. "You lucky!" She mouthed the word 'bitch.' "I don't disrespect my elders."

"No, you lucky. You got that off. Right now I'm worried about your brother. I don't have time for this petty shit. We will see each other again, bitch. My college is only a minute away from where you be at. We *will* see each other again." Heat snapped.

"Yes we will. Believe that!" Iyana walked out the bathroom. "Mercedes, what did Samad's lawyer say?" Iyana yelled, before closing the bathroom door.

Chapter 12
Focused

January 18, 2001. . .

"Hey, big head," Heat said. "You hear me talking to you." Heat had just pulled up in her paved driveway. She noticed he had shoveled the snow off the driveway. She smiled.

"Hey, what's up, sis?" Aaron replied.

She grabbed her books and bag as she got out the gray BMW truck and locked her door. Her brother was sitting on her porch eating a bowl of cereal. "That's a nice leather bubble jacket. It goes perfect with your Timberlands. I like that color."

"It's peanut butter. Thanks. How's your college classes coming along?" Aaron noticed Heat's thick school books in her arms. He stood up to help her with her books.

My psych class is very interesting. Communications is easy. So far so good. Since I took a couple of pre-requisite classes my senior year of high school, I'm ahead of the game. So I'm good so far."

"I'm proud of you. It pays to do right in high school."

"Yes it does. So much so, my guidance counselor pulled some strings and secured me an internship also. This way I don't need to wait until my junior year. I can do my internship right away."

"That's great, little sis."

"Thanks for shoveling that little bit of snow in the driveway."

"Aww, come on, you already know."

"But anyway, how did you get in, Aaron?"

Aaron held up a key in his hand.

"Oh, that's right. I forgot Samad told you to make a copy for yourself when you finalized the paperwork."

"Yeah, since he wasn't here to meet with the real estate agent during the closing I acted like I was Samad. You know they think we all look alike anyway. So she didn't even know I wasn't Samad when I gave her the cashier's check and signed the papers."

Aaron smiled as he munched on the cereal. "That's my man, and you are my little sister. Of course I was going to step up and make sure this went through. I knew he was serious about you, and I know what kind of man he is. He came to me like a man about you, knowing that you are my sister. I gave him my blessing man to man."

"Thanks, big bro."

"Family is everything to him, and you and him are starting a new family." Aaron pointed at Heat's belly. "He wanna make sure y'all are okay with a roof over your head, even if he's not here."

"I love you for that. Thank you for handling the closing. Lord knows with this baby and my hectic schedule . . . Hmph . . ." Heat smiled inside, thinking of the many nights Eli had talked about buying a brownstone and taking care of her while she went to college.

"No doubt, sis. You know Mommy feels a way about you movin' out. But she knows you're growing up, and you're no longer her baby, technically. But I assured her you'd be okay because you're responsible and handling your business. I told her I would check on you from time to time."

"Thank you for that. I'm going to always be her baby, but I have my own life to live."

"I hear you. You're right."

"But on another note." Heat pointed at the large bowl of cereal. "You do not be playin'. You make sure you eat every chance you get. Outside in the cold too. Super ghetto!"

"That's right!" Aaron joked. "And by the way, I like how y'all got this brownstone hooked up. I gotta salute Samad for buying this. It's beautiful, little sis."

"Thank you. It's nice and cozy."

Aaron hugged Heat and rubbed her stomach. "Wow, your stomach's getting big."

Heat hugged Aaron back. "I know, right? I gained five pounds. This baby is growing fast."

Aaron stuck a spoonful of cereal in his mouth.

"You always eating up everybody's food! Your chicks not feeding you? As much as you eat, you never get fat."

"I stay in the gym to keep my weight right, sis. I'll train you when you drop that baby to get that fat off you. Ha!" Milk dripped down his chin and Aaron wiped it away

"Ahh. Whatever. Eeeew! Nasty, talkin' with your mouth open." She held her hand out to Aaron. "Gimmie some of that big money. I'm still your little sister, ain't nothing changed." Heat laughed.

"Stop begging!" Aaron laughed and went in his pocket, pulling out a stack. Turning away from Heat, he peeled off five 100 dollar bills.

"Even though you don't need my money, you're still going to always be my little sister, and you can get anything from me. You got that."

"Run that," Heat said, keeping her hand out.

"Shut up!" He handed her the five bills. She grabbed them and put it in her wallet.

"Heat, drop me off real quick," Aaron said.

"Where's your vehicle? One of those girls got it?" She laughed and walked off, not waiting on his response.

"I crashed on the Vanwyck in Queens. I fell asleep driving home from this chick's house. Let me hold your truck real quick. I'm coming right back. I swear I'll be right back!"

"Oh, hell no, Aaron! The last time I let you hold my ride, you did not come back for three days. You made me miss one of my doctor's appointments. I had to drive Samad's big ol' Suburban. You cannot get my ride."

"Speaking of him, what they saying about his sentence?"

"Just a bunch of mess. He gotta do the entire five years. He won't be home until Summer 2005.

"Wowww!..Word?"

"Yeah, he violated his probation. Also they charged him for assaulting that police officer, and the drugs they found in his barbershop."

"Damn! So they did give him the entire five?" Aaron shook his head.

"Yes they did. Even though I can't stand his sister, she called me on the three-way for him. Like she didn't just jump on me in the bathroom. Iyana phony. But I gotta deal with her though—that's his blood. He already knows how we feel about each other, and she's friends with Mercedes. I told him to write me letters, or call the house directly."

Aaron munched on his cereal and talked with his mouth open. "Heat, you know that chick Mercedes just started working at the jail he's locked up in. So just be prepared when you go visit him. She be giving all his visitors a hard time."

"Oh really?" Heat looked at Aaron.

"Yeah, but she's nothing to be worried about. The only reason he deal with her, is because she let him sneak drugs in the jail. The guys in there behind the wall already know her reputation from the streets. They just use her as a mule for smugglin' drugs. That's the only reason everybody be nice to her. Just try not to let her push your buttons. Don't worry about Samad behind that wall either. I'm sure his money long enough to pay whoever off to get him whatever he needs in there."

"Hmph!" Heat said.

Aaron stood in front of Heat. "But for real, sis, back to your vehicle. Let me hold the truck. I was waiting for this chick to come scoop me. She taking too long."

"No! I ain't messin' with you like that no more, Aaron! I'll drop you off from now on, until you get your car back. Where you going anyway?"

"To Baltimore to handle some business."

"Maryland? B'more? Ooooh no! I thought you was gon' say around the block, to the hood or something. You talkin' 'bout outta state. I'm not drivin' you to Maryland! I'm not feelin' good. This baby got me sick every day."

"Rent me a car then."

"Let me think about it. I will let you know. Bye, Aaron. I love youuuu," Heat replied with a song in her words.

She walked to the door, but turned back to face Aaron. "Hold on. I need to make a few runs to get some things for Samad. But gimmie a minute."

"How long? I really need to do something right quick."

"Not that long. Just gimme a minute."

"I'll be right here on the phone. All right, lil sis?"

"All right."

Aaron held the bowl up to his mouth and drank the milk from the cereal. He walked to the door where Heat stood. "Here, take your little fancy bowl back in the house."

Heat's phone rang three times.

"Answer your cell. That's a corny ring tone."

"Shut up, boy! Hello? Hello?"

Click.

Heat looked annoyed. "Somebody keeps calling me from blocked unknown numbers. Restricted, unavailable, or ID withheld private numbers keep poppin' up! I didn't answer blocked numbers before, but when Samad be calling my phone, blocked numbers be coming up. Sometimes it's him. Like when he can't reach me in the house. That's why I got that ring tone on my cell for blocked numbers only. Somebody's been playin' on my phone. They keep calling and hangin' up."

"Probably one of Samad's bitches!"

Heat shot Aaron a cold look.

Aaron laughed. "I'm just playing."

"Don't get him beat up," Heat replied, taking the bowl out of Aaron's hand.

A black Range Rover driving by caught their attention. The windows were tinted and she and Aaron couldn't see inside.

"Who's that?" Aaron said, walking to the end of the driveway.

A Dodge Intrepid pulled up in the driveway, taking his attention away from the black truck.

"Who's that in the car, Aaron?" Heat asked.

The driver blew the horn three times.

"Well, it's about time. Took you long enough," Aaron said to the girl driving. "I thought you wasn't coming."

"I told you I had to pick up my cousins. They riding with us to B'more."

"Who are all those people?" Heat asked Aaron, getting a good look at the driver as well as the passengers.

Aaron turned to Heat. "Neeka just a chick from around the way."

"Hmph!" Heat replied.

He glanced in the car at everybody and gave them a head nod. "Hold up a minute."

"Damn, if I knew all these people were going to be riding, I would've told her just give me the car. I could've driven myself. This that bullshit."

"Well, I can take you if you can wait a little while."

"Nah, that's okay, lil sis. I need to leave right now. You need to rest with Lil Samad inside you. I'll see you when I get back. I love you." Aaron opened the door and got in. Neeka drove off with tires screeching, headed to the highway.

Heat's stomach dropped and roiled. "It's too many people in that car. I bet they get stopped by the cops. I hope Aaron ain't holding nothin'," Heat said out loud. *Please God, don't let anything bad happen to my brother.*

CHAPTER 13
Behind the Wall

February 14, 2001

"I can't deal with this bullshit driving back and forth to no jail, and I'm pregnant too. School is keeping me busy; this baby got me hot and sweaty all the time," Heat complained. "Oh hell no!" Heat sat in the truck that Sunday morning after what seemed like forever driving to the jail.

"It's Valentine's Day. Pssst." Heat let out a loud sigh. She opened her letter from Samad before going inside. This was her first time visiting him since he was found guilty. She looked down at the letter and read part of it again.

I heard about the fight you had with my sister at the trial. I spoke to Iyana about that too. I'm not getting into no girl fights, but she knows better now. I told her when it comes to Mercedes to mind her business. But I want you and her to squash whatever it is going on between y'all. An apology is in order so you two can get past the bad blood.

Mercedes told me she saw you in the hallway. That girl is obsessed with our life and our love. I don't even know why she was there. Heat, don't let that fake toy cop Mercedes get to you when you're coming through security. She just don't get it. Once I found out she was a slut, I cut her off way back then. She's trying everything in her power to win me back, so while

I'm in this jail I'm going to be cordial to her for now . . . I can't wait to see you, and I'll see you soon.

Love,

Samad 7400

She folded the letter and stuck it in her glove compartment.

Heat felt dizzy and lightheaded after driving around and finally finding a spot in the crowded parking lot. So she wouldn't have any problems getting past the metal detector, she emptied her pockets of any loose change, keys, and all metal.

After checking her bag and removing her ID, she put her bag in the passenger seat. She picked up her leather jacket, then wiped sweat off her face. "Wheww, I'm hot." She put the jacket across her arm then stepped out the vehicle locking the door behind her. She pulled up her blue stretch pants, hating the fact that she couldn't fit any of her jeans anymore. *I need to get some maternity clothes. This baby is growing inside me faster than I imagined. I can't believe I'm already three months. The only thing I can fit on my thighs and butt is leggings.*

A line was forming at the doors, and she hurried out the car to join the others. A woman standing behind Heat tapped her on the shoulder. Heat turned around.

"I don't think they'll let you in with that shirt on, or those leggings. This must be your first visit here."

"Why do you say that?" she asked, wearing this naïve look.

"They're very strict on their dress code when visiting inmates. They might let you get away with the leggings, but the shirt—the shirt I just don't know, sweetie . . . It has to be long. It can't be a certain color that the inmates wear inside. The shirt has to be long enough to cover your butt. No see-thru with lace on your shirt. None of that sexy stuff you got on showing cleavage. This one female corrections officer be trippin' too. She don't let nothin' slide."

"Oh, I didn't know." Heat looked at the way everybody was dressed, then looked down at herself. Everybody had on long T-shirts covering their butts.

"Maybe you should put on the jacket to cover up, but then again they gonna tell you to put your things in the lockers."

"I'm having hot flashes. I'm not putting this jacket on."

"Okay, if you say so." The woman shrugged, then moved up following the line.

The guards walked out toward the door ready to let everybody inside.

"Everybody in this row, line up against that wall. Once you get inside, walk down the hall and put your things in a locker in the room on your right. The lockers are fifty cents. Then have a seat until the person you are visiting comes down," the first female corrections officer yelled to all the women standing in line coming through the metal detectors.

Heat followed the line. This was new to her, so she didn't know what to expect.

"Thank God the line's moving fast today," the woman standing behind her said.

Heat ignored her, too worried about her clothes. *I hope they let me in. I'm not beat for the fuckery. .*

"Next person step up."

When Heat walked through the metal detector, the machine beeped.

"Step back and try it again," the guard said.

Heat stepped back out, then walked through again without the machine beeping.

"What you're wearing is not allowed," a female corrections officer said, looking Heat up and down.

Heat recognized Mercedes. *This bitch. Damn, I didn't want no drama today. I'm not feeling good. Aaron was right. She is a big, tall bitch. Speaking of Aaron, why can't I get in touch with him? I'm worried about him. That's not like him to not come by the house or call to even check on me.*

The correction officer repeated herself. "What you're wearing is not allowed."

"I drove all the way here to visit my man. I didn't know what I could and could not wear. But thank you, I will know next time."

"No, you don't get it. You won't be allowed in to see anyone wearing that today." Mercedes snarled.

"Well, I'm not leaving. Because I wasn't aware of a dress code until now. I need to speak to your superior."

"I am the one in charge over here today," Mercedes replied. Her gaze translated to Heat clearly. *Bitch, I know who you are. You not gettin' in here today. How 'bout that!*

Heat rolled her eyes. *Here we go.* "Well, you're gonna have to escort me out because I'm not leaving."

"That's not a problem. I get paid for this." Mercedes grabbed Heat and pulled her out of line.

The other women gazed at the commotion.

"Get your fuckin' hands off me!" Heat snatched her arm away.

"We can do this the easy way, or the hard way." Mercedes grabbed Heat's arm tighter.

"Like, for real, all this extra stuff is not necessary. Bitch, don't put your hands on me! I know why you're doin' this. You just mad that my man played you, and you're still bitter because you want what we got."

"Please, this has nothing to do with Samad. You're just not getting in here with that on." Mercedes removed her hands from Heat's arm.

"Officer Johnson, can you tell this visitor that she can't be dressed like that for a visit and she needs to change? She thinks I'm singling her out."

"It's not that bad, Best," Officer Johnson responded. "She probably didn't know."

"Johnson. Is she, or is she not violating the dress code policy?" Mercedes asked plainly.

"She is—but—"

"No buts. She's gotta go. I'm not dealing with uncooperative visitors. I'm leaving in five minutes to get breakfast, so let's make this a smooth transition. The easy way or the hard way!"

This toy cop bitch is obviously starting trouble with me, Heat thought. "You are being extra."

"Just like your outfit. Let's go."

Heat knew she wouldn't be able to get past Mercedes. "Fuck it then." Heat turned and walked out of the line. "Bitch!"

Mercedes walked behind Heat out into the first hall where nobody could see them. The two women were alone. Mercedes pointed to the exit. "Sorry, but next time dress appropriately when you come visit an inmate." Mercedes offered a devilish smile as Heat walked out the building. "Have a great day."

Heat exited the building upset. Exhausted from the baby, she sat in her truck listening to the radio and eating the apple and then the orange she left in a paperbag. She pulled out Samad's letter again.

Still hyped up about the incident, Heat pulled her notepad from her bag and wrote Samad about what just happened. The moment she finished penning all her aggression and frustration, she looked up and spotted Mercedes walking near her car.

"Well, well, well . . . Let's see if she's as tough on this side of the wall." *Can't stand this dirty bitch.* Heat got out the truck and raced toward Mercedes. As she placed her hand on her car door, Heat yanked her hair, turning her and startling her.

"Oh shit!" Mercedes said. "Bitch, go 'head on before I fuck you up."

Heat threw a punch that landed on Mercedes' jaw. "Fuck you, bitch! That's for playin' on my phone." The jab rocked Mercedes and sent her stumbling backward. She hit the ground and rolled over. Seeing the damage, Heat turned and walked to her truck.

It took Mercedes thirty seconds to reach Heat. She gripped her by her clothes and flung her like a rag doll. She cursed as she travelled across the cold, icy pavement and slammed to the ground on her stomach.

"Now you gotta buy a new shirt anyway, bitch!" Mercedes waved Heat off. "You lucky I didn't shoot you." She waited to see if Heat would get up, but she hadn't. "Sweetie, don't be mad at me 'cause I didn't let you in. You will not be seeing *our* man Samad today."

Heat placed both of her hands flat on the ground and pushed up. That's when Mercedes turned and walked away.

In seconds Heat was on her knees once the pain from the fall subsided. "Bitch. You think you bad because you have that uniform on?" she yelled as she hopped to her feet. She rushed Mercedes' from behind and flung her to the ground by her arm. Heat threw a left that connected with her cheek, just below her eye.

"I'm sick of you!" Mercedes screamed and kicked Heat in the stomach. She stood to her feet.

"Oooh!" Wincing and grunting, Heat doubled over in pain. For a moment Heat lost her breath.

"Go home, slut! You're not dressed appropriately."

Heat charged Mercedes, then grabbed a handful of her hair, and punched her face repeatedly.

"Get the fuck off me, bitch!" Mercedes yelled as she fought Heat off and tried twisting out of her grasp. Instead of facing Heat, her back was toward her from all the tussling.

Heat kicked her in the back and she fell forward. The hard contact with the concrete dazed her long enough for Heat to get away.

"Now bitch. Tell Samad I said hello when you see him." Heat rushed inside her truck and drove off fast.

CHAPTER 14
Be Very Clear

Where the hell is Heat? Inside the day room, Samad waited patiently to go downstairs for his visit to begin. He looked through the glass outside and saw only Pezo.

Mercedes walked out of the room marked 'infirmary' and headed to the day room. She stopped at the glass and stared at Samad as she continued to wipe her face with the baby wipe. She placed the drink holder filled with orange juice and the McDonald's bags down on the table.

To the right he saw Mercedes through the glass. It looked as if she was wiping something off her face. *Fuck wrong with her? Look like she been in a brawl.* Samad stared at her, but he did not crack one smile. *I hate this girl.*

Mercedes sent another officer to take him to the room in the back, the same room they always fucked in.

"Come with me. My superior told me to take you in that other room over there. I guess you must be somebody important," the officer joked as he gestured to Samad to follow him.

Samad looked this new rookie corrections officer over. He stood up and stretched, already knowing the routine. Even though he didn't like Mercedes, he never turned down the opportunity to fuck her, or let her suck his dick while he was in jail.

The officer handcuffed Samad's left hand to the bar near the bench, then left Samad in the room alone, closing the door behind him.

Mercedes walked in the secret room and closed the door. She unlocked Samad's cuffs and kissed his neck. Samad moved his head away. She gave Samad a flirty look with love in her eyes. She handed him the McDonald's breakfast sandwich. He ate the sandwich fast and sipped the orange juice quickly.

"The only reason I'm tolerating you behind this wall is because you're just a piece of ass while I'm locked up. And you let my workers slip drugs through. So be very clear on what this is," Samad said with ice in his words.

Mercedes did not care. She loved Samad and wanted any piece of him she could get. "I know that. You told me already. I hear you. That's what your mouth says. But that's not what that says." She pointed at his dick and smiled as infatuation gleamed in her eyes.

Filthy slut, Samad thought. "Nobody outside can know about us." He dropped his pants and underwear to his ankles.

"Your boy Pezo downstairs in the visit room waiting to see you. Let's hurry up. No managers or supervisors are here. I'm the one in charge today. I just got back from picking up this breakfast. I don't want to be away from my post downstairs long." She pulled her pants down with no panties on and sat on top of Samad, fucking him raw. "Happy Valentine's Day, daddy."

Samad stood up from the chair and turned her around. He bent her over the table and rammed his dick in her pussy.

"Ahhh," Mercedes moaned while Samad stroked deeper inside her, fucking her forcefully with no emotion.

Today, Samad finished quickly, busting his nut and pulling out, letting his cum explode on her back. He abruptly stopped and pushed Mercedes off when Heat's beautiful face popped in his thoughts. He fixed his clothes, then reached inside the McDonald's bag and pulled the concealed drugs out from under the food, stuffing it down his boxers, securing it between his balls.

Mercedes fixed her clothes and walked out of the room first. Samad waited a moment until the officer returned to escort him downstairs. He walked quietly ahead of the officer to the visit room.

Once he reached the large area, he looked around at all the other inmates visiting with their family. He searched for Heat but spotted Pezo in the corner seat. As he walked through the room, he gave dap and a few handshakes to other inmates he knew from the streets.

"What's good, Pezo? Where's Heat?"

"I spoke to her last night, and she said she was going to drive up here on her own. She's probably tired from her classes. Maybe she will come up here on the afternoon visit. I gave her the directions and the times of your visits."

"Okay. Thanks for taking care of everything for me. Make sure you check on Heat when you leave here."

"Of course, I'm going to check on Heat, no question. Maybe she left me a message or something. My phone's downstairs in the locker.

"I need to get out of here and get back to my life outside."

"Weinstein will be here today to go over what's going on with your case."

"Yeah, I know. Mike been in touch with my lawyer too. Him and Will been coming up here to visit, keeping me in the loop with everything. I heard Moe and Bono had some words back and forth. What's going on with that?"

"Yeah, they having problems in their camp. I don't have all the details, but I will report back to you when I come up here next week. But what I can tell you is, they losing a lot of money, so no need to worry about them. Everything is good on our end. That's all you need to worry about, boss man. Business is great."

"I need to get out of here and get back to my family. But let's get down to business. You got the stuff?"

"Yeah." Pezo went in his pants and pulled out a small bag and handed it to Samad under the table. Mercedes turned her back.

"I gotta leave right away and take care of something out there. My peoples following up on that Born situation. My connect out in Miami not answering his phone, so I need to check on that situation too. Something's up."

"Okay, thanks, Pezo. Yeah, let me know what's going on with that Miami situation. I'm going back upstairs, so I can give out this work. Good looking. Be safe out there."

"Be safe in here," Pezo said as he stood and hugged Samad.

Samad hugged Pezo back. "I'm good in here, trust me." He looked over Pezo's shoulder, glancing at Mercedes through the glass.

CHAPTER 15
Blood on her hands

Heat stopped at the traffic light, angry after driving back home for over two hours. "I can't believe that bitch turned me around after I drove to this damn jail!" She banged on the steering wheel. "I wasn't even allowed to visit my man, the father of my fucking child! I can't stand that bitch!" Tears fell as she pressed her foot down hard on the accelerator. " . . . Bitch get on my nerves!" She wiped away a few tears that fell. "Wait until I have this baby. I'm gon' whoop her ass how I really want to."

Realizing that a cop might be anywhere, she slowed her speed and let the teardrops fall. She felt a few dull pains in her stomach and winced. The longer she drove, the stronger the cramps became. After another ten minutes of driving, Heat felt wetness between her legs. She put her hand between her legs, looked at her hand, and saw blood. "Oh my God!" She panicked, feeling even sharper stomach pains.

She got off at the next exit and turned on Lakeview Street, realizing she was only five minutes away from Saint Matthew's hospital.

Heat parked in the visitor parking lot by the emergency room. "Ahhhh," she moaned as another sharp pain shot through her belly. She felt so alone. No one was around to help her. While looking out the window she spotted a familiar face walking out of the emergency door.

Although Samad mentioned Moe as being one of his enemies, and warned Heat to stay away from him, she didn't see the harm in asking for his help right now. She beeped the horn to get his attention.

Moe squinted and approached the vehicle. He smiled when he recognized Heat. She rolled the window down.

"Hey, Heat. What's goin' on? What you doin' here?"

She grunted before speaking. "Moe, I'm having really bad cramps in my side. I just came from visiting Samad at the jail, and I got into it with one of them corrections officers. She used to fuck with Samad. Ahhh." Heat grabbed her stomach.

"You must be talking about Mercedes. Crazy bitch." Moe shook his head. "Let me help you." Moe was surprised Heat knew that much about Samad's past. He opened the door and helped her out of the car. She wrapped her arm around his firm back and they slowly walked toward the entrance.

"What are you doing up here?" Heat asked, breathing through another strong cramp.

"I'm visiting my aunt. She broke her foot. She's going to be here for a while."

"Ay yo!" Moe yelled at the EMT workers walking toward the entrance with a wheelchair. "Can somebody bring that wheelchair over here, please? She's having pains in her stomach."

The EMT rushed over to them and placed Heat in the wheelchair. "How long have you been having pains, ma'am?"

"Almost an hour. I'm three months pregnant and leaking blood."

"How bad is the pain?"

Moe looked at Heat's stomach when she said three months pregnant. "Oh wow! I didn't know that," Moe said, going with her to the kiosk.

After a few more questions from the nurse, Heat was placed on a bed and sent up to a room immediately. Her temperature and blood pressure were too high and her back was killing her.

The doctor examined her, and two hours later he informed Heat that she'd lost the baby. The sheets had to be changed several times after she'd passed several blood clots and finally the fetus. Moe stayed the entire time, waiting quietly outside. She was given a sedative and slept for a few hours. Once she awakened, she spotted Moe on her right sitting in a chair.

"Heat, did you get a chance to call somebody on your way here? Your girls Unique and Ebony? Your mother? Aaron?"

"Yes. I called my man's friend, and I left him a message telling him where I am. He should be on his way. Thank you for staying here with me, Moe."

"You're welcome. Sorry about your loss. I hope you feel better."

Pezo walked in the room.

"Speaking of the devil," Heat said. "Thanks for your company, Moe."

"No problem. Feel better." Moe stood. "What's up, Pezo?" he greeted.

Pezo glanced at Heat, then turned his focus on Moe. "You being in here is what's up," he replied.

"I'm glad somebody was here to help me," Heat said, ending the stare down between Pezo and Moe.

"I'm outta here. Take care, sweetheart." Moe made his exit from the room.

Pezo stood next to Heat's bed. "What the hell is Moe doing anywhere near you?" he asked.

"I'm doing fine, Pezo. Oh yeah, I just lost the baby a few hours ago. I also had a fight with that bitch Mercedes at the jail—but thank you for being concerned," she replied sarcastically and wiped away a tear that fell.

"I'm sorry, Heat. Damn . . . How long have you been here?"

"About three hours."

"Sorry . . ." Pezo grabbed her hand and squeezed it. "I came as soon as I left visiting Samad. I listened to your message. That's fucked up Mercedes was trippin' and wouldn't let you in."

"Fuck that bitch! I'll deal with her another time. I left a message on my mother's phone. I can't get in touch with her. Can you call Ebony and Unique for me?"

"I already called them when I heard your message. They should be here by now, or on their way."

"Thanks. How was Samad?"

"He was in good spirits. Upbeat, you know how he is. Nothing gets to him."

"Ahhh. I got more pain meds. They need to hurry up with some more pills."

"Sit tight, Heat. Let me get you a nurse."

"Okay."

Unique and Ebony entered as Pezo was leaving out. They exchanged a few words and Pezo left. Heat smiled at the sight of her girls showing up right away.

"Hey girl," Ebony said, kissing Heat on her forehead. Unique did the same.

Heat wasn't in the mood for a pity party, so she got right to the matter at hand. "Girl, me and that bitch Mercedes—Samad's old bitch—had a fight at the jail. On Valentines day!"

"What!" Ebony said.

"Oh, hell naw. We gon' get wit' that bitch!" Unique said.

"Yeah girl, and she didn't let me in to see Samad. This was my first time going to the jail—haven't seen him in three whole months—and this bitch said I couldn't get in because of what I had on."

115

"Girl, your hair looks a mess," Unique said as she pulled Heat's hair up in a ponytail and put a rubber band on it.

"Thank you, Unique," Heat said sarcastically, trying to keep a straight face, but winced as a sharp pain struck.

"What's taking them so long with the pain meds?" Ebony asked.

"I don't know. That's why Pezo went out there to the nurse's station."

"I'll be right back," Ebony said, leaving Heat and Unique alone.

Unique sat down beside Heat. She stared at Unique for quite a while.

Her face looked as if she attempted to cover up a black eye with make up, but she'd done a terrible job of it.

"I had a miscarriage, Unique," Heat finally said.

Unique looked at Heat, surprised. "Oh my god! For real?"

"Yes. Can you believe I lost my baby on Valentines day. This holiday is *never* going to be the same for me. I'm in sooo much pain. Ahhh," Heat grunted through another stabbing cramp.

The nurse came in and gave Heat two white pills and a cup of water. She asked Heat if she needed anything else and left once Heat nodded no and thanked her for the pain relievers.

"Can I be honest with you, Heat?"

"Of course. Why you ask me that?"

"'Cause I don't want you to get mad at me."

"I won't get mad. You must got something smart to say." Heat rolled her eyes.

"Not smart. But you gon' think it's mean. But . . . I don't know . . . since being in a relationship with Sean, I think different about stuff than I used to."

"Go 'head, Unique. What is it?"

"Maybe having a miscarriage wasn't a bad thing. I mean . . . I've heard some things about Samad."

"Like. What?"

"Not to make you upset or anything, but I heard he's very controlling, and he's got abusive tendencies. So maybe losing the baby wasn't a bad thing. I mean, not saying it like that . . . but—"

Heat cut Unique off. "What! You sound crazy right now, Unique. My child just died!"

"I know, Heat, and I'm really sorry about that. I really am. But I'm just saying . . . I'm glad you met him, and he took your mind off Eli, but are you really ready for a baby? I mean, you're going to school to become a psychologist one day. On top of that, I hear a lot of girls be calling him, and he's got a lot of bitches fighting over him."

"Look, Unique, I'm not in the fucking mood for that right now."

"Well, damn, Heat. I was just saying—"

"Well, don't just say. Keep your comments to your motherfuckin' self!"

"I'm sorry." Unique got up out of the chair and walked to the window. Heat heard her snifling. *I'm the one who should be crying. My baby's gone.* The more Heat thought about Sean beating up on Unique, the less mad she became. *She deserves to cry too. She deserves someone better than Sean's trifling ass.*

Ebony returned to the room.

"The nurse came in already, Ebony," Unique said.

"I'm going to fuck that bitch Mercedes up for making me lose my baby," Heat said.

She stared at Unique as her harsh words echoed in her head. *Maybe having a miscarriage wasn't a bad thing. I mean . . . I've heard some things about Samad. Not to make you upset or anything, but I've heard he's very controlling, and he's got abusive tendencies. So maybe losing the baby wasn't a bad thing . . .*

Those comments left Heat pondering the condition of their friendship. *Would a real friend say that to another friend? Does she really have my well-being at heart? I don't think so. Who's been feeding Unique all this bad shit about Samad?*

CHAPTER 16
Hospital Fever

Four days later . . .

"Like I fuckin' said. Don't question me on who I went to Miami with, boy. I told you I was in Miami with a friend of mine. He's just a friend! Fuck you too then! Hello? Hello? Oh, this nigga mad and wanna hang up," Ebony said with a tight frown on her face. She'd just walked into Heat's hospital room and bumped into the doctor.

"Oops. I'm so sorry." Ebony smiled as she passed him.

"Take those two pain pills. I'll be back later." The doctor told Heat, then turned and walked out the door.

"Hey, Heat. How ya doin' today, mama?" Ebony gave her a gentle hug.

"A bit better. Still hurting though." *Who was she arguing with all loud on the phone? I heard her big mouth in here. When did Ebony go to Miami? I'm so out of it; I don't even know how long I've been here. I don't even have the energy to ask her about her shenanigans.*

"I picked up your mail from your post office box." She handed Heat her mail. I just came to drop it off. I can't stay long. I gotta go handle some business."

Heat took the mail out of Ebony's hand. "Thank you. You're starting to sound like Samad and Aaron," Heat said, hoping Ebony took her comment to heart.

"Yeah right. Sooooo, I spoke to your mother. She said she got your message, and she's been calling up here, they've been giving her the run around. Her doctor advised her to stay in bed, walking pneumonia is serious. She wants you to know not to worry about her, and she wants you to get your strength up, and feel better. I drove your truck to Aaron, he parked it for you he got your keys. I saw him when I went by the barbershop. He told me to give you this in case you need anything while you're up here. He said you know how he feels about hospitals, and for you to call him when you get situated."

Ebony handed Heat three hundred dollars. Heat took the money and laid it on the nightstand. She placed the large stack of mail on her lap, then pulled the rubber bands off all the mail.

"Later y'all. I got a cab waiting for me. Let me let some light in here first." Ebony opened the blinds to let sunlight in the room. Heat waved good-bye.

"I'll call you later, Ebony," Unique said as she squinted from the bright sun now shining in the room.

Heat tried to reach the pain pills the doctor left on the tray. Unique saw her struggling and knew she was still in pain. "Let me move the tray closer to you." Still pissed over the comments Unique made about Samad and the baby, Heat did not reply.

She rolled Heat's tray closer to her bed anyway, so she wouldn't have to strain and reach for the tray. Unique realized Heat was still deep in her feelings. Heat finally had enough of the silence.

"Unique, where are you getting information about Samad from, especially the things you told me?"

"Heat, right now is not a good time. Just relax. You've been through a lot. We can talk about that another time."

"Hmph." Heat cut her eyes at Unique. She flipped through the mail and the magazines and stopped when she saw Samad's letter. She placed the rest of the mail on the side of the bed and opened Samad's letter.

Dear Heat,

I hope this letter reaches you in the best of health, baby. I miss you and I love you.

I heard about your visit up here at the jail and that bitch Mercedes blocked you from coming in here to visit me. I should have warned you about what to wear. They don't play when it comes to the dress code. I didn't think she would give you a hard time either.

I'm sorry I wasn't able to protect you from a fight with this bitch. She's beneath you. I can't believe this bitch is the reason you had a miscarriage. You don't even know what I'm feelin' right now about the baby. Sorry I can't be there to comfort you.

Also I heard from my man, Pezo. That nigga Moe was at the hospital with you the day you lost the baby? How did you bump into that dude? What was he doing in your room? I will deal with that too.

Take care of yourself out there.
I love you.
Samad 7400

Heat closed the letter, then reached for the two sedatives near the food tray and lay on her side. After fifteen minutes, she drifted off, fast asleep.

She awoke and looked around the room. Ebony was going into the bathroom with the pitcher of water. Unique was asleep on the lounge chair near the window. Heat drifted back to sleep.

Her room door opened.

Moe entered and walked over to Heat's bed and kissed her on the forehead. He walked to the door, ready to exit.

Ebony walked out the bathroom wearing a surprised look when she saw Moe. Unique woke up from the movements in the room.

Moe surprised them both. He held a bouquet of flowers and a teddy bear in his left hand.

"Hey, Moe. What you doing up here?" Ebony asked.

"I'm on my way to see my aunt down the hall. She's on the same floor. I just wanted to stick my head in here and say hello."

Ebony walked to the door. "Now is not a good time. She lost her baby," she whispered in a low tone.

"Yeah, I know. I was here during the whole thing, and I'm really sorry to hear that," Moe said with genuine concern.

"Oh really? I didn't know you were up here with her?" Ebony looked over at Heat sleeping peacefully.

"Who are the flowers and teddy bear for? Heat, or your aunt?" Ebony asked.

"I was going to give this to my aunt, but here, give Heat this teddy bear when she wakes up. I'm about to go see my aunt before the rest of the family comes up here. When she wakes up, tell her I said I hope she feels better." Ebony took the teddy bear.

Unique stood and walked to the bathroom. "Moe, that's sweet of you, and thank you for checking on her."

"The doctor just gave her some pain pills, so she's going to be out for a while. She needs to rest anyway."

"I understand. Let me get to my aunt's room. Take care of her," Moe said.

"We will," Ebony replied with an interesting smile. She placed the teddy bear on the side of Heat's bed.

As Moe was leaving, Pezo entered Heat's room. Moe walked by without a word to Pezo.

"This is the second time I saw this nigga around Heat. I know Samad won't like that." Pezo pointed his thumb as he took a seat at Heat's bedside.

"What's up, Pezo?" Ebony said.

Unique walked out of the bathroom. "Good morning," she said.

"Hey, what's up, y'all?" Pezo looked at Heat asleep on her side. He saw the teddy bear sitting on the bed and frowned.

"What the fuck is Moe tryna pull? I gotta holla at my man, Samad."

CHAPTER 17
Playing with Fire

I got some major decisions to make. Maybe I wasn't ready to have that baby after all. Maybe Unique was right. Maybe it wasn't meant to be right now. What am I going to do with my life? Here I am 18 years old. I lost my baby, my man's still in jail locked up. What am I going to do with my life?

Heat sat on the edge of the bed and glanced over at her clothes neatly folded. When she looked at the flowers, she smiled and thought how nice Moe had been since she'd been hospitalized. Every day she woke up to a fresh bouquet of flowers, or a dozen roses, and a teddy bear.

Heat twisted the top off the bottle water and took a sip. The door opened. She thought the other nurse was coming in to clean up. "Thank you for everything. I put the dirty sheets and towels in the—" Heat stopped talking at the sight of Moe. She smiled. "Moe?"

He smiled also. "Good morning, beautiful." Moe glanced down at the slightly opened overnight suitcase. Her clothes were packed. "Oh, you leaving today?"

"Yeah, I'm ready to go. The other day one of the doctors told me I was leaving Monday. But the doctor that came in here earlier said he was releasing me today."

"I know you ready to get out of here."

"Yes. Ready to eat some real food." She pushed her food tray away.

"Ahhhh." Moe laughed. "You got a ride home? Is somebody picking you up?"

"I left a message for Ebony and Unique before I got in the shower, letting them know I was getting out of the hospital today instead of Monday. I can't get in touch with my brother. And I didn't want my mother to come up here. She's still sick."

"You call anybody else?"

"No. I didn't call Pezo yet to tell him they changed my release date. I might just take a cab home."

Moe nodded. "Well, don't worry. It's no problem for me to take you home. I just came from visiting my aunt down the hall. Her foot wasn't healing right. She won't be leaving this place for another week."

"Oh, I'm sorry to hear that."

"She'll be a'ight." He broke their eye contact and looked at the floor. "So how are you feeling, Heat?"

"Better. I'm so ready to leave this place."

"Well, since I'm here, it's no problem for me to take you home. I mean, if you want me to drive you home. It's no problem to me at all."

Heat smiled, then looked around the room. "I am ready to go. Thank you. I'll be ready in five minutes."

After driving in an unfamiliar direction, Heat finally asked. "Where are you going?"

"Whole Foods. You need organic healthy stuff. My treat."

"But you don't have to—"

"I want to," Moe said, pulling into the Whole Foods parking lot.

Forty minutes later, Moe and Heat walked back to his car and put the two bags of food in the trunk.

"You really didn't have to take me to Whole Foods and get all of this stuff. Thanks though. I do appreciate it."

"It's only two bags of groceries. It's not a lot. I just want to make sure you're taken care of—I mean—I just want to make sure you are okay, being that you had to eat that nasty hospital food."

"Yeah, yeah, yeah." Heat smirked.

"Ahhh." Moe laughed. "You know it tasted like cardboard."

"Ahhh." Heat laughed. "You're right. But my girls brought me some food up there too."

Heat wiped protein powder out of her hair. You must be bad luck or something. How did that protein powder in the plastic container spill all over me? It's all in my hair." Moe brushed the rest of the powder out of Heat's hair.

"Ha. That wasn't my fault." They shared a quick laugh.

Moe opened the door and let her in the passenger side. Then he walked around to the driver side to get in. Heat leaned over to unlock his door, and she pushed the driver's side door open so he could get in.

As Moe got in, he tried to suppress a smile and started the car. The music came blasting through the speakers. He turned it all the way down.

"I like that Usher song. Turn that up a little."

Bobbing his head, Moe turned the music up. "Okay, you ready to go home?"

"Yup." Heat put her seatbelt on and rested her head against the seat.

They rode off listening to Usher's song, "You Make Me Wanna."

Moe pulled up in front of her house. Heat stared out the passenger window looking for her brother's black jeep to no avail.

"Nobody's home. Thank you for the flowers and teddy bear. My girls told me you left them for me when I was sleep." Heat avoided looking at Moe. She glanced up and down her block. It was empty of people and traffic.

"No problem. I'm glad you feel better." Moe touched Heat's hand catching her off guard and sending a chill up her spine. She turned to face Moe. They stared at each other for a moment. Silence filled the car. Heat turned away.

"Thank you again." She took her seatbelt off and got out of the car quickly.

Moe smiled. "Let me help you with the bags."

She grabbed her overnight bag from his backseat, then closed his door. He walked Heat to the front porch.

"Thank you for making sure I got home. I really appreciate all of your help."

Moe smiled. "You're welcome."

"So what's on your agenda, now that you are no longer pregn—" Moe caught himself. "So what's your plans moving forward?"

"Well, I start my classes Monday—got a lot of make up work to do, and right after that I start my internship."

"Oh, that's great. Is it too soon for you to, you know, move around and stuff? How does your body feel?"

"I feel fine. That's the reason they kept me in the hospital so long, to make sure I healed properly. I felt a little cramping, but the doctor said that's normal. It should subside. He gave me pain pills."

"Oh, okay. If you need anything just call me." He handed her his card. Heat took it and stuffed it in her jacket pocket.

"Well, tell me about this internship, Miss College Lady," Moe said.

"Well, it's a paid internship learning firsthand under both a high level social worker, and a well-respected psychologist. One of my guidance counselors from my old high school plugged me in to some people she knows very well. A few college professors are looking out for me, too.

"At least I will have my own money coming in since . . . I mean, I gotta do something for myself."

Samad flashed in her head. "Look, I gotta go. Thanks again, Moe." She opened her front door.

Moe stepped inside the house right by the doorway, placing the two bags down on the table against the wall by the front door. "Take care of yourself, Heat." He gently kissed her hand.

Blushing from embarrassment, Heat couldn't hide her smile. "I will. Bye, Moe." Heat turned and walked in her house, closing the door behind her. But someone was holding the door, keeping it from closing.

"Oh, this nigga Moe playin' with fire," Pezo said, staring at Heat's surprised expression. "Whatever the fuck you doing, you better cut this shit out!" Pezo warned.

"Were you here when I called you, Pezo?" Heat felt anger rising. "Were you? Huh?"

"Naw, but I'm here now."

"Late as shit!"

"I'll remember to tell Samad you said that."

"Fuck you, Pezo! Tell Samad! Do what you gotta do." She rolled her eyes. They both watched Moe slowly pull off.

"This mutha—" Pezo said as Moe's Porsche turned the corner.

"When you tell Samad about Moe, make sure you don't leave out the part that you played—being late instead of helping me get home right away so I can start the healing process. Ugh!" Heat walked inside, preparing herself for the letter Samad would write her about consorting with his enemies. It was as if no one gave a fuck about her losing a child. No one.

"Fuck Samad, too," she mumurred. He was miles away probably watching TV, shooting dice, or playing cards. "Tell him that too, Pezo!"

CHAPTER 18
Welcome Home

Five years later . . .
Summer 2005

"Where do you wanna go first?" Mike asked a newly released Samad.

"To a few spots so I can get fresh, and then I'm going home to see Heat."

"I checked on a few of your stores and checked the books. Some of your business wasn't handled right by Pezo. I'm not really sure how close Heat was watching him. She's been busy with finishing school, so her mind was not on your business like it was supposed to be. A lot of money is missing. Also, one of your stores got broken into."

"Oh really? Heat didn't tell me that."

"Yeah, also I told him to give me ten stacks so I can pay some of your other workers on the lower east side Harlem. Some workers still didn't get their money this week. Heat was supposed to go over there and meet Pezo and everybody, but she left them hanging."

"Oh word?"

"Yeah. She thought Pezo was going to handle it since he was already there in Harlem, and he thought she was going to handle it. They weren't communicating. She stopped returning calls and just let

Pezo handle stuff. I think she felt some type of way when Pezo told you Moe was hanging around her at the hospital back when she lost the baby. She's been holding a grudge against him ever since. I heard Moe was in the crowd at her college graduation too. I don't know if she knew he was there, but you need to watch him around her, boss man."

"Thanks for that information, Mike. Heat was supposed to follow up and make sure everybody was paid."

"Aaron really stepped up to the plate though, S."

"That's what's up. Aaron always been a stand-up dude."

"Yeah, he filled your shoes and made sure everybody was on point doing what they were supposed to do. We got worried one time when we couldn't get in touch with Aaron. We thought something happened to him. But he didn't have his phone charger with him. Also, he didn't know anybody's number off hand to call from another phone. His phone was dead. But when he got back, he made sure he remembered *everybody's* number by heart." Mike laughed.

Samad didn't. "Yeah, that's good. Because in this business if you don't make contact once you reach your destination, everybody always thinks the worst."

"True . . . very true. We were worried for a moment."

Iyana sat in the backseat texting on her phone. She interrupted their business talk. "I'm glad you home, big brother. I missed you. I don't know why you with Heat. Mercedes is the one for you. She will always be my sister. I like her better anyway."

Mercedes, who also was sitting in the backseat smiled. "Iyana, you know your brother's not gonna ever let me go. I don't care how many years it's been. Samad is, and will always be my man. We got history together. I loved you then, and I still love you today."

Turning, Samad looked at Mercedes and Iyana. One day he was going to kill Mercedes for making Heat lose their child. He needed to wait for the right moment. *As soon as I get all of my money this bitch been holding for me it's a wrap for her.*

Samad flashed a fake smile at Mercedes. "That right there will always be mine." He pointed at her pussy.

She giggled.

"Eww, get a room!" Iyana complained.

Mike had grown closer to Heat, although at first he thought he'd have to murk her. Now he couldn't stand Mercedes. Even though this was Samad's call to have Mercedes ride with them, he couldn't wait for this ride to be over.

As soon as Mike turned the corner, a cop put his siren on. He spoke through the bullhorn. "Pull over."

Samad turned and looked through the back window. "They just tryna fuck with me because I'm out now. Do these motherfuckers get it on their texts when

134

real niggas like me come home?" Samad reclined back in his seat.

Mike pulled over. The cop walked over to the driver side. "Do you know you have a broken light in the back?"

"No, I didn't know that," he replied.

"May I have your license and registration?" the officer asked.

Mike reached over to the glove compartment to retrieve his information. The cop leaned in to see who was in the truck. Samad looked the cop right in his eyes. The cop turned away from Samad and looked in the backseat. He recognized Mercedes.

"Best, how are you today?"

"Good, how are you, Rizzo? These are my people. They're okay."

Mike handed him the registration and license. The cop just looked at it. Then he handed it back to him. "Make sure you get that light fixed."

"Sure," Mike replied.

"Have a good day." The cop walked back to his car and sat there until they drove off.

"I can't stand police," Samad said.

Mercedes cut her eyes at Samad.

Mike continued to drive for another twenty minutes before reaching his destination.

"Roll the windows up," Samad ordered. "Good, you got tints on the windows, so nobody in the barbershop will know it's me. I'm not ready for anybody to know I'm home yet."

Mike parked by the barbershop, rolled all the windows up, then turned the AC on. Iyana got out of the truck and waved good-bye. Mike made his exit as well. Samad slid over into the driver's seat, and Mercedes climbed from the backseat into the front passenger seat. She reached in the backseat and grabbed the duffel bag, placing it on her lap.

Mike stood by the driver side window. Samad rolled the window down a little. "I'ma need these wheels for the week to make my rounds. I need to get fresh and make a few pop up visits to a few people. Shit about to get real serious now that I'm out. I got a lot of loose ends I need to handle. A lot of shit about to change. Watch what I tell you."

"Go handle your business, boss man. Holla at me when you get yourself settled."

Samad looked over to Mercedes, who sat there cheesing her face off. "I'll hit you a little later when I'm done," he told Mike.

"Later," Mike said, smirking at Mercedes. He walked off murmuring something under his breath.

"One." Samad rolled the window up, then drove off.

Mercedes turned to Samad. "Let's hurry up, so I can deposit this money. The bank closes in five minutes."

Samad looked at the bag of money on her lap. "I understand you want me to keep all the money you made behind the wall in a separate lockbox. Why didn't you ask Heat to put it in her account? I mean, she is your girl and all . . ."

He shot her a deadly glare. "Don't worry about that. I told you never mention Heat's name. Ever!"

Mercedes received satisfaction from already knowing Heat didn't know about her and Samad after all of these years. "I love you, Samad. And I always will."

Looking at the watch on his arm, Samad hit the steering wheel once he glimpsed the traffic ahead. He made a left turn off the main street and took the back street coming around to the side of the bank. He pulled up slow, realizing he had just missed the banking hours. He saw the locked doors then pulled off.

Samad drove to a local hotel off the highway and pulled around back. "Go pay for the room," he ordered Mercedes. She put the bag in the seat and stepped out the truck heading to the front desk.

As she walked away, Samad kept his snarl intact. His hatred for Mercedes grew with her every step. He reached over and grabbed the duffel back and unzipped it. When he saw the stacks and stacks of money, he smiled and closed the bag and zipped it back.

Mercedes returned ten minutes later with the room key and handed it to Samad. "Pull around to room 702," she said.

He located a parking space, parked the car, and hopped out the truck. Mercedes followed. Samad unlocked the room and walked in kicking his boots off. She strolled into the room already knowing what time it was. In seconds she stepped out of her pink sundress and was down to her bra and panties.

Roughly, Samad grabbed her and ripped her bra as he tugged on it. He turned her and pulled her panties down, then bent her over the lounge chair.

"Ahhh," Mercedes moaned as Samad rammed his dick in her pussy from the back. After a few minutes, he pulled out, then pushed his dick in her ass, fucking her forcefully.

Mercedes bit her bottom lip as he whispered in her ear, "You better never let Heat know about this." Samad pulled her hair. She thrust her ass back as Samad pounded her out until he exploded.

"I love it when you fuck me in my ass. Ooh, yes daddy!"

He growled and grunted like a wild animal. Pumping in and out of her tight asshole. He felt himself about to cum and pulled out, exploding on her lower back covering her tattoo and all over her ass.

Samad entered the bathroom and turned on the shower, washing up thoroughly but quickly. He dried off and dressed in a hurry. Mercedes walked in the bathroom as he was walking out. He kissed her on the mouth and smacked her ass.

"I left you something on the bed, Samad. Welcome home."

"I'll be in touch when I'm finished running around."

"Okay, daddy." She beamed as she walked in the bathroom, turning the shower on.

Rushing to the bed, Samad opened the duffel bag that Mercedes had been carrying. He smiled. Besides the stacks of cash she held for him over the years, she included a bottle of Polo cologne, his favorite. He sprayed a lot of the scent on his neck and all over his clothes. He wanted to make sure he did not have Mercedes' smell on him, even after his quick shower.

Satisified with the amount of cash, he stuffed some of the money in his jeans pocket, closed the bag, and grabbed his keys. He left Mercedes in the hotel room.

One hour later, Samad drove across town through the streets in a trance, reminiscing about the time he'd lost and the years he missed out of his life. He promised himself he would never go back to jail. Thoughts of all the years he fucked Mercedes at the jail, and even though he couldn't stand her when he first went in, he had to admit over the years he'd grown a soft spot in his heart for her. She was loyal. He decided he would keep her close by for now until she got out of pocket. That would be his secret. As he drove through his blocks, his next moves were his only concern. *I'm back now,* Samad thought. *I'ma deal with that nigga Moe real soon.*

Chapter 19
Pure Silence

"Where is he?" Heat asked aloud, looking at the clock on the cable box again. "It's 7:00 p.m. See, I *knew* I should've gone with Mike. Talkin' 'bout he don't want me to see him as soon as he step out of jail until he get fresh and get a haircut." *I saw him when he was sleeping, clean, dirty, snot-nosed. Boy, please! I've seen him at his worse!*

Every time she heard a car, she ran to the window. Only to see it was one of her neighbors pulling into their own driveway, or opening up their own gates. Samad's release made her reminisce about the baby she had once carried but lost. *If I hadn't lost our baby, our baby would be four years old now, turning five. It's all good though. Everything happens for a reason. Things are going great. I finally got my degree. Samad is finally out of jail. We can finally move forward with our life.*

Click.

The lock turning made her heart beat faster, and then it dropped! She knew Samad was fumbling with the keys. Heat smiled and went in the kitchen to make him a plate of his favorite food.

She heard him carefully walking around in the living room, and pictured him scanning the newly redecorated house equipped with brand new, state of the art electronics and appliances.

"Yo!" he yelled out. "Ma! Nobody home? What's good?"

She heard him in the bedroom kicking his Timberlands off and decided to stay in the kitchen until he got settled in. "In a minute, baby. I'll be right out. I'm making your plate," she replied.

"Smells good too! I need a home cooked meal!"

"Damn, after missing my baby, you'd think she would have a king's robe and slippers ready and waiting at the door!" he said playfully. "Where's my dinner, woman? I'm starvin'!" he teased. "I miss you. Where you at? Damn, I need to see your face." He went looking in every room, peeking his head in and out of the rooms while walking through the house.

"Hello?"

She walked out of the kitchen and down the hall. He stopped in his tracks upon seeing her. Staring at her, longing for her touch, her kiss. "Finally."

"A vision of beauty. A sight for sore eyes." His voice dropped to a whisper. "Damn, I missed you, mamí! Come to daddy."

Heat melted from his sexy voice and the look on her man's face. She noticed his beautiful body was more sculptured and toned. She admired his wonderful physique up top, muscles bulging through his white wife beater.

Samad held a light blue Tiffany jewelry box with a white ribbon in his right hand. She ran to her baby. Everything seemed to go in slow motion. He wrapped his arms around her waist, lifting her up in his strong arms. Heat wrapped her arms around his neck, and Samad buried his face in her neck, inhaling her familiar scent.

"I missed you too, daddy!" she whispered, matching his soft tone. They embraced. He ran his fingers through her hair. Tears of joy filled her eyes and raced down Heat's cheeks.

He felt her warm tears on his shoulders, dripping down his arm. Although Samad was a 'manly man' who 'never cried,' his tears slid down the back of her neck. She didn't turn to look him in his eyes, letting him have his moment. He gently stroked her hair while she sobbed softly. They needed to release the years of emptiness they held inside while being away from each other. Memories of Heat losing the baby flashed through Samad's mind. When they hugged they felt complete.

"Oh, baby. You're home." She began kissing his neck, cheek, and then gently bit his bottom lip. Slowly, Heat slid out of his arms and rubbed the sides of his body, feeling muscular ripples under his clothes.

"I missed you so much!"

"I missed you too, baby."

Gently, he placed both hands on her face, cupping her chin and lifting her head to meet his gaze. He wiped her tears away and gazed intensely into her beautiful, brown eyes. Samad planted small kisses on her nose, forehead, then her cheeks. Placing his lips on her lips, he playfully teased her with his tongue, kissing her passionately and hungrily.

She kissed him back ravenously, sucking his tongue. She knew her kisses *always* sent something throughout his entire body. Straight to his dick. Heat felt his hard dick brush against her stomach through his jeans. She dropped down to her knees, unzipped Samad's pants, and slid them down. His dick was poking out of the slit in his boxers. She smiled wickedly, then pecked the crown. Eager to satisfy her man, she swirled her tongue around it until pre-cum oozed out. She deep throated Samad right where he stood.

Holding her throat still, she tightened her throat muscles, then released them. Tightened them again, turning her head side to side, up and down, making circles with her head, letting the tip of his dick grind against the back of her throat. Pleasing her man the way he liked it. "Mmmmm," Heat moaned when she tasted her man, missing him in her mouth.

Bobbing up and down, she opened her mouth wider, letting the juices run down her mouth and along the sides, making sure it was nice and sloppy wet— sloppy-toppy, the way he liked it. She tightened her mouth.

Samad's eyes rolled in the back of his head. "Hmmm. *Yeah*, just like that Heat," he sang.

She repeated her technique, ready to bring him to climax. Heat slurped, kissed, licked, sucked, grinded, and tightened her throat muscles, letting him feel the back of her throat again. She knew he was about to bust.

Staying on her knees, she stopped moving, relaxed her throat muscles and swallowed his cum as it exploded in her mouth. Samad gripped her hair and held her head, looking down at her as he came. Heat wiped her lips.

"Damn, girl. I missed that!" he said, pulling Heat up off her knees and kissing her mouth. Samad pulled his pants up and zipped them.

Heat hugged him and kissed his cheek. "I know you do." She turned and walked to the bathroom. Samad slapped her on her ass.

"I just want to take a long hot shower in my own bathroom, get something to eat, fuck all night, and fall asleep in my own bed. I'm staying in the house with you."

Samad walked in the kitchen and saw his plate of food. He walked over to the stove, lifted the lid on each pot and inhaled. Although some of the food was burnt, he loved her for putting forth the effort, and making sure he was always fed. Heat was not that great of a cook, but she tried, and he loved her for that.

"My favorite." He ate a few forkfuls off his plate, then set the plate down on the table.

Samad remembered what Mike said about money being messed up. He headed to his safe in the other room. *Let me see what's going on in here.* His eyes were fixed on his safe. He turned the dial left, then right, then to the right again until he heard a click. The safe opened. Samad's face twisted up when he noticed a few stacks missing. He examined the contents and counted out fifty stacks.

"It was more than this when I left." He cursed. "Heat!" Samad yelled. "Come here!"

Heat walked out of the bathroom with her robe on and her hair wet from her shower. She stood by Samad near the safe.

"I know you said you used some of the money to pay the bills and redecorate, but damn! How much did you use?"

"Not that much. I needed to handle my business out here while you were locked up. What did you expect me to do for money?"

"I know you needed money to maintain, but not for you to go fucking crazy on a spending spree! When some of my workers aren't paid, and it's money missing, that makes me wonder what you were doing all this time."

"What you mean, Samad? I was handlin' your business. Also, uh hello! Did you forget my college tuition? School kept me busy all these years. How about a congratulations on your Sociology degree Heat, instead of all of these questions. So what, I went shopping here and there, and treated myself to a few day spas, manicures, and pedicures. Not to mention redecorating this place." She gestured her hand around the room. "But I handled what needed to be handled."

He shook his head. "That's not what I heard. When's the last time you sat down with Pezo and went over the books." He looked at Heat when she hesitated to respond.

Heat looked down when she spoke.

"You about to lie. I can see it coming a mile away," Samad said.

"No I'm not." She could never look Samad in the face when she lied.

"So when was the last time you and Pezo hooked up to go over the books?"

"Last week. I was supposed to meet him in Harlem, but I got caught up."

"Caught up doing what? You're never supposed to be too busy to pay your workers. Whenever you have unpaid workers on your team, that's the moment you leave them open to start wondering about you. That is when problems come in. Always make sure the team is fed! Anything other than that—that's when the bullshit starts. Everybody supposed to eat on your team."

"Yeah. I know, Samad. You're right. But do we have to do that right now?"

"Yes. Why didn't you tell me somebody broke into one of the stores?"

Heat looked him in his eyes. "Because Samad, I did not want to worry you."

"I got people I pay to worry about that. I need to know shit like that."

"You just came home. I miss you." Heat leaned in and kissed him on his neck. "Mmmmm." She inhaled his cologne. "I don't want to talk about this right now. Can we enjoy each other?"

Samad watched as she walked to the kitchen. He moved the money back and lifted another compartment and counted five guns. "Who did you have in this house while I was gone?"

"What? Nobody. Don't start with that paranoid shit."

Samad closed the safe. "I got a lot of catching up to do. It's going to be a long night." Samad closed the safe. "Where's my nine and my forty caliber?" He noticed two guns were missing.

Heat's reply was pure silence.

CHAPTER 20
Quality Time

"Smells good, baby. You got a tray full of my favorites: banana pancakes, beef sausage, grits with cheese, and scrambled eggs with diced onions in it, and wheat toast and orange juice." *Now that's what's up,* Samad thought. *Breakfast fit for a king!*

"Wake up, sleepy head! You hungry, baby?" Heat sang.

"I ain't sleep! I see you. Been woke. Took a shower already. Did some push-ups, pull-ups, made your closet rack over there my dip bar." Samad pointed to the rack. "Feels good taking a hot shower at home, walking around my own home in my boxers. I just got back in the bed. This bed feels real good. I was laying here while you were sleeping earlier."

Heat set the tray down on his side of the bed. "Oh okay. So what were you doing all this time?" she asked.

"Just flipping through the TV. I been woke—just laying here thinking. I smelled the food cooking, and I heard you when you got up. I didn't want to interrupt, but I didn't want you to burn my food. But I see you burnt my pancakes a little. I hope my eggs all right."

Heat tilted her head and twisted her lips, smiling as he teased her.

149

"You know you can't do two things at the same time. Like walk and chew gum," Samad joked. "But it's all good. Thanks, baby. I appreciate you."

"Oh, you got jokes early in the morning? Don't be teasing me about my food."

"Nah, I'm just joking with you, ma. Next to my mother, your cooking is the best!" Samad put a fork full of eggs in his mouth.

"Hmph!" she mumbled.

"Sike, I'm only playin' ma-ma! You the best, baby!"

The home phone rang, interrupting their quality time. "Answer that, baby!" Heat said as she walked out of the room.

Samad picked up the house phone and hesitated to speak. He remained silent. The person on the other end spoke.

"Hello?" a woman said.

Samad did not respond. "Hello!" he finally replied.

The woman hung up.

Samad looked at the phone, puzzled. He recognized the woman's voice. *Why is Mercedes calling Heat?* He hung up.

Samad walked to her computer desk, and looked through the paperwork in the folders on the side of the desk. *Damn.* He thought.

Heat walked back in the room. "Who was it?" She sat down in the middle of the big king-sized bed and pulled her tray of food to her lap. She ate her breakfast and flipped through the TV channels.

"I don't know. They hung up," he lied. Samad placed the phone back on the charger. He reached over to the tray of food and sampled everything, then took a long sip of the juice. He pushed the tray away then stood up. "Let me ask you a question."

Heat heard the seriousness in his voice and stopped eating. She laid the remote down on the bed and met Samad's gaze.

"What the hell was so important that made you careless about handling my business?"

"What?"

"You heard me!"

"First of all, my college classes took precedence over that street shit."

"Well, if it wasn't for this *street shit*—them fucking college classes would not have been paid for!"

Heat stared at Samad. "I've still yet to hear congratulations from you." She moved the tray of food and stood up, ready to walk out the room.

"Don't go no where. We're going to deal with this right now."

"I'm not dealing with shit. It's too early in the morning for this. If anything, you should be happy you have a woman that held it down and waited for you to get out of jail. On top of that, my career and future is important to me, which by the way, you don't seem to acknowledge. Do you plan on being in the streets all of

151

your life? Huh, Samad? You should be lucky you have a woman that handled your business for you this long while you were locked up."

"Well, according to Mike, the business wasn't handled right. Workers were not paid. Just sloppy business. You slacked off."

"Fuck you, Samad! Fuck Pezo, too!"

"Oh yeah, that's right. I forgot you still mad at Pezo for telling me about Moe visiting you in the hospital."

"Well, you weren't there. You should be happy somebody was here to take care of me that day when your fucking hoodrat ass ex-girlfriend and I had a fight when I came to see you at the jail. The same bitch who's responsible for our baby dying. You should thank Moe for making sure your woman made it in the hospital all right!"

"What the fuck your smart ass say?" Samad moved closer to Heat and grabbed her arm tight.

"Get off me!" Heat yanked her arm, trying to get out of his grip.

"Say that shit again!" Samad drew his fist back.

Heat stared at him, tilted her head sideways, shocked by his gesture.

Samad caught himself and let her arm go. "There are two guns missing out of my safe. Who did you have in this house while I was gone?"

She kept staring at Samad as he moved away from her, still shocked by his actions. "I didn't have nobody in here, Samad. You got me all the way out here in the woods. Nobody even knows I'm here. The only person who's been here was Aaron. Or did you forget you told him to make a copy of the key for himself in case he needed to come here while I was away? Did it occur to you to ask him if he had your fucking guns! I'm sooo tired of this shit. Welcome home!" Heat walked out the room slamming the bedroom door behind her.

"Aaron," Samad said as he looked at the safe.

CHAPTER 21
Ungrateful

"Tell the fucking truth, Heat! Did you or did you not have that nigga Moe at this house?"

"Look. I'm not going back and forth with you, arguing all day about something that did not happen. Also, I'm not arguing anymore about what I did *not* do while you were gone, Samad."

Ding!

The doorbell rang.

"I'm going to take a shower and go to the day spa. I need to pamper myself."

"According to these receipts, that's what you've been doing everyday for the past five years. Going to the spa!"

"Fuck you, Samad!" Heat rolled her eyes and waved her hand at him. She walked out the room.

Samad stared at her back as she walked out. He laughed and shook his head. "That girl knows how to spend some damn money!"

Walking toward the security cameras, Samad leaned over to look at the small TV monitor to see who was outside the door. Aaron stood there talking on his phone.

Samad smiled when he saw Aaron and pressed the button to speak through the intercom. "Where your key at, play boy?"

"Let me call you right back." Aaron ended his phone call. He looked up at the camera and smiled. "I left it in my other jacket. I was already out the door. Welcome home, baby!"

Samad hit the buzzer. The lock clicked. Aaron bent down and picked up two garbage bags off the ground, pushed the door, and walked in. Samad pulled out a few stacks of money and placed it on the desk. Aaron walked in the house and stood in the doorway of Samad's office.

"Your sister's in there. Close that door and lock it too, so I can holla at you real quick."

Aaron locked the door then placed the two bags on the floor. "First and foremost, welcome home, baby!" Aaron and Samad hugged, giving each other genuine brotherly love.

"What's good with you, baby? I heard about what you been doin' while I was gone. I heard you really stepped up to the plate."

"Yeah, I mean you was gone, so I had to hold the fort down. You would have done the same for me. That's what real niggas do!"

"You right."

"I just made sure everything was handled smoothly, making sure money continued to flow. But anyway . . . that's what I'm here for. This is for you." Aaron pointed at the two garbage bags. He picked up the bags and dumped the contents on Samad's desk.

Stacks and stacks of money fell out the bags onto the desk.

Samad's eyes got big. "What's this from?"

"When I noticed the money was being mishandled by Pezo, I stepped up and took over his position, pretty much. Him and Heat was back and forth, all in their feelings. I told Heat to focus on school. Leave her out of the business side of things anyway." She had a lot on her plate. When she lost the baby she didn't take it well. I stayed here at night waiting until she fell asleep before I bounced. Then I came back before she woke up in the morning."

"Good lookin' out." Samad extended his hand to Aaron. He was thrown off by this new information. Pezo had told him that Heat was messing up. All along it was Pezo.

"I'm about to make a few moves out of town to handle a few things for you. The last time I went to B'more, the chick that drove me—her peoples that was in the car with me plugged me into another connect down there too."

"Okay, no doubt. Hit me when you touch down."

"I just wanted to stop by to give you this and return these two guns. I needed them for something."

Samad looked at his two guns, the nine millimeter and the .40 caliber that went missing from the safe. They were in Aaron's hand. "Do they got—"

Aaron cut him off. "No, they don't got bodies on them. Luckily everybody handled their handle, and I didn't need to use 'em."

"They loaded?" Samad took the guns out of Aaron's hands.

"No. Here's the ammo." Aaron handed him a small black pouch filled with bullets.

Samad took it out of his hands and walked to the safe, placing them back inside.

Heat knocked on the door.

"Hold on," Samad replied.

Aaron put the money back in the bags and put it under Samad's desk. Samad let Heat in.

"Why is the door locked?" Heat's face lit up with a smile. "Hey, Aaron!"

"Hey, baby girl. How you been, sis?"

"I'm good." Brother and sister hugged. "I missed you."

"You the one been busy, Miss College Graduate."

"What you doing here?" Heat asked as Aaron pulled papers out his pocket.

"I needed to drop these papers off to you and Samad. I had these mixed in with my papers. Y'all gonna need this. The guy said whenever y'all ready to have the big black security gates built around the house. These are the contractors you guys need to contact."

"Oh, okay thanks." Heat took the papers out of Aaron's hand and looked them over.

"He said when you call, let them know you would like an early Saturday morning appointment, because if they get here early, they will be working all day and they can complete the job in one day."

Samad took the papers from Heat and looked at them. "Thanks, man."

"Where you going, Aaron?" Heat asked.

"Out of town. I need to go to B'more to handle some business. My ride picking me up."

Samad cut his eyes at Aaron. He hated people knowing where his spots are. "That's the reason I'm getting those black security gates."

"I know, man, I know man. The driver good peoples though. That's her on the phone now saying she outside. I would ask you two to let me hold one of the vehicles, but the last time I went out of town, the same chick Neeka drove me there and her peoples riding with us. She knows exactly where I need to go, and she knows the guy I need to see."

"Just be safe, Aaron. Last time I was worried when I couldn't get in touch with you. Make sure you have your phone charger."

"I'm good, little sis. No need to worry about me. I'm out."

"Hit me when you get there safe." Heat glanced at her vibrating phone. Five missed calls from Unique. *Damn, wonder what she wants.*

"No doubt."

"Later."

Heat walked Aaron out the house. She looked in the car and noticed the same faces from before when Aaron went out of town. They were in the same car as before. They all waved. She waved back.

"Be safe. Call me when you on your way back, so we can go eat lunch."

"Later, baby sis. You worry too much. I love you."

"I love you too." Aaron walked off to the car.

She had this funny feeling in her stomach, a violent turning and twisting. "It's too many people in that car like I told him the last time. They should've rode in two cars instead. I bet they get their asses stopped by the cops today. Aaron knows better," Heat said out loud. *God, please keep Aaron protected today.*

Heat closed the front door, ready to enter round two with Samad. She didn't want to argue with Samad in front of her brother, but now was the perfect time. She stormed down the hall to Samad's office.

He had just put the money in the safe that Aaron gave him. Then he pulled out the bag from under his desk and dumped the money inside the safe also. It was the money Mercedes gave him the other day at the hotel. He watched Heat on the small TV monitor walking toward his office and timed her. The moment her feet were at the door, he closed and locked the safe.

Heat pushed his office door open. "Look, let me just say this to you, Samad. I don't appreciate—"

159

He cut her off. "I want to apologize. First of all, for accusing you of not handling my business. Second, for raising my hand at you." Samad hugged Heat.

"What gave you a change of heart?"

"After talking with Aaron, he filled me in on a few things. I need to go handle some business with Pezo."

Heat looked at the safe behind Samad's back as he hugged her. She noticed money hanging out the bottom of the safe. Her phone vibrated again, and she glanced at the display. She let Unique's call go to voice mail figuring she'd call her later. *What's up with all this extra money?*

CHAPTER 22
Back to Business

"Let's get ready to rumble!" he shouted at the top of his lungs and nodded to the beat. Samad drove through his old hood, blasting Red Man's classic song "Time for Some Action." He swerved in and out of traffic, gliding through the streets pushing his new 150 Bentley GT continental as the wheels hugged the road. He was in his zone. He had business to get back to. Out of all the years of him being in the streets, he only had two enemies. Bono and Moe. In his line of business, that was two too many.

He switched the music to Notorious Big's classic song, "Who Shot Ya." Biggie Smalls' distinctive voice came blasting through his speakers. He sang along to the music in a low tone. "Separate the weak from the obsolete, hard to creep them Brooklyn streets. It's on niggas."

As he passed an open fire hydrant, kids were running in and out of the spray. All the kids began running to the ice-cream truck that parked near the curb. The sight took his mind back to his younger days and he smiled. He too used to yell up to the window and ask anybody in his house if they could drop down some money so he can get an ice cream. Samad parked behind the ice-cream truck and sat for a moment. He laughed while remembering one or two times the money got stuck on the roof when the wind blew in a different direction. He would eventually run to one of the older heads on the block who had money. Now, he was that old head the kids ran to for money.

"Samad! Samad! Samad!" All the kids yelled his name as they ran to his car. He rolled down the passenger side window and smiled at all the smiling faces. Samad loved the kids in the neighborhood.

"What's up, y'all? Where y'all rug-rats going?" he asked as he handed all the kids a twenty dollar bill. About fifteen kids surrounded his car. They each grabbed the money and ran to the ice-cream truck.

Inhaling the fresh air, he took in the familiar aroma of his old neighborhood and smiled when he smelled the delicious pizza from the corner store.

"You see the dice? What it land on? Four, five-six, nigga. Pay up!" a loud voice said. The disruption came from the direction of the dice game against the brick wall near the mailbox. "This game is called cee-lo. This is not a daycare! Why you babysitting the money? While you're at it, stop babysittin' the dice!"

"Fuck outta here. It hit his foot! Let me roll again!"

"Nigga, pay up!"

Same cee-lo game. Familiar voices, but now with a hint of maturity. He knew whose voices they were. *Same niggas,* Samad thought as he pulled up. None of the guys noticed him sitting across the street behind the ice cream truck watching them. They were busy focusing on the dice game.

Mrs. Alexander sat on her porch smoking a cigarette. She spotted Samad in his car and waved. He waved back. Mrs. Alexander watched half of them grow up.

"Hey, baby!" she yelled with a toothless grin.

"Hey, Ma! How you been?"

"Oh, I'm all right, baby. If you see that grandson of mine, tell him to come here. I need him to go to the store for me."

"Yes, ma'am. I will!" He noticed the same mailman from his childhood walk by delivering mail. He smiled when the twins Dave and Derrick zoomed by on their motorcycles.

"Them lil' niggas got big as hell!" he mouthed, inhaling deeply and then exhaling. Samad felt content, and he felt at home. The smell of the air, the energy of the people, and the smells from the diners nearby welcomed him. He took it all in.

Again he looked at his watch wondering where his two soldiers Mike and Will were. They both were supposed to meet him right here before he surprised the rest of the team.

Mike and Will finally walked around the corner. Samad saw them in the rearview mirror walking in his direction. He smiled and stepped out the car greeting them both, and closing the door behind him. Mike, Will, and Samad headed to the guys standing in a huddle over the dice.

"Time to play catch up!" Samad said as he walked to the crowd of guys.

Samad hugged Will. "Welcome home, boss man," Will said as he let Samad go.

"Thanks. Glad to be home."

"Look at you, Samad. Your skin all clear! Got ya weight up! Got your glow back!" Will laughed.

"I never lost it, baby," Samad replied as he hugged Will on the left side of him and hugged Mike on the right side of him. They walked to the team.

"Oh shit! Look who's home!" one of the guys shouted.

The crowd of guys huddled around Samad.

"Damn, they let you out!" Pezo said as he picked the dice up off the ground and collected his money. His face lit up with a warm smile.

"Oh shit. Samad! What's good, baby? Damn, they let my nigga out? They fucked up now!" Pezo stood between Samad, Mike, and Will. "Why didn't you tell me you was coming home?"

Mike smiled. "He wanted it to be a surprise to everybody." He put his arms around both Samad and Will's neck, and he walked them through the crowd of guys.

"Yooooo!" Mike yelled to get everybody's attention on the entire block. "Look who's back!"

"Who the hell let you out?" one of the other guys yelled. The crowd of guys looked in their direction.

"Samad got that glow. That G-L-G! That 'good living glow,'" Mike said. "It's gon' be some shit now. Lock and load!" shouted Mike.

"When you come home, Samad?" Face asked.

"Today!" he lied. "Everything's good out here?" Samad asked, raising an eyebrow, looking Pezo directly in his eyes.

"Yeah, why wouldn't it be, nigga? You already know!" Pezo responded. "You don't have to hold our hands, nigga. We can stand on our own two. It could be five years, or fifty-five years!" he snapped, playfully throwing punches Samad's way.

Samad dipped left, then dipped right quickly. Shadow boxing toward Pezo and catching him in the side with a hard blow to the body

Pezo stumbled backwards. "Nigga! What the fuck is wrong with you? Hittin' me like you a boxer, motherfucker. Damn! What the fuck you was punchin' behind that wall?"

"Nigga, you slippin'. Your new girl got you whipped, Pezo. You pussy nigga!" Samad laughed.

"Pussy? Oh, we not gon' talk about whipped! Let's not talk about how Heat used to have you holding her purse in the mall that time!" Pezo yelled.

"Yo, y'all remember that shit? We turned the corner, and this nigga had Heat's Gucci bag in his hand like he's the fucking hired help and shit!"

Samad stopped laughing and got serious. He stepped closer to Pezo's face. "Yo, you might wanna watch what you say."

"Damn, nigga, that jail got you sensitive?"

Samad grabbed Pezo's neck. "Yo, watch your motherfuckin' mouth like I said!"

Mike grabbed Samad's hand. Samad closed his fist, about to hit Pezo.

Will stepped between Pezo and Samad, pulling Pezo away.

"Yo chill," Will said. "Tempers is flaring. Both of y'all relax. We on the same side."

"Are we?" Samad replied as he cut his eye at Pezo. "Let me talk to you for a minute." Samad nodded his head at Pezo gesturing for him to step aside.

"Yeah." Pezo shot Samad a menacing stare as he rubbed his neck.

"What's this I'm hearing about the money, and business wasn't handled right. I heard a lot of money got fucked up. Aaron stepped up and di the job *you* was supposed to be doing."

Pezo hesitated to respond..."With all due respect, we can sit down, and I will be happy to go over everything with you. Not right here in front of everybody. It's a long story. Grant me that respect boss man."

Samad stared at Pezo. Then he looked around at his crew a few feet away from them. "Let me just enjoy this love right now. Yeah, you right." Samad flashed a crooked smile staring at Pezo. "We could talk about this another time."

Mike interrupted the stare down.

"Yo!" Mike yelled at the guy washing his car. "Look in my trunk and get that box of Cohibas out the back, and a box of matches, my dude!" He tossed one of the rookies the keys.

Samad smiled and took a deep breath, feeling the love all around and taking it in. The rookie returned with the box of cigars and matches. Mike passed a cigar to all of his men.

"It feels real good to be around my niggas. My real niggas who I *know* got my back out here in these streets." *I don't know about Pezo no more.* He thought. Samad took a long pull on the cigar then looked around at his boys taking a long pull off their cigars.

They all shouted in unison, "Till the casket drops! Not even death can separate us! Till the death! Kill or be killed! Welcome home, nigga!"

Samad felt someone staring, and he turned to look over his shoulder. A black car drove by slowly. He could not make out the driver or passenger because of the dark tinted windows. When the car turned the corner, the glare from the sun showed three shadows inside. None of his boys caught that. He blew a cloud of smoke out of his mouth and stared at the car. Samad looked around at his boys, and realized they got too relaxed instead of being on point. Some of them were distracted by texting on their phones, or just not as focused like they were before he left.

"Yo! Y'all better keep your eyes open at all times! Cars ridin' through here and y'all didn't even catch that." He watched a few more cars driving through the block.

Someone other than his men knew that Samad had just been released, or maybe things on the street were a lot worse than he was told.

CHAPTER 23
Denial

"I been trying to reach you all week. I see you called me five times. Where you at?" Unique asked Heat.

"I'm sorry, Unique. Something came up with Samad's ass. Right now I'm at World's Finest Hair with Ebony. Just got my hair done. Now I'm with the nail tech. Ebony's still under the dryer." Heat put the phone between her shoulder and ear to avoid messing up her nails. She placed her hands under the fan so she could finish drying them.

"So what's up?"

"Not a whole lot now. I needed you when I called the first five times."

"I really do apologize. But what's this I'm hearing today about you having cuts and scratches on your face, Unique?" Heat put the phone on speaker so her stylist, Classy, could hear the conversation. Classy told Heat about the most recent fight Unique had with Sean. Two days ago Unique came to World's Finest Hair to get a sew-in because Sean dragged her by the hair and pulled a plug of hair out.

"I don't have no cuts and scratches on my face. You heard wrong! Somebody lying to you," Unique replied defensively.

Classy smirked and shook her head. "Mute your phone real quick," Classy whispered. Heat pressed the mute button.

"She's lying! I saw Unique with my own eyes. And so did everybody who work in this shop. Sean kicked her ass good. Ask anybody in here."

The shampoo girl added, "He sure did. Unique looked terrible. Make up was a mess. Didn't hide nothing. Black eye, bruises, scratches, you name it."

She un-muted the phone. "You a dumb bitch if you stay with this bum ass, woman beater. I heard it from more than one person. Everybody can't be lying. Why you covering for this low life?"

"I'm not covering for him."

"If this nigga hit you and you not telling nobody, how you expect somebody to help you? He's the reason you stopped taking your classes. You're like two semesters away from becoming a teacher."

Unique sighed. "Oh boy, Heat, here we go with this again."

"Oh boy nothing! I understand Sean's your child's father. But you've had better men in your life in the past, and to let this bum ass nigga put his hands on you—"

Unique interrupted. "If he was hittin' me, I would tell somebody." She paused for a few seconds. "He's just goin' through somethin'. On top of that, he's not workin' or hustlin' right now." Unique paused before finally admitting, "I love him. He's just stressed."

"So, what does that have to do with him puttin' his hands on you, Unique?"

"Nothin'. I'm just sayin' . . . Business is slow.

Shit happens in relationships. We don't all have a perfect relationship like *you and Samad*."

Heat intercepted Unique's sarcasm and rolled her eyes. "Nobody has a perfect relationship, but I'll be damned if I let a man put his hands on me and hide it from my friends."

"Friend? I don't really feel like your *friend*. Heat, I haven't seen you in months since you've been holed up with Samad."

"What you mean *holed up*?"

"Just what I said. You've been in that house for over four years now, and I haven't been there once," she complained. "That doesn't sound like friendship to me. Even Ebony said the same thing."

Heat couldn't help but glance at Ebony sitting under the dryer. *Have they been talking about me behind my back?*

"All of a sudden, it's all about Samad now! Last year you missed my son's fourth birthday. Fuck your friendship with us, huh?"

Suprisingly, Heat didn't have a response for Unique. "Where Sean at anyway? And Lil Sean?" she asked, letting Unique's accusations sink in.

"Sean's in the shower. The baby's sleeping." Unique sighed. "Heat, I'm about to go. Thank you for being concerned though, but he is not hitting me."

"You can believe your own lies if you want to."

Unique chuckled slightly. "I'm not lyin'! Look, everything's been good between us, until this last fight."

"Last fight?" Heat shook her head in disgust. "But you just said everything is good between you two."

"The fight was nothin' big though; it was more like an argument," Unique lied. "Earlier in the week I got mad and wanted you to ride with me to get my things from his mother's house. Anyway, that's why I was calling you. But I got my stuff already."

"So you all right now?"

Classy whispered in Heat's ear again and pointed at the pregnant woman occupying the dryer two seats down from Ebony.

"Yeah, I'm good now. Did you speak to Ebony?"

I know I just told her Ebony was under the dryer. Heat shook her head, realizing Unique was deflecting.

Classy headed back to her chair to start on another client.

"She's under the dryer. But anyway, back to Sean. Like I was sayin' . . . You need to get rid of his no-good ass. I been hearin' things about him in the streets . . . foul shit. Samad even told me some shit about him."

"Samad . . ." Unique laughed hearty. "Mmph, mmph, mmph! So anyway, ummm, I'm about to go to this after hours spot with Gwen. Tired of sitting in this house . . . Sean letting me go out tonight to get some fresh air. He's staying with the baby."

"Whatever, Unique. You just make sure you let me know if that nigga puts his hands on you. Samad got dudes out here on the streets that'll handle his ass."

"For the last fuckin' time, Heat, he is not puttin'

his hands on me! My business is my business; your business is your business. Let me handle mine over here, and you worry about Samad over there, all right!"

"Tell her about Marrisa," Classy said loud enough for Unique to hear over the speaker phone.

"What about Marrisa?" Unique asked.

Heat couldn't take Unique's denial anymore. What she had to say was going to hurt Unique's feelings, but she needed to know. "Sean got a girl named Marrisa pregnant, *and* he be paying her bills. She's sitting right here right now." She glanced at Marissa, who sat under the dryer texting on her phone.

"What the fuck that bitch say?" Heat heard Sean ask in the background. Unique must've had her on speaker phone too. "Hang up on that dumb bitch. Tell her to worry about her own man. She act like she want me anyway. Watch ya' friends, Unique."

"Fuck you, Sean!" Heat replied, storing his comment about Samad for later. "And fuck you too, Unique, if you wanna be stupid! That washed up, bum ass nigga! Fuck him! I hope he heard that too!"

"You know what, Heat? Fuck you and ya cheatin' ass man. Check ya own shit before you check mine." Unique hung up.

Heat slammed her phone down on the table with the tightest screw face ever, after arguing loud enough for the entire salon to hear her conversation. Her thoughts took over. She never understood how some females let a man come between friendships. *That's some good ass dick when a nigga got you turning on your own family and friends.* She couldn't believe her girl let this guy manipulate her mind and their friendship of many years like that.

On several occasions Heat bumped into Sean, and at the mall he blew a kiss at her. At the carwash he licked his lips and blew another kiss. At the corner store he bumped into her, brushing up on her ass from behind while Heat was getting milk out the freezer. That's the day she slapped the shit out of Sean.

Every time he flirted with her, she held her own, or dismissed his advances and kept it moving. She didn't think twice about letting Unique know then, because it didn't mean anything. *Oooo she stupid!* Heat thought.

Classy walked over to Heat…
"Did they find out if that nigga guilty or not guilty—the one that killed Ebony's mother and her uncle Breeze and snitched on her father?"

Heat looked over at Ebony under the dryer texting on her phone.

"They didn't go to court yet, Classy," Heat responded. "But Ebony don't like talkin' about that. She really gets depressed. Especially about her mom's death."

"I hear you, that's why I asked you while she's under the dryer. But you know the streets talkin' already. But I'm gon' leave it alone."

"They go back to court in about two months."

"I hope everything work out for the best."

"Yeah me too."

"Lata girl there go my other client.See you next time."

"Later classy."

Heat walked over near where Ebony was by the dryers. "I still can't believe Unique trippin'."

As she sat waiting on Ebony's hair to dry, Heat reminisced on their childhood. All three girls used to play games on guys together. Get whatever they wanted from any guy in their presence. Never once did they question one another.

She laughed at the fact that Unique always, always was the one who used to say, "Ain't no nigga gon' come between us! If y'all ever see me slippin', y'all better slap the shit outta me and wake me the fuck back up!"

Well, I guess I got a lot of slapping to do! Wake the fuck up, bitch! She shook her head. "My, how things have changed." *Here we are, older, evolved women, brighter, and this chick forgot the rules over the years. Unique needs retraining in Niggas 101! Or Streets 101! Some things you just aren't supposed to forget! Common sense is never out of style! It never changes! Wait until I tell Ebony this bullshit.* Heat laughed, and as she got up and sat next to Ebony, she knocked on her dryer.

"What's up?" Ebony answered, pushing the dryer off her head.

"Girl, listen. I just called Unique and our conversation about that cheating bum Sean went left real quick."

"Oh yeah? I knew that was your loud ass, so I tuned you out. But you should have told her dumb ass about all the times he flirted with me too."

"Girl, I didn't even get to you yet. The call went all over the place real quick." She glanced to Ebony's right and whispered, "I even told her about Marissa who's supposed to be pregnant by Sean. Ain't that her sittin' right there?"

"Yeah, that's her. Girl, I'm not surprised. Fuck Unique. She been actin' funny lately."

"She got all defensive and flipped it on me. Saying I'm not around that much no more since Samad's been home, and she didn't feel like we're still friends."

"Unh." Ebony tilted her head and gave her that 'Unique hit that one right on the head' look.

"What?" Heat scrunched up her face.

"You haven't been around."

"That was because of school. Not Samad."

"School's been over, Heat."

"True. Okay, maybe it is because Samad's home. I just miss him." She took a piece of gum from her purse and put it in her mouth." She offered Ebony a piece, but she declined.

"Oh, but wait! Let me tell you this! She talkin' about Samad's cheatin' on me."

Heat expected Ebony to say something, but Ebony exhaled and rolled her eyes and pulled the dryer back over her head. Seeing Marissa sitting there gave

Heat the perfect opportunity to get to the heart of the matter. Heat walked over and tapped her arm, and Marissa pushed the dryer up.

"Excuse me."

"Yeah."

"Do you know Sean Johnson?" she asked, without being polite. "I just want my friend to know the truth."

"Yeah, I know Sean. Very well. You see my stomach, don't you?"

CHAPTER 24
Secrets and Lies

Two months later . . .

How did this bitch get my number? Heat thought, seeing the name 'Mercedes Best' on the screen. She loved her new phone. It wouldn't allow restricted, unknown, or blocked numbers through, and it showed the person's name.

After a very short debate with herself on whether she should answer the phone, curiosity got the best of her. Heat picked up after the third ring.

"Hello?"

"May I speak to Heat, please?"

"Who's this?" Heat asked, already knowing the answer.

"This is Mercedes. I'm sorry for calling your phone, but I needed to let you know what's going on with *our* man."

"Oh?" Heat asked, raising an eyebrow. "Our?" She sat up, getting comfortable on the bed, wondering what she could possibly be telling her about Samad. Her mind wandered back to when they had the fight at the jail. *What this bitch want with me?*

"Hello! . . . Hello! . . . Heat, are you there?" Mercedes said.

"I'm here! What do you have to tell me about *my* man?" she asked.

"Did Samad tell you that he and I have a son?"

"Excuse me!"

"Did. Samad. Tell you that he and I have a son? There's a lot you don't know, so let me get you caught up."

"Mercedes, why you calling me playing games? I'm too old for this."

"This ain't a game. When we had that fight, they admitted me in the hospital and ran all these tests. That's when I found out I was pregnant. Oh, by the way, he told me about your miscarriage. You lost the baby four years ago. Was it from the fight we had?" Heat knew this bitch Mercedes was smiling, already knowing she was the cause.

Silence loomed for several seconds.

"Anyway, sorry about your loss. When my pregnancy test came back positive, I knew Samad was the father. I wasn't fucking anybody else during the time I worked at the jail. That's the reason I gave you a hard time when you came to visit him. Because I had, and still *have* feelings for that man since we were teenagers. Just seeing him with another woman, I'm not comfortable with that."

"How do you know your baby is Samad's?"

"Well, before I got fired from my position as a correctional officer—that was right around the same time when you and I had that fight—one of the inmates snitched on me, telling my superiors that I was involved in a relationship with one of the prisoners. They also found out you were the girlfriend of the inmate that I fought. I was placed on suspension, pending further investigation. After speaking to several visitors who were there that day, I was eventually fired."

Heat's call-waiting beeped, but she ignored it.

"When I told Samad I was pregnant, he denied it at first, but then he said it could have been one of the other guys I was fucking."

"Bitch, I don't believe you. You done fucked half the niggas in your hood."

"Excuse me. It's Miss Bitch to you. No, I have not fucked the niggas in my neighborhood. But I did fuck *our* man. As a matter of 'fuck' I had him first. So really, you're fucking my sloppy seconds. Fact!"

"Obviously, you wasn't fucking him right, if I still got him all these years later."

"You sure you got him, sweetie? By the way, I hear he hits you. Is that true? Are you two fighting in your relationship? He's never hit me." Mercedes laughed.

"It's none of your business what's going on in my relationship with Samad, but that's neither here nor there. Anyway, what about a blood test? Did you get a blood test to prove it's his kid?"

"We had a blood test, three blood tests at that! The first one was administered by the doctor in the jail, but paranoid ass Samad thought I paid the doctor to say it was his child. So he had his lawyer, Mr. Weinstein have another paternity test done in Brooklyn. Then he had his boy Pezo set up another doctor's appointment to have it done in D.C. All three tests came back 99.99%, proving him to be the father for sure."

Heat's silence only confirmed that Mercedes' plan was working.

"Look, I'm not using Samad being the father of my son as ammunition to break up y'all relationship. This is not about my child giving me leverage. I just want you to know what's going on and how I feel about him." Mercedes cleared her throat.

"That's exactly what you're doing, but . . . whatever!" She wanted to cry because deep down she knew Mercedes wasn't lying.

"Samad thought he could keep my baby a secret. His plan was to move us far away, but I always came up with excuses why we couldn't leave New York."

"Did he ever bring you to our house?" Heat asked.

"Yes, I have been to your house before. I guess you were out of town somewhere in Virginia that week around Presidents Day holiday. That's what Samad told me. Was it business, or pleasure?" Mercedes laughed.

Heat was shocked that she knew about her trip out of town to Virginia. "Not that it's any of your business where I was, Mercedes, but I was out of town at a funeral. Family friend. Just so I'm clear, you were at my home? My house, Mercedes?"

"Yes. Your house. Not the whole week though, only that first night. The next morning I guess he was feeling guilty or something. We checked into the Trump Hotel. I was with him when he brought you that platinum tennis bracelet with the yellow diamonds." Heat looked down at her wrist.

"As soon as you walk in your house, your dining room area is sunken with marble on the floor in the little sitting area. There's a beautiful high vaulted ceiling. I could see the sky through the skylight. You got a three-piece light tan, suede living room set. On the floor underneath that is a dark tan carpet. You also have a bunch of sweet smelling candles all over your living room. I believe strawberry, or watermelon scent. Smelled nice." Mercedes laughed. "When you walk down the hallway, there's a small room right there with exercise equipment in it."

This bitch has been inside my house!

"The bedroom is similar to a wine color. A lot of baby pictures of Samad and you are on the walls. There's a king-sized bed and a sliding glass door to walk out onto the patio right from that first bedroom. The bathroom's on the left of that room. Look . . . He's trying to act like my son does not exist. It is not going down like that!"

I'ma have to kill this bitch! Heat had heard enough. She knew Mercedes was not lying about Samad bringing her to their home. She glanced over at the picture of her and Samad on the dresser. *I'm going to fuck this nigga up too.*

"Can I see your son?" Heat asked.

182

"Yes, sure you can see me and Samad's son."

"I can meet you right now if you not busy," she replied, waiting for an answer.

Mercedes hesitated, knowing she had the upper hand. She basked in the glory, letting Heat eat on air. Heat suffocated on the silence. Mercedes knew she controlled the situation. After a brief pause, Mercedes finally spoke.

"I guess I could meet you right now. So where do you want to meet?"

"By Junior's Cheesecake in Brooklyn," Heat suggested.

"Okay, I'll be there."

Heat hung up the phone. She already had it in her mind that even if the baby boy was Samad's son, she was determined to punch the shit out of Mercedes off GP for all the bullshit. Heat slipped on some jeans, one of Samad's big T-shirts, and some sneakers. She wrapped her hair up in a doobie and grabbed her purse, then raced out of the house, off to her destination.

She located a parking spot and shut the engine off. Once she walked inside Junior's, she looked around trying to spot Mercedes. On the right, Mercedes was sitting with a small boy, but his back was turned. So Heat couldn't see the boy's face. She took her sunglasses off as she walked to where they were seated.

The moment Mercedes spotted Heat walking in her direction, she smiled and stood up. Heat looked her up and down, noticing the designer heels and short black dress— like she was about to go to the club. Heat reached the table without saying a word. She looked down at the child, who was eating cheesecake.

Mercedes tapped her son on the shoulder. "Samad Jr., look up." The child looked up at Mercedes. "This is Heat. This is your father's friend."

Heat stared at the boy and she saw Samad's face. Mercedes was not lying. This was Samad's child. Even down to the dimple, cleft chin, and the same shaped head, everything was identical. Heat knew it in her heart.

"Now, was I lying?" she asked with a stout smile.

Heat yanked Mercedes' weave with her left hand and punched her repeatedly with her right hand. Caught off guard, Mercedes swung back.

"Bitch, this is for all them times you gave me a fucking hard time coming to that jail. This is for you making me lose my baby, bitch!" Heat pounded Mercedes' face until she saw blood.

The little boy stood up. "Get off my mommy!" he shouted, trying to get Heat off his mother.

Heat uppercut Mercedes, who kept swinging to back away from the solid blows.

The guy from behind the counter and other people in the store were startled by the disruption. The workers came to break up the fight. Heat punched her one last time, then kicked her so hard in the stomach Mercedes flew backward with her son.

"Trifling bitch!" Heat turned and walked away as workers rushed from the back to break up the commotion. Heat hurried to her car looking over her shoulder. Police sirens wailed nearby as she got in her car and drove off.

"Bitch! Fuck you, Mercedes! And you too Samad!" she yelled.

The cop saw Heat speeding and turned her lights on. The officer busted a U-turn, following Heat until she pulled over.

"Oh shit!" She panicked, pulling over and putting the car in park. "I'm about to go to jail for assault." She left the engine running and put her hands on the steering wheel.

The female police officer stepped out the car with her hand on her gun. "Do you know how fast you were going?"

Heat's hands shook; she was obviously nervous. "No. I-I-I'm sorry. I have a lot on my mind. I just found out the man I am with has a baby by another woman."

"Okay, well calm down. Let me have your license, registration, and insurance card." The officer remained stone faced.

Heat reached in the glove compartment and retrieved her documents.

The police officer looked at Heat's paperwork, then leaned over inspecting the windshield sticker. "I see all of your paperwork is up to date. I'm going to let you go with a warning, only because I understand how that feels. I was in a situation myself, so I do empathize. The things we women go through . . ."

"Thank you. I'll make sure I drive at a normal speed."

"Slow down, Ms. Jordan. You have been warned." She handed Heat her documents. "Driving when you're upset is the last thing you need to do. Go home and call a friend over and vent. And don't reduce yourself to childish, violent antics over someone who hasn't evolved to your level. We're good at blaming the other woman instead of the man. We have to grow up and stop doing that. More than likely, he's just not the one for you. I had to learn that the hard way. So I'm not just talking to be talking. Men only do what we allow. Always remember that."

"Thank you. I appreciate it."

The female police officer got back in her car and drove away.

Heat shook her head and beat the steering wheel. "Fuck you, Samad!"

Chapter 25
The Elephant in the Room

"Hello!" Ebony said, hearing Heat crying. "Heat?"

"Mercedes has a baby with Samad." Heat sniffled. "I just saw the baby. I met her at Junior's Cheesecake by your house. That boy looks just like him."

"Are you okay?"

"No. I'm in Brooklyn coming to your house. Come downstairs. I'm around the corner."

"Okay. I'm on my way downstairs."

Heat pulled in front of Ebony's house and spotted Ebony on her porch and gestured her toward her car. She slid over to the passenger seat and pointed to the driver's seat once Ebony was at the car. "You drive. I just can't right now."

Ebony got in. "Where you wanna go?" she asked.

"Just drive for a minute," Heat said, uncertain of a destination.

"Okay. I'm going to the store to get a few things. Unique's on her way over here. She said she'll be here in an hour. Her and Sean had a really bad fight. She didn't want me to tell you about it."

Heat did not respond. She was in her own feelings thinking about Mercedes, Samad, and that baby . . . Heat rolled her eyes at the mention of Unique's name. She still hadn't spoken to Unique after the big argument they had about Sean.

Ebony drove to the store as Heat sat in the passenger side crying.

Thirty minutes later, Ebony put the bags from the store in the truck. "It's going to be a'ight," Ebony said, trying to comfort her friend.

"Fuck Samad! Fuck that bitch, Mercedes! Fuck that child!"

Ebony took a deep breath. "The child is innocent, Heat. He don't got nothing to do with this bullshit. He didn't ask to be here. It's not his fault. That's Samad fault. He's the one fucked that bitch."

Heat knew Ebony was right. She turned away from Ebony and looked out the window. Ebony started the ignition and they rode in silence.

At some point, Heat had dozed off. After driving another ten minutes, Ebony parked in front of her building.

"Wake up, sleepy head." She shook Heat. "We're here."

Looking around, Heat tried to focus as she wiped her eyes. She yawned and stretched and stepped out the truck. Ebony was already walking around to the passenger's side when a couple of guys getting out of a Monte Carlo grabbed her attention.

Ebony yelled out to one of them, "What's good, Face? Where the loud at? I need to smoke." She put her hands up in the sky as if saying what's up.

"Damn, E, just tell the police I got the smoke!" Face looked over his shoulder, then tossed her a bag of smoke in a small Ziploc bag. "You tryna get a nigga locked up? Be easy." He spotted Heat getting out of the car. "What's up, Heat?"

"Hey, Face," she replied with no emotion as she grabbed a few bags out the backseat.

"What's up with you, girl? When you gon' stop frontin' on me, and give me a shot?"

Ebony interrupted. "She don't want you, boy. Ya young ass! You better not let Samad hear you playin' like that, talkin' to his girl."

"Who said I was playin'?" Face replied in a low voice. They didn't hear his comment.

"You be having these little hoodrats fighting over you." Ebony laughed.

"Stop hatin'," Face retorted. "I can't help it if the pipe game right! These chicks know what it is." Face laughed.

"Nigga, please!"

"Yo! Face!" somebody called. "He want six. Let me get three, and you take the other three," the guy yelled.

"A'ight bet. Hold up, Bizz! Yo, I'm out. Later E. Take care, Heat!"

From a distance they all heard gunshots. "Yo, y'all better hurry up and get outta here. It's a lot of shit going on."

"You don't gotta tell me twice. I already know," Ebony replied. "Later, Face."

Heat waved and followed Ebony into the building. They stood in the foyer waiting for the elevator. Heat's phone vibrated. She rejected Samad's call, sending it to voice mail.

Ebony and Heat stepped in the elevator and Ebony pressed the number five. Silence filled the air. Ebony pulled the bag halfway out her jacket pocket and glanced down at it. She tried to make small talk. "Face got that good smoke! I got enough wake and bake to smoke for a month. Face getting that gwop too!" Heat didn't respond.

Ebony put the bag back in her pocket. "Heat, I know that shit about Samad's son got you fucked up, so I'm just gon' shut up."

The elevator stopped on Ebony's floor. They waited patiently until the door opened. Unique stood right outside the elevator by Ebony's front door. Heat glanced at Unique, who turned away and finished texting. Then she put her phone in her jacket pocket and proceeded to take one of the bags out of Ebony's hands.

Ebony put the key in the lock, then glanced from Heat to Unique, feeling the tension.

The girls walked in the house headed to the kitchen. Ebony and Unique set the bags on the kitchen table. Heat sat down at the table and pulled out her phone.

"Do you have any peroxide and Band-Aids, Ebony?" Unique walked over to the cabinets to get a glass. Her hair was a mess. Her ponytail was crooked and some of her hair was out of place as if a big wind machine blew it all over her head.

"No. But what we need to talk about is the elephant in the room. You and Heat are like my sisters. When one of us has a problem, we talk about it. We don't keep shit bottled up inside, letting days or weeks go by without mending our friendship."

"Damn, bitch, do you have peroxide and Band-Aids or what? Yeah or nah? I didn't come here to get the third degree!" Unique barked as she took off her sunglasses, revealing a twisted face, and looking like the victim of a facelift gone bad.

"Damn!" Ebony said. "What happened to you?"

"Nothing. I ummm . . . I was in a fight." She put the glasses back on.

"With who, Unique?" Ebony asked, already knowing the answer.

Unique ignored her question and went in the refrigerator to get something to drink. Heat was too busy texting and arguing with Mercedes to pay them any mind.

Ebony repeated her question. "Who did you have a fight with, Unique?"

"Them bitches up the block from me," she lied. "They jumped me, all right? It's nothing. I'm okay. I'm all right."

Heat could not be quiet anymore. She put her phone down on the table and stood up. "That nigga Sean probably did it. Don't fucking lie!" She turned her back on Unique and reached for a glass from the cabinet.

"Bitch, mind your business. First of all, you need to worry about your own man, Samad. I'm hearing shit about him too. So none of us need to be judging others."

"Don't think I forgot all that slick shit you and your dirty ass baby daddy was talking on the phone. You dumb bitch. I called you to fill you in on what the girl Marissa told me about your baby father. And to confront Sean right in front of you while he was there, but your dumb ass chose to side with him. Fuck you, Unique!"

"Fuck you, Heat!"

Heat threw the glass at Unique's face and Ebony ducked. The glass broke against the wall and Heat and Unique came to blows. Finally, Ebony stood between the two trying to break it up.

"Ebony pushed Heat away from Unique, and Unique fell into the fridge. "Both of y'all wildin' the fuck out! Stop it!" Ebony turned in Heat's direction and pushed her again. Heat fell against the sink.

Unique grabbed her stuff and turned to leave. "Fuck you, Heat!"

"Fuck you, bitch!" Heat yelled. "Dumb bitch. Go be with your dirty ass baby father. You dead to me, Unique."

Unique stuck her middle finger up and walked out the door, slamming it behind her.

"You and Unique need to get y'all shit together," Ebony said, huffing and puffing with three layers of skin wrinkling her forehead. She had her own problem to deal with, and it was much larger than the minor bullshit they had going on.

CHAPTER 26
Cut Off

"I can't stand this bum bitch. I need to let her know once and for all what the fuck it is!" Samad pulled his phone out of his pocket, and scrolled through the names until he came to Mercedes. He shook his head and placed the phone to his ear waiting for Mercedes to pick up.

Mercedes recognized Samad's number right away and answered on the second ring. "Hey, big daddy. I miss you."

Samad twisted his face up. "Look, it's not that type of phone call." Mercedes answered with ten seconds of silence and finally a soft sigh.

"Look, I'm with Heat now. Whatever we had in the past is in the past."

"Well, Heat knows about Samad Jr., and do you know this bitch had the nerve to fight me at the cheesecake spot in front of our son?"

Samad didn't respond. It was no secret to his boys that he didn't have any feelings for Mercedes, and he never showed any love or affection toward Samad Jr.

"Like I said, whatever we had is in the past."

"So you think your son is in the past? Your son is right now. I've been meaning to call you and—"

Samad interrupted her. "Look. Like I said. What we had was in the past. I'm with Heat now. That's my lady. You need to respect that."

"But what about us, Samad? Huh? What was all that shit you was saying?"

"There is no us; it's about Heat."

"Ooooh. Okaaaay. In the jail when you were fuckin' me and I was suckin' your dick. It wasn't about Heat then."

"One of my men will be in touch with you to make sure your son is taken care of."

"What the fuck you mean one of your men will be in touch with me to make sure *my son* is taken care of. This is *our* son. I didn't make this baby by myself, and I'm not taking care of Samad Jr. by myself."

"Somebody will be in touch with you to make sure he has what he needs." Samad hung up and dialed another number. The person picked up on the first ring.

"Hey, boss man. What's the word?" Mike answered.

"Same shit, different day." Samad sped through the red light. "I'm tryna see if my man, Aaron, made it down there yet. I haven't heard anything from your people, or anybody for that matter."

"Nothing yet. I'll make sure I call you as soon as I hear something."

Another call was beeping on his phone. "Okay, I need to answer this. This is my other man down there. Let me chop it up with him."

"No doubt. Later, Samad. Oh, one more thing before you go. About that other thing, you know what I'm talm' 'bout'?" He spoke in code. "Yeah, that other thing—the other guy. It was confirmed. He was murdered in Miami."

" . . . I heard . . . We'll talk later. One." Samad answered his call waiting.

"Yo Samad. I'm returning your call. Still didn't hear anything on your man Aaron. So I can't even call it yet, baby."

"Damn," Samad mumbled. "Okay, make sure you hit me as soon as you hear anything."

"I will."

Samad clicked END and tossed the phone on the passenger seat. He drove faster through the streets wondering where Aaron was.

"After this big move, I just wanna leave this state with Heat," Samad said out loud. He let out a loud sigh and rubbed his hair, stroking his waves forward. Music filled the car as he drove.

He pulled up to his sister Iyana's house, hit the horn, and waited for her to come outside.

"I'm coming down!" Iyana yelled out the window.

"Hey, big brother," she finally said, getting in the car some ten minutes later. She reached over and hugged Samad. He kissed her cheek.

"Hey, little sis. How you been?"

I'm good. Thanks for agreeing to drop me off, so I can pick up my car."

"No problem." Samad turned the music down. He turned to Iyana. "I need you to understand something . . . Heat is my woman. I know you cool with Mercedes, but you're my little sister, and I need you to respect Heat."

Iyana turned her head and looked out the window.

"Look at me, Iyana!" Samad yelled, making her jump.

"I hear you."

"No, I really need you to hear me, hear me." Samad stared at Iyana with intensity in his eyes.

"I understand Heat is your woman. I'll respect that."

"Good, because it's a lot of stuff going on that you don't understand. I got a lot on my mind, and I don't need to be no referee dealing with no female drama. I got enough to worry about out in these streets."

"I understand, big brother."

"Good. Before I drop you off, I want to pick up these balloons and a small cake to surprise Heat. Her 23rd birthday is coming up soon, and she said she doesn't want a party since her mom will be out of town for some lawyers' conference. But I am her family."

"Hmph!" Iyanna said.

Samad glared at her. "She's not expecting it, so I'm going to just surprise her and take her out later. I just dropped her off to get her hair and nails done. So I got time to get everything now and drop it off at the spot. They're going to serenade her and everything."

"I can tell you must really love her. You've never been this way before with any woman, as far as I know. Okay, I will even pick out the cake and balloons to show you I know how to bury the hatchet between us." Iyana faked a smile.

Samad tilted his head like 'yeah right.'

"Besides, they said my car won't be ready for another hour or so. Let's go." Iyana turned the music up as Samad drove off fast through the streets. "Poor Mercedes . . . I don't understand how dudes just treat women any kind of way. Don't you know karma comes to visit every once in a while?"

"That's why I'm tryna do right by Heat."

"Just fuck Mercedes and Samad Jr., huh?"

"Samad Jr. is going to have his needs met. Me and his mama are done. So it is what it is," Samad replied.

Iyana sat back and closed her eyes. "I hope you can say the same thing to karma. 'Cause when she comes, she's coming strong too. One day . . ."

CHAPTER 27
I Need Answers

"I hate Samad's lyin' ass! How could he! He can go to hell for all I care! I need to move in a different direction with my life!" Heat inhaled, then exhaled loud. "I got a headache." She had just woke up on Ebony's couch and lay in the same spot staring up at the ceiling. She reached over to her phone, which was vibrating again. Nineteen missed calls and nine text messages. All from Samad. He called Ebony all night looking for Heat. Ebony lied and told Samad she was looking for Heat also.

By text, Heat learned that Ebony went to the store and now was going to check on Unique afterward. After reading Ebony's text, she plugged her phone up to the charger, then shut her phone off.

Even though Heat had her own problems, she was worried about Unique. Over the years they argued as best friends do, but she never put her hands on a person she called a friend, especially one who was close enough to be a sister. Although they were mad at each other, they shared an unbreakable bond. The three girls had developed a friendship that's hard to come by these days. Heat decided their friendship *was* worth repairing. She also decided she was going to deal with Samad another time. *He got his coming.*

Heat picked up Ebony's house phone, buried her feelings deep down inside, and tried to push the baby situation to the back of her mind. Once Heat dialed a number, she waited as the phone rang on the other end.

"Thank you for calling National Domestic Hotline that offers help for women. All of our representatives are currently assisting other customers. Your call is very important to us. Please do not hang up, and your call will be answered in the order in which it was received." The recording played on the phone.

Heat waited.

"Good afternoon. This is Sarah. How may I help you?" The representative came on the line cheerful, full of energy, upbeat and bubbly.

"Uh, umm, uhhh . . . hi, good afternoon!" Heat stuttered.

"May I have your name please?"

"Umm, it's umm . . . uhh . . ."

"It's optional. You don't have to give your name."

"Tammy James," Heat answered.

"How may I help you today, Ms. James?"

"Can I ask you a few questions, please? Sarah, you said, is it?"

"Please do so. Ask me anything you want. Yes, ma'am, it's Sarah."

"I'm actually doing research on a case study. I'm a social worker, studying to become a psychologist, and I've recently received my degree."

"Congratulations."

"Thank you. Maybe I'm missing something. Can you please explain how you can tell if someone is being abused? Or, umm . . . uhh, how can I get someone to admit they are being abused?"

"That's the difficult part, ma'am. The denial."

"Umm . . . is it abuse if someone is yelling at you? Er, umm, uh—if somebody keeps you in the house, and they won't let you go anywhere, or ummm . . . if you don't see any marks, but you know somebody is being abused. How can you umm . . ." Heat let out a long sigh. "I don't know what I'm really trying to say, Sarah."

"Well, ma'am, there's several types of abuse: substance abuse, mental abuse, verbal abuse, emotional abuse, sexual abuse, and the obvious: physical abuse. These are the most familiar forms of abuse. I'm not a licensed doctor, so I can't get into all the legalities with you over the phone. However, I can assist you as best as I can, and possibly point you in the right direction— connect you to the right people locally in your zip code, so you can get help. Your phone call today is one step in the right direction, talking about it, and admitting the abuse."

"Oh, it's not for me. I'm calling to help a friend out. Can you explain what some of the behaviors of an abuser are, please?" Heat asked in an innocent child-like voice.

"Well, if someone is controlling your every move, as you mentioned—the isolation and verbal abuse eventually leads to physical abuse once escalated. In addition to that is a dire need to know where you are and what you are doing every minute, checking up on you and controlling your entire life. Isolation, as I mentioned, is definitely a big red flag! The abuser will try to cut off everybody around you—all communication—so they can have you all to themselves."

Heat shook her head and thought about how aggressive Samad had become when he first told her they were moving, and he didn't want any of her friends popping up at their house until she ran it by him first.

"Can you give me some more examples of verbal abuse, please?" Heat quizzed.

"Well, for one, the verbal abuse starts with statements like: 'You're never gonna make anything out of yourself,' or, 'I hate you.' In some cases, the name-calling begins with statements such as: 'You're dumb, or fat, or stupid'—just to name a few. That can stem from a cycle of abuse he or she experienced as a child, and sometimes he or she repeats the cycle. Maybe something heard in the home mixed in with the mental abuse, which can internally scar a child if he/she hears it long enough growing up. It will manifest into their world."

"Funny. I always thought name-calling didn't hurt because we're taught to ignore it."

"Untrue. Those negative words will eventually get inside their head and take root. Then sooner or later, the person suffering from the abuse might start believing them, and it'll eventually chip away at their self-esteem. They'll believe they are nothing and nobody wants them. Then they'll start believing they are ugly or fat, which can sometimes lead them down a dark path. This is when low self-esteem or substance abuse comes in, and sometimes even suicide."

Heat shook her head because she didn't agree. She remembered when Samad cursed at her plenty of times before, hurting her feelings, calling her names. But she dismissed it as him just being mad. "To my understanding, if a guy hits you, then that's abuse, but if he says little hurtful remarks, I don't see nothin' wrong with that. I don't think that's abuse if your man is arguing with you, or calling you out your name. No couple is perfect. Everybody fights in their relationship," Heat replied.

"I agree that no relationship is perfect. But I do not agree with your significant other calling you out of your name, or belittling you, or making you feel inferior to a point where it changes your perspective about yourself and makes you feel inadequate. Yes, it slowly chips away at your self-esteem. That is not a healthy relationship. That is a form of verbal abuse."

"Hmph! Well, I don't consider that abuse," Heat replied. "I told my professor the same thing. And I know what the textbook says, but opinions are just that— opinions."

Someone knocked at Ebony's door, interrupting Heat's conversation.

"Hold on one moment, Sarah."

"Sure, no problem."

"Who is it?" There was no reply. Heat walked to door and looked out the peephole. Someone had their back to the door.

Heat asked again. "Who is it?"

Face turned and she opened the door. He stepped inside the apartment before Heat could say anything.

"Hey. What's up? Ebony here?" Face asked.

"No. ."

"Damn, I gotta get something from her. She was holding for me."

Heat noticed Face kept looking out the window, then looking at his phone. He paced in a circle as if he was worried about something. Sweat beaded up on the bridge of his nose. *What's wrong with his nervous ass?* she thought.

"Well, she's not here, and I don't know how long before she gets back."

"Let me call Ebony real quick to see if she can tell me where she put my stuff. I'll only be a minute."

"Okay." Heat watched as Face walked to the window and looked out. *Why he acting funny?*

"Hello, are you still there?" Sarah interrupted Heat.

"Yes, I'm still here." She watched Face with the phone pressed close to her ear.

"Yes, ma'am, with all due respect, like I said that is not a healthy relationship. That *is* verbal abuse. Kids today face all kinds of abuse in the form of bullying on the Internet, via slander on social media sites, and on the playgrounds. Abuse comes in many forms. We need to make sure we are aware and sensitive to other people's feelings," Sarah stated firmly.

"Most kids are tough these days. Most of them just shake it off," Heat said.

"They may be tough, and they may appear to shake it off, but we don't see the tears once they're alone, or the little 'talks' they have with their conscience when it speaks negatively about them. Or maybe they self-mutilate. So, it's still abuse, and words can be just as damaging as a knife or a bullet. A lot of people are not aware of that," Sarah continued.

But that would mean that I . . . Heat refused to say it aloud.

"Regardless if it's in a relationship, or being done by peers in school. Most people overlook this form of abuse because no physical harm is done, like hitting a person with your hands. Unfortunately, name-calling can be more harmful and detrimental, particularly to younger children during their most impressionable years."

"It does make sense, but I was raised to let words go right by me. But I guess it didn't really work because if you said something foul to me back then—you better believe a mouth shot was coming." Heat laughed.

"Ms. James, we're supposed to communicate when someone has hurt us. As a future psychologist, you know that."

"I do, it's just . . . old habits are hard to break." Heat was thinking about her fight with Unique. "Now what about psychological abuse?" she asked.

Face overheard some of Heat's conversation. "Yo, who you talkin' to on the phone?" Face asked. "My man Samad be hot-headed." Heat ignored Face.

"Here's a rundown, Ms. James. Let's say you have an adult who threatens their loved one—to kill them one minute, then the next minute proclaim their love—it messes with a person's mind. That's definitely psychological abuse, which can also scar a person long after. Words definitely hurt."

"They do," Heat said. "Hitting is a no-brainer. We recognize it as abuse right away."

"That's correct. It is the obvious, Ms. James. Physical abuse occurs when the perpetrator puts his or her hands on you—lashing out in an act of violence and sometimes making sure they only hit you somewhere not noticeable to your family members or friends, at first. Until eventually, the marks will become visible, like a black eye, or a busted lip, or a broken arm. It almost, always escalates, and gets more violent as time goes."

"Well, thank you for your time, Sarah."

"Ms. James, may I ask which zip code you are in?"

"Uhh, no thanks. Have a nice day, and I appreciate your help," Heat said, disconnecting the call.

Face walked to the front door. "I'm about to leave. She's not answering her phone. It's going to voice mail. I'll be back after I get in touch with Ebony. If she calls, tell her to call my phone."

"A'ight." Heat followed Face to the door and locked it once he left.

She released a loud sigh. *I'm up here talking about Unique and Sean, and Samad ain't no different from him. Sooner or later me and Samad will be fighting.* "Hmmm. I never thought I would say this, but . . . I am in an abusive relationship my damn self!" she admitted.

CHAPTER 28
The Cover Up

"Hello?"

The loud ringing house phone awakened Heat. She'd fallen back to sleep on Ebony's couch for at least an hour. Recognizing Ebony's name on the display, she picked the cordless phone up and walked to the window, looking outside. "Heat!" Ebony called her name, sounding panicky.

"Ebony?" she asked. "Face came by—"

"Girl, I been callin' you on your phone. It keeps going right to voice mail. Somethin' happened with Unique."

"Like what?"

"I'm at her house. Just come over here, but come next door to her neighbor Gwen's house. We need your help. Park around back when you get here."

"Why? What happened? Why you talking so fast?"

"I can't say it over the phone. Just come here."

Heat's eyes narrowed. "Okay. I'll be there."

They hung up. *This can't be good.* She put on her sweatpants and jacket and zipped it up in five seconds. After putting on her sneakers, she grabbed her iPhone off the charger, along with her keys and ran out the door wondering what could have happened to Unique.

Remembering her run-in with the officer after the fight with Mercedes, Heat kept her speed at the proper level, and within fifteen minutes she was pulling up to Unique's building. She drove around back and spotted a parking space near the end of the lot. She texted Ebony to let her know she was outside.

Ebony appeared in the doorway, but then turned and walked away, leaving the door open. Heat walked to the front of the building and looked up and down Unique's block. Empty. *What the hell is going on?*

"It's breezy out here." Heat closed her jacket.

She went to the back and entered the building, locking the door behind her. Heat made her way to Gwen's apartment next door.

Anxious, she rushed into the living room. Unique sat on the long brown leather sectional curled up with her knees folded to her chest. She rocked back and forth with her arms wrapped around her legs. Blood spotted Unique's orange T-shirt and jeans. Heat smelled trash. *Gwen's house stinks,* she thought.

"What's going on in here?" Heat asked in a low tone.

"Come here. Sit down right here," Unique said, patting the couch beside her.

Ebony looked at Unique and asked, "Do you want me to tell her?"

"Tell me what? Come on now. Y'all tweekin'. Woke me up outta my sleep. Somebody better tell me something!"

"Do you want me to tell her?" Ebony asked again.

209

Unique nodded yes. Heat slowly turned her head toward Ebony, while looking at Unique out the corner of her eye. Unique's dark, beady eyes looked zombie-like. Her hair was messy.

Ebony took a deep breath and let out a long sigh. "Well, Unique and Sean were fighting. He came home from the club pissy drunk, poppin' pills—them mollys and God knows what else. He started arguing with Unique for no reason. Just came in flippin' on her."

Unique kept rocking and sobbing with her head down. "He smacked me while I had the baby in my arms," she interrupted Ebony. "Lil Sean was sleeping, thank God. He almost fell when Sean hit me, so I walked away to lay him down. Sean started screaming at me from the kitchen to come make him something to eat. He said when he got back from the store I better have his food ready or else.

"At that point I was gonna leave as soon as I heard him leave. I was tryna find my ID and keys and stuff that he hid, and I ran across some x-rated videos of him and other chicks. The icing on the cake was the pictures I found of him and some girl hugged up. Marissa was in the pictures. He had his hand on her pregnant belly." Tears raced down her face as she spoke.

Ebony hugged Unique to calm her trembling arms.

"I had so many emotions running through my veins. I was hurt, and all those scared feelings I used to have, went out the window. My mind wandered back to all the times he hit me and mistreated me. I took Lil Sean over to Gwen's because I knew things were gon' turn out fucked up."

"I wish you had just left," Heat said.

"I can't say the same, Heat. I really can't . . . I was too far gone at that point, so I slid a pair of thin black socks on my hands and loaded Sean's gun and screwed the silencer on it. And I waited. I felt different with that gun in my hand, and I stood against the wall bracing myself. I was beyond being tired of his bullshit. I put up with a lot.

"After a while I heard him banging on the front door. 'Bitch, let me in! Open this door. My food better be done, you whore!'

"His voice snapped me out of wherever the fuck my mind had wandered to. It was like having an out-of-body experience while all of this was going on. I saw it happenin' and I heard everything around me. It was . . . as if . . . it wasn't me. His drunk ass entered the hallway and approached the kitchen. I stepped out and aimed the gun at him.

"Don't fucking move! Do not come towards me! Do not take another step in my direction. If you even *look* like you about to flinch, I swear to God, word to my son, I will kill you!

"Sean tilted his head, looking me dead in the eyes. 'Please put the gun down, baby . . .'"

"Did you call the police?" Gwen asked.

Heat, Unique, and Ebony looked at her, dumbstruck.

"What! Okay, the answer's no then."

Unique continued. "He begged me to put the gun down.

"Oh my God, Unique. Tell me you didn't—" Heat said.

"Funny how having a loaded gun changes a person's behavior. Sean's words were no longer filled with hatred. His voice was soothing and warm, as if he were talking to Baby Sean.

'Unique, please put the gun down, baby. We can talk about whatever you're upset about.'

'No we can't. It's too late,' I said. Images of him hitting me, and of us arguing and fighting, and him embarrassing me . . . All that stuff flooded my brain . . ."

None of the women knew what to say to comfort Unique. Bursting with the finale of how things came to an end, Unique stared ahead revealing her truth.

"Baby, I love you. I'm sorry for whatever someone told you about me. You know they're all lies! You know how people try to get in our business. They jealous of what we got; they just mad at what we got. I hope you not believin' the lies. Baby, I love you," Sean begged.

Tears streamed down Unique's face.

"Please, Unique, hand me the gun!" The smell of alcohol on Sean's breath shot straight to her stomach.

Numb of any emotion, she didn't hear his supple voice. All she heard was the same Sean yelling at her, smacking her for no reason, just because he was in a bad mood. The venom he spat at her, and the severe beatings he gave her. Him demanding she stay home and cook and clean while he ran the streets doing whatever. That was the voice she heard.

She no longer saw the sparkle in his eyes like when they first met some years ago, before his true side came out. Unique saw abuse in his eyes, and the word 'abuser' tattooed on his forehead. They were in two different worlds, and neither of them realized it. She remembered girls coming to their house asking for Sean, and how he'd lie about them wanting to cop drugs, or that they were his cousin's friends, or 'his manz' girlfriends.

Unique now understood how stupid she had been all of these years putting up with his bullshit. Sean always had an answer that seemed like a lie, and even the facts never added up. Yet, she dismissed it and went against her own instincts and believed his every word. Even if she saw the lies with her own eyes, he would somehow twist what she just saw or heard, and still manage to convince and manipulate her into believing that her eyes were playing tricks on her.

The phone started ringing, bringing her out of her trance.

Ring! Ring!

She turned in the direction of the loud, non-stop ringing. As she turned, Sean reached for the gun. Unique turned back and let off a shot.

Chirp!

The silencer muffled the sound.

Chirp!

Sean stumbled backward and fell to the floor. His body convulsed, and his eyes rolled in the back of his head, as if having a seizure.

Heat placed her hands on Unique, comforting her. "I did nothing to save him. I wanted him to die," she cried. "I watched him reach for me, but I stood frozen in that very spot. I don't know where the bullets struck him. I just know I shot him. His body shook, then there was no movement. I walked over to Sean to see if he was still breathing, and to see where I shot him. Blood was gushing out of his chest and his side. I turned and walked away. He grabbed my leg with both hands, digging his nails deep in my left ankle, leaving this mark. It's still bleeding." She pointed to her ankle.

Ebony walked to the bathroom and came back with a washcloth. She wrapped it around Unique's ankle to stop the bleeding.

Unique continued. "When he grabbed my ankle, I turned and shot him again. This time I unloaded one right in his head and another in his chest. His eyes were open, looking straight at me. He kept a tight grip on my ankle. Sean made this weird sound, like he was gurgling on blood, and his body shook one last time before it went limp.

"He lay dead on our floor, and I left him there. No matter which way I walked through the house to gather my things, I kept looking at his body . . ."

"Ugh!" Unique said, getting the chills just thinking about it.

Ebony stood up. "Where's the gun? We gotta do something with that gun. Get rid of it first and foremost. Stash it somewhere. It's empty, right? Any more bullets in it?"

Unique shook her head no. "I already emptied the gun and wiped my fingerprints off, even though I had my hands covered."

"You sure you wiped your fingerprints off?" Heat asked Unique.

"Yeah, I'm sure. I scratched the serial number off the gun too. I need to get this gun far away. "

"We need to get you out of here. I know some people in Atlanta who owe me some favors. I'll give them a call," Ebony said, walking toward her phone. She dialed a number, and then disappeared into the other room.

Heat turned to Unique and said, "It's gon' be all right. I spoke to a professional, and she answered some questions I had about abuse. That'll be your defense. What's interesting was, I called for you, trying to get some answers to help you in your situation, and I found myself in what she described as abuse was going on in my relationship with Samad. I was embarrassed to open up to you and Ebony about me and Samad fighting. I thought just because we fought behind closed doors, that it was okay because nobody knew." Heat lowered her gaze, pushing back the tears welling up in her eyes.

Unique rested her head on Heat's shoulder and began to cry again. This time she didn't stop. Heat stroked her hair, comforting her best friend, whose silent nightmare had just come to an end. Unique hugged Heat back, comforting her as well.

Sean got what he deserved, Heat thought, hugging Unique tighter.

Ebony walked back in the room, tossed her phone on the other couch, and sat beside Unique. "I made a few phone calls. Don't worry about it Unique. Everything's going to be all right.

With Heat sitting on the other side of Unique, the three girls sat hugging each other, sharing a familiar bond. Secretly all three girls wondered if Unique would eventually go to jail for killing her baby daddy.

CHAPTER 29
Damage Control

"Flight 404 to Atlanta boarding on gate three!" blasted through the loudspeakers at the airport.

"That's us!" said Heat.

Ebony, Unique, and Heat stopped at the security area and set their bags down on the floor near the x-ray machine. Ebony walked through first. The metal detector beeped.

"Please step back through and try again," the TSA said.

Ebony stepped back and walked through again. The machine beeped once more. "Please step aside and let me check you with this handwand. I need to check for any metal you may have on you. Something is setting the machine off." Ebony stepped aside. The security guard pointed at the small table next to the conveyor belt. "Empty everything out of your pockets and place it in those plastic containers right there," the small woman demanded in a surprisingly harsh tone.

"Heat and Unique, go ahead. I'll catch up to y'all in a minute."

"No, we not leavin' you," Heat said as she and Unique stood at Ebony's side. Unique talked on her cell phone.

"Let's go over there to that McDonald's to get something to eat first. We only got thirty minutes before our flight leaves," Heat suggested.

217

"Okay," Ebony replied.

"I need to use the bathroom anyway," Unique chimed in.

The security guard repeated herself and pointed at the small table next to the conveyor belt. "Empty everything out of your pockets and place everything in those plastic containers.

Ebony twisted her face up. "I don't have nothin' in my pockets. You not checkin' me."

"If you want to come through this security area and board the plane, you will be checked." Ebony glanced down at her bag on the floor.

Heat whispered to Ebony. "Do you have anything on you that's making the machine go off?"

Ebony whispered, "Yes. I'm dirty right now."

"Girl, what!" Heat whispered as other people walked around them going through the metal detectors. They talked in hush tones. "Dirty?" Unique said.

Ebony shook her head. "Yeah. This toy cop must not be in the loop."

"Girl, I heard rumors about you doin' certain things, and I always defended you, giving you the benefit of the doubt. Girl, what the fuck is wrong with you? Who the fuck do you think you are? You gonna go to fuckin' jail, Ebony! Don't you know we at the airport—"

"I'll explain another time." Ebony ignored Heat and looked around again to see if she saw her contact.

After the TSA agent finished searching the large

crowd of people that went through, she noticed Ebony, Heat, and Unique still standing and blocking the walkway through the metal detector. She saw a new line forming.

"Pssst." The TSA agent sucked her teeth, annoyed with the fact that they were now holding up her line. She wasn't in the mood for annoying passengers today.

"Well, you have a choice before you can come on this side. I can either check you, and you can go ahead and catch your flight, or you can refuse to be checked. You do have that right. However, you won't be able to go pass this checkpoint. You can leave the airport."

Ebony snarled, looking the TSA up and down. With one swift move, she grabbed her bag and abruptly turned away from the security area. Heat and Unique followed her. They went to McDonald's and ate their food quickly.Afterward, they made a detour to the bathroomand checked each stall to make sure they were alone. Heat and Unique checked the other side to be certain the stalls were empty. Ebony pulled her cell phone out her jacket pocket and checked her messages for her airport connect.

"Girl, did you think this thing through, Einstein? Bringing shit through an airport knowing they on high alert across the fucking nation!"

"I know Heat, but when I was at security, the person who's supposed to be checking us was not on her post. I said I'll explain it another time."

"Girl, you a fuckin' trip! Ain't much more to explain!"

Ebony received an incoming text message. "Hold on, that's him hittin' my phone now. He just texted me saying he was in traffic, but now he just clocked in. So, let's go back to security while he's there; his people are in place."

Heat turned and looked in the mirror. "I cannot believe your ass. What else have you been hiding from me?"

"Nothing. Let's go," Ebony replied.

Heat shook her head while turning on the faucet and splashing cold water on her face. Again she wet her hands, putting some in her hair. She pulled a brush out the side zipper of her bag and brushed her hair up into a ponytail. Then she put on her large round sunglasses.

Unique came out of the stall and washed her hands. She grabbed her McDonald's bag off the top of Heat's bag, and they all exited the ladies room.

They headed back to security without incident.

Heat, Ebony, and Unique were finally boarding the plane to Atlanta. They found their seats, placed some of their bags above in the overhead compartments and finally got comfortable. Heat kept one of her carry-on bags with her.

The flight attendant walked up and down the aisle passing out peanuts, crackers bottle water, and can sodas. She also made sure everyone had their seatbelts on.

"I need to use the ladies room. I'll be right back," Heat said, walking to the back of the plane.

"Heat? Is that you?" a masculine voice asked.

"Moe?" Heat answered with a surprised look.

"How are you?"

"I'm good."

"How's your mother? And Aaron? I haven't seen or heard from your brother in a minute."

"Everybody's good. How are you, Moe?"

"Better, now that I see you," he said.

Heat blushed and lowered her gaze.

"I have not seen you since, since . . ." Moe looked up. "I have not seen you since you were in the hospital."

Heat heard all the stories about Moe from her brother Aaron after she questioned him. She never told Samad how well she really knew Moe. Aaron introduced her to Moe back when she was dating Eli. Moe bought Aaron his first vehicle because he earned himself the top dog spot in Moe's eyes by selling his bricks faster than anybody, making Moe rich. Moe surprised Aaron on the block with a brand new black jeep for being one of his top soldiers.

Aaron was always the go-to guy when anybody wanted to get at Moe. Samad took a liking to the way Aaron handled his business and offered him his own situation working alongside him. Moe took that as disrespect, and that was the beginning of the fallout between Moe and Samad.

Even though Moe knew Aaron was a loyal dude, he never wanted Aaron to remain working under him. He looked at Aaron as an up and coming Boss. He felt like Aaron was manipulated by Samad. Moe knew Samad wanted Aaron to work under him so he would always answer to Samad instead of becoming his own Boss. Samad's manipulation worked, making Aaron switch sides.

Moe leaned in and hugged Heat. "Damn girl, you look even sexier than I remember."

Heat smiled, remembering how nice he'd been when she lost her baby. Before she could resist his hug, Moe gripped her waist tight and pulled her in close. "Mmmmm, you smell good too."

Heat hugged him back, feeling the muscles on his chest press against her face, and his large upper back muscles brushed across her embracing hands. Mercedes and Samad's young son's face flashed in Heat's thoughts.

"Thank you, Moe. You smell good too," she replied. Heat smiled and took a step back out of his tight grip.

She looked Moe up and down. You look good, Moe. Your skin's glistenin'. Looks like you've been in the gym liftin'. "Fit and in shape and you always, always dress nice."

"Thank you. Watch out now." Moe blushed in his cool way.

"So how you been? You married yet? Got any

kids? What you been up to?" Heat asked.

Moe couldn't hide his smile and beautiful teeth. "Me married? Nah, not yet. I haven't found that special one yet. And I don't have any kids. But I want a daughter." He gazed at her with admiration and lust.

"What about you, Heat? You married yet? Any kids?" he asked, already knowing she and Samad had lost a child and currently didn't have any kids. Even though Samad tried to keep his child with Mercedes a secret, Moe knew about him.

He knew the other side of Samad and heard about all the killings in the streets ordered by Samad. He wondered just how much Heat really knew about the man she was with.

"Who're you with on this flight? Where you staying when you get to Atlanta? You gotta go out with me while you're in the ATL. Okay?" Moe shot off question after question without giving her a chance to reply.

Heat turned and look toward the front of the plane. "I'm not going down to the A for pleasure. I-I-I'm going down for business," she stuttered.

"Well, make it your business to get at me while you're there, okay?" he replied with a devilish smirk and handed her his card.

She looked down at the card. "I will." Heat took it out of Moe's hand. "So what are you going to the A for?" she asked.

"I'm on my way to my boy's video shoot in

Buckhead. He's doing the cafe scene tomorrow. Then he's doin' a few scenes in the strip club." AR was sitting in the aisle behind Moe's seat on the phone texting and listening to messages. The popular rapper had been making much noise on radio air waves and TV.

Moe made introductions. "This is Heat. Heat, this is AR."

AR took his earplugs out of his ear, then extended his hand. "How are you doing, Heat? Nice to meet you." He smiled and she took his hand and shook it.

"Hello, nice to meet you, AR," Heat answered softly. She let AR's hand go, then turned back to Moe.

"It was nice seeing you, Moe. Let me get back to my seat with Unique and Ebony."

"Ebony told you that I ask about you a lot?"

"Nope!" she lied, knowing she had to stay away from Moe because she knew he was Samad's enemy. She also knew Moe liked her ever since back in the day. And the fact that Pezo told Samad about Moe being at the hospital during the time she lost the baby meant Moe was off limits.

"Excuse me, ma'am! Excuse me, ma'am!" a woman said, walking up the aisle trying to squeeze by Heat. The lady impatiently brushed by and sucked her teeth with two small children in tow. One of the kids touched Heat's soft, baby blue crushed linen pants, leaving a handprint of chocolate. She looked down at her pants.

"Shit!" she cursed, looking into Moe's brown eyes. "You're bad luck, Moe! Every time you're around it's under crazy circumstances! Something always happens!" Heat giggled.

She began brushing the chocolate off. Moe kneeled and rubbed the chocolate with napkins from the food tray, which only made it worse. He stroked Heat's leg in a sexual way. She realized what he was doing and stopped him.

"You're smearing it. You're making it worse. I got it."

"I'm sorry."

"See, now I have to change!" she said, pointing to her carry-on bag on her shoulder. "I need to go to the ladies room. We planned to go out and have fun before I leave the A, I guess I gotta put on my club outfit I planned to wear."

Moe raised an eyebrow. "Where did you say you were staying in Atlanta?"

"With my cousin. Unique got a job interview with a school in Clayton County as a substitute teacher," Heat lied again.

"What's your cell number? Can I call you?"

"Ummmmm, I just got that phone and I don't know the number. But you just gave me your card."

"Yeah, but I got three phones. One for business, one for family, and one for friends. So what's your number?" he asked again.

"I'll be right back!" Heat abruptly left him

225

standing there. She headed to the bathroom and glanced back at Moe, who was still watching her.

Once inside the small box of a bathroom, Heat filled Ebony in via text on what she told Moe, so they could be on the same page. Quickly, she changed clothes and rushed out to get back to Ebony and Unique. *I don't trust myself with Moe. Right now I'm in a vulnerable state of mind. Even though Samad had a baby with that bitch Mercedes, I know better. Two wrongs don't make it right.*

"Please take your seat. Keep this area clear," a flight attendant announced as she walked down the aisle.

Moe stepped inside close to his seat, waiting for Heat to walk past. "Damn! See, you ain't right. You ain't even playin' fair! Lookin' like one of them models in *Straight Stuntin* magazine." Moe smiled as he admired her tight fitting one-piece body suit showing off all of her curves. He smiled when he looked down at her pretty feet in her open toe shoes.

"I brought this outfit with intentions to wear to one of these clubs before leaving the A."

He grabbed her arm and stopped her from walking. They stood face to face. "So when you gon' give me some of your time? We can just eat lunch or something. Me and you, away from everybody. No entourage, no interruptions. When you gon' stop running from me?" Moe asked with a serious expression and a slight grin.

Heat was thrown off. She didn't know how to respond. "I gotta go to my seat, Moe. Since Ebony already got all of your contacts I'll get them from her." She glanced at his hand and he released her arm.

"I want y'all to come to my man's video shoot if that's possible. You could wear something like what you got on now. I wanna link up before you leave Atlanta, okay? Let's make it happen!"

Heat nodded okay. Moe hugged Heat and held her in his arms.

"So who you fuck with, Heat?" Moe whispered in her ear, his lips tickling her ear lobe.

"Who *you* fuck with, Moe?" she whispered also, suprising him.

"What lucky guy taking up all your time?" He kept her close to him, leaving no gap between them. Moe already knew the answer to his question, but his luck depended on her reply.

"What lucky girl taking up all your time?" She flipped it back on him and didn't break their close contact.

Moe smiled. "Nobody! I'm single. I'm tryna fuck with you heavy! You got a nigga chasing you," he whispered.

"It was good seeing you, Moe."

"You too. I hope to see more of you." Moe loosened his grip.

Heat turned to walk away, ending their flirting game.

"No mention of Samad. Today must be my lucky day," Moe said, although Heat had not heard him.

CHAPTER 30
Secrets in Atlanta

Hartsfield Airport
Atlanta

"She's still throwing up in the bathroom, Heat," Ebony said as they stood near the baggage carousel.

"Yeah. Unique said she's pregnant," Heat replied.

Ebony shook her head and continued texting. "I'm gon' get us a cab. Come out of those doors right there!" Ebony said, pointing to the exit as she walked off.

"Okay. Cool."

Unique walked out the bathroom and joined Heat. "I'm good now."

"You sure, Unique?"

"Well, I'm good for now."

Heat approached the carousel and grabbed her and Unique's luggage.

"Oh shit! There goes Sean's sister Angie. They found me!" Unique panicked.

"What! Where?" Heat turned in her direction.

"Right there!" Unique pointed at a woman approaching them.

"That's not his sister, Unique."

"That looks just like Angie coming right towards us."

Heat's heart dropped and she looked around, noticing the cops standing on the right side. The woman strolled right by them, minding her own business.

"Girl, you paranoid. And you know the airport always have police here. Relax. Calm down, Unique. You making me nervous now. Damn!"

Unique took a deep breath then let out a loud sigh of relief. " Let's just hurry up and get out of here. Where Ebony go?"

"She went to get us a cab. Grab your stuff and come on."

Heat and Unique walked to the exit, hoping Ebony got the cab.

Ebony called Heat's phone.

Heat picked up. "We coming out right now."

"Where y'all at?" Ebony asked. "Our ride waiting for us! What y'all doing in there? Come on! It's scorching hot out here!"

"Our ride?"

"Yeah. Moe."

Heat went silent.

"Hello? Heat?"

"Yeah, Ebony, we coming right now." Heat hung up. "Come on, Unique. You sure you feel okay?"

"Yeah, I feel better now. After splashing cold water on my face, I'm good."

The big glass doors opened automatically. They spotted Ebony outside.

"Come on, girl. They dropping us off at the hotel!"

"Move your vehicles!" the cop yelled through the bullhorn, grabbing their attention.

Everybody walked quickly to the vehicles, and drove off bumper to bumper until they reached Crowne Plaza Hotel. Moe led the way inside.

"Moe, how many rooms do you have reserved in here?" Ebony asked.

"The entire top floor."

Everybody headed toward the elevator and piled inside. The doors finally opened on the eighth floor and everyone exited.

Heat and Unique looked to Ebony for their room key. "Unique, we're at the very end of the hall," Ebony said, passing Unique a key.

"Heat, your room is right there!" Moe interrupted, pointing toward room 801 and handing her a key-card.

She walked to room 801 and realized her room was right next door to Moe's. Room 802. " . . . Oh, no problem."

Moe looked at his key-card. "Eight-o-two. Looks like AR got some pull up front. He put me right next door to you." He smiled as he looked at his key. Then he looked at hers.

Heat smiled. *Mmm hmm. How convenient.*

"So what's on the agenda for tomorrow?" Moe asked.

"Nothing much right now. We'll be here for a week taking care of a little business. Our schedule's a bit hectic! But I'll call you. I need to freshen up," Heat replied, trying to brush Moe off, staying smooth away from him. She knew there was strong chemistry between them.

"Me too!" he replied. "I need to get out of these clothes. It's hot and muggy as hell in Atlanta.

"Okay. Later Moe," Heat said, watching Ebony enter her room and close the door.

"I'm for real, Heat. Just don't leave Atlanta without making a little time for me," he said, holding up his index finger and thumb, gesturing a pinch of salt.

Heat tried not to smile, but she couldn't hold it in. "I hear you, Moe."

"That's all I'm asking for is a small spot from you to fit me into your life. Ahem." Moe cleared his throat. "Umm I mean, fit me into your schedule," he said with a sexy smile. "Is that too much to ask?"

"No, that's not too much to ask, Moe. Let me go unpack." When she thought of Samad, she realized Moe was asking for way more than she could give. Any more than the conversation they just had would only result in trouble. That much she knew.

Heat walked in her room and let the door close behind her. Too tired and frustrated with this week's events. Her mind was racing. She tossed her bag on the bed, dropped the key on the dresser, missing and sending the key falling to the floor. She waved her hand at it as if to say 'I'll get it later.' She walked toward the bathroom, removed her sunglasses, and set them on the compartment above the vanity.

She looked at her reflection in the mirror for a

moment, placed her hands on the sink, resting on her palms.

Tears welled up in her eyes. She held in her tears but let out a loud sigh.

Heat noticed a red beam reflecting off the mirrors. Her mind wandered back to the daily talk shows she used to watch about peeping toms putting surveillance cameras in their neighbor's house to see them undress. She laughed at herself for being paranoid when she noticed the sink had a sensor on it, her hand motion activated the red beam when she placed her hands on the sink.

She continued looking in the mirror, staring into her own soul. All the turmoil in her life was taking a toll on her. Her heart was weary. She blinked back tears, turned away from the mirror, and faced the shower. Turning the shower on full blast, she jumped back as a bit of water splashed her hair.

"Shit!" she shrieked, pulling the clip out of her hair and letting her long tresses fall to her shoulders.

Slowly, she unzipped her one-piece body suit, and stepped out, then let it drop to the floor feeling a cool breeze between her legs.

The steam from the shower began to rise, engulfing the room, fogging up the mirrors. She stepped in the shower, letting the warm water caress her body, and the pain that overwhelmed her. Heat pictured Samad's face, and she could not stop thinking of how much the toddler was a spitting image of Samad. *How could he go to sleep every night in the same bed, knowing he had a child out there somewhere? How could he betray me?*

She leaned against the wall underneath the shower nozzle, drowning her sorrows away and crying softly, which immediately turned into uncontrollable loud cries. Letting go of all the pain and hurt inside, she bawled as the water washed her tears away, down the drain.

She tried to gather her composure to feel at peace. *I' have to deal with Samad when I get back to New York City. I can't live like this.*

While water beads pelted Heat's skin, she failed to notice Moe entering the bathroom and watching her naked reflection through the glass. He smiled at the fact that his enemy was in another state, and his woman was right here alone crying. Moe moved closer making a sound on the floor. Heat turned, startled.

A few seconds passed without a word from either Moe or Heat.

"How did Samad end up with a beautiful, smart woman like you? You shouldn't even be with Samad anyway. I want you for myself, Heat. Always have." She stared at Moe and allowed the tears to fall.

As the reality of her situation with Samad and Unique's murder of Sean came to the forefront, Heat turned her back to Moe and wept violently. Slowly, Moe unbuttoned his cufflinks one by one, keeping Heat in focus. He then unbuckled his jeans. One of his diamond cufflinks dropped on the plush carpet. He pulled down his boxers and stepped out of them. Fully erect, his dick poked out at attention. Determined to rid her of her sadness, he pushed the glass door back and stepped in the shower, gently tracing a line up the middle of her back. He reached under her hair and gingerly grabbed her neck and turned her to face him.

"You shouldn't be here, Moe," Heat whispered softly, with no conviction in her voice. He smiled, knowing she didn't mean it.

Moe pushed the stray strands of hair away from her face. His touch calmed her and her tears stopped. He placed his other hand around her waist and pulled her toward him. She didn't resist. His lips touched hers, and she kissed him back passionately, placing her hands around his neck, and pulling him closer.

Gently, he lifted her in his arms and placed her against the wall. She straddled his waist, wrapping her legs around him tighly. They continued kissing, enjoying each other's taste.

Slowly, he entered her raw, feeling how tight she was. Her body tightened as he went deeper. She kissed his neck, riding him.

"Ahhhh," Moe moaned, feeling himself about to bust. "Damn!" he then groaned.

Heat enjoyed herself, letting go of all the hurt and pain. She was so caught up in the moment with Moe. Dropping her head back, the water splashed all over her face. He began sucking and gently biting her neck and breasts, leaving dark red bite marks on her flesh.

As the water began to cool, they both reached their climax. Moe exploded inside her, although it wasn't intentional. It felt too good to pull out.

"Ughhhh!" Moe grunted as he came.

Heat's body shook as she came also. "Mmmmmm," she whimpered.

He slowly placed her on her feet and rested his hands on the wall right above her. Moe looked down at her breathing heavily while trying to catch his own breath. She buried her face in his chest, breathing her warm breath against him.

Reality sank in and guilt crept into Heat's mind. She couldn't look him in his eyes, and she stepped out of the shower. He grabbed her arm.

"Heat," he whispered. "What's wrong, ma?"

"Nothing's wrong," she replied, dropping her eyes to the floor.

"Don't feel guilty. What we just did was beautiful."

She reached for the white plush robe and walked out of the bathroom, stepping over Moe's clothes. She turned on the television and quietly lay on the bed.

Moe stepped out the shower and grabbed the white plush towel to dry off. He dressed in the bathroom with the door open while Heat watched him. Fully dressed, he stepped in her space, and she turned over on her side getting comfortable on the bed.

"You okay, ma?"

She didn't answer him, but shook her head yes.

He walked toward her, leaned over, and kissed her on her forehead. "Get some rest, mami!"

She lay in the bed wondering how she and Samad had gotten to this point. They both broke one of their own rules: seeking comfort outside of their relationship.

Heat pulled the cover over her head. *I'll never allow myself to be in a vulnerable situation like this again! I need to stay away from Moe! This will be my little secret!*

CHAPTER 31
GUILTY

"I need to check on Unique and make sure she got there safe," Heat said the next morning at 8:00 a.m.

The phone rang twice before Unique picked it up.

"Hello," she answered eagerly.

"Hey, Unique. This Heat. I just wanted to make sure you got there safely."

"Yes. I'm good now. I met up with Ebony's people. We in Buckhead. Remember when we had the pool party for Ebony last year? I'm safe. Tell her thanks."

"Oh, okay, I know where you at now. Good. How's baby Sean?"

"He's good. Safe with Gwen."

"Glad to hear that. So what's the plan?"

"They're going to hold me down while I'm here in Atlanta. I don't want to keep making phone calls. I'm staying away from phones, off the grid for a minute."

"Yeah, you do that. I'll be in touch with you when everthing is okay."

"Okay. Later, Heat."

"Okay, take care, Unique. Relax."

"Thanks. I'm in good hands though."

Heat hung up the phone, and then checked her messages. She deleted all of the ones from Samad.

He can't deny he's the father of that child. He's his spitting image! Heat wanted to look Samad in his eyes when she confronted him. *I need to see his eyes up-close.*

237

Hear his words. The sound of his voice, the tone. "I know Samad like I know myself."

The thought of what awaited her at home drowned her spirit, and she decided she wanted to be alone and headed to her room. She sent Ebony a text:

HEAT: *Have fun at the video shoot today. I'm gonna stay here by the pool & get sum R&R B4 we leave 2nite.*

EBONY: *Girl U crazy. U gonna miss out on the fun but Ok I guess. I'll hit U l8r 2nite.*

Heat felt she owed Moe an explanation for being a no-show, so she texted him as well:

HEAT: *Don't feel up 2 going 2 the video shoot. Not N the mood 2day. Not feeling well. Thanks 4 the invite, but I'm going 2 pass. Sorry.*

Someone was knocking on her door a minute later, but she ignored it. Whoever it was would get the hint and leave. She tiptoed to the door opening it halfway and looked out the door. Ebony was walking down the hall. She watched Ebony stop by AR's door and insert the key card, and enter A.R's room. Heat closed the door.

Heat twisted her face up. *What's Ebony doing going in AR's room? Oh well, I guess they hit it off.* She climbed back in bed, pulled the covers up over her head, and reassessed the state of her life. After a while, her eyelids lowered and she dozed off.

The moment she awoke, she called the front desk to change rooms. She left strict information with the front desk to inform anyone calling her that she checked out with no forwarding information.

Heat showered quickly and afterward, put on the plush white cotton robe hanging on the back of the door. She walked to the big window and pulled the blinds back to let some light into the room. Staring out the window, she wondered if breaking up with Samad would be better for her. *It's time to move on. Samad can stay with that bitch Mercedes and raise their son together. Fuck Samad!* Tired of crying, she closed the blinds.

"Let me get dressed and go home," she mumbled. "I'm ready to face Samad today." She called the airlines and changed her flight.

Heat grabbed all of her things and stuffed it in her suitcase, including the hotel's white cotton HIS and HER robes hanging in the closet. On her way to the small closet, she spotted a manila envelope sticking under her door.

"What is this?" She bent down to pick it up. Heat opened the letter and noticed it was written on AR's stationery from his record label. She sat on the bed and read the letter.

Heat,

I just want you to know I'm here for you. Last night happened for a reason. I can't get you off my mind. I don't regret anything that happened. I don't know what the situation is right now between you and Samad, but something's going on. Something's got you so upset. I just want you to know you don't have to go through whatever it is alone.

What we shared last night in the shower is something I

will never forget, and I don't want you to forget it either, or feel guilty about it. I have to leave early to do a few things before the video shoot. I did call your room, but there was no answer. I had to use a few tricks to find out where you moved to so fast. At first I was going to text you this, but I wanted to write this in my own handwriting, so you'd know it's real. I wanted to see your pretty face before I left Atlanta.

I'm going to be busy, so if you come to the shoot with your girls and you don't see me, just get one of the interns to come find me in the trailers, or call my phone. 212-777-0000. Stay in touch, Heat. I noticed the bite marks on my neck, and I see you left your mark. I left a few bites on your neck too. Making love to you was all I ever thought it would be. Got a nigga writing letters instead of texting. That should tell you something. Lol. I was caught up in the moment.

I don't want our special friendship to end. This could be the beginning of something good. Although you and I know there is someone else in the picture, where do you and Samad stand? Are you two still together?

Moe

Heat bit her bottom lip smiling when she thought about their episode in the shower. She stood with the letter still in her hand and walked to the mirror to look at the bite marks. Big, red bite marks, like tattoo footprints lead from her neck down to her breasts. She leaned her head back, counting all the bite marks. "Damn, Moe," she said. "I can't let Samad see these."

She walked to the bathroom to get her toothbrush and mouthwash. Before she could step through the threshold, she stepped on something sharp. "Ouch!" she screamed, and hobbled to the door to catch her balance. She grabbed the doorknob and glanced at the object on the floor.

Upon closer inspection, she thought it was a piece of glass, but when she bent down to pick the item up, one of Moe's monogrammed platinum cufflinks blinged its brilliance. She rinsed the cufflink off in the sink, then poured alcohol on her foot and put on a Band-Aid. Heat placed the cufflink inside an envelope and sealed it shut, dropping it into her robe pocket.

I told you, Moe. You are bad luck. First the chocolate on the plane, now this. Always crazy circumstances.

Heat decided to hang out at the hotel pool while Ebony attended the video shoot. She lay poolside in a red, green, yellow and blue chair enjoying the alone time and the sunrays.

That evening around 6:25 p.m., Heat texted Ebony: *Meet me @ the airport in 1 hour. Going home.* She went back to the room and packed her things and took a cab to the airport.

Heat spotted Ebony standing by the wifi lounge area at 7:43 p.m.

"Girl, why you got this worried look on your face?" Ebony asked.

"I'll fill you in on the plane," Heat said.

"Last call for flight 973 to Newark's Liberty Airport," erupted through the loudspeaker.

"Come on, girl. We're going to miss our flight!"

Heat grabbed Ebony's hand as they raced to the security checkpoint.

"Do you have anything on you that I need to know about?" Heat cut her eyes at Ebony.

"No. I'm clean," Ebony said. They made their way to the gate quickly.

Heat wished she could say the same thing regarding her conscience.

CHAPTER 32
The Big Fight

Despite Heat's continuous bubble guts during the short flight, they reached *Newark Airport* safely at 10:30 p.m. Ebony grabbed her bags from the overhead compartment and shook Heat's arm. "Wake up, girl. We here."

Heat gathered all of her things, stood up, stretched, and yawned. She was so ready to get home, but so nervous about what would happen once she brought up Samad's son and Mercedes.

They walked off the plane. Ebony was still stunned by Heat's confession. "Girl, you are always the voice of reason, always telling everybody what they should and should not do, and here you are letting Moe knock it down in the hotel. You got a man. What you need to be all up in another man's face for?" Ebony mocked.

"I can't with you. I need to hide these bite marks from Samad. Even though this nigga had a baby by that bitch, to add one more thing to this fucked up relationship to argue about."

"Here. Wrap this scarf around your neck, girl. That will only save you getting in the house safe, but after that ….You on your own! You better not let Samad see those bite marks. Girl, he is going to kill you! Just keep your guard up, avoid him seeing your neck. Get up early, and let's go to the gym before he wakes, this way you will be gone out the house all day tomorrow." Ebony said, handing her a red scarf.

"Well, thank you for the vote of confidence and the moral support, Ebony!" Heat said sarcastically.

"Shit, you know that nigga crazy!"

They gave each other a hug.

"Bye, girl. Get home safe."

"Bye, Ebony, you too."

Heat got in her cab and looked out the window, seeing a guy in a black truck pull up for Ebony. Heat rolled down her window. "Who is that, Ebony?"

Ebony turned to answer her, but before she could reply, Heat's cab pulled off, jerking her backward in her seat.

"Well, damn!" Heat cursed at the driver as the cab sped to her destination. She checked her phone and deleted Moe's text messages.

"Oh shit!" Heat panicked when the cab pulled up to her house forty-five minutes later. For some reason when she saw Samad's Bentley GT Continental in the driveway, her heart dropped. She took a deep breath.

"Pull over right here by the gate. I need to disable the alarm," she said, aiming the key in the direction of the metal black gates and causing them to open.

"I can get out right here. Thanks."

"Seventy-six dollars and eighty cents," the driver said.

"What? Well, I only got fifty-five dollars."

"What do you mean? The fare is seventy-six

dollars and eighty cents."

"Well, I'm just getting back in town. Come back to my house tomorrow, and I will give you the rest. I live right here. Where am I going? Look, it's been a long day."

"Why the hell did you get in my cab if you did not have all the fare?"

"Look, I'm not for no drama today. I didn't know it was going to be that much." Heat tossed the money through the partition and opened the door. She slammed the door behind her.

"Bitch!" the cab driver said.

"You toooo!" She watched as the driver sped down her driveway. Then she hit the alarm on her keychain again, enabling the alarm.

The black metal gates closed.

Heat let out a long sigh. With a nervous gait, she walked up the stairs and into the house. She stood by the door listening for any movement and caught a glimpse of the television light flashing in the living room. Also, she heard the TV on in their bedroom and walked in the room expecting to see Samad awake. He was asleep fully dressed, Timberlands and all.

"Whewww! Good." She breathed a sigh of relief. "I cannot do this tonight," she said, looking at the plate of food on his side of the bed. The pillow lay halfway in the chicken and macaroni and cheese and collard greens. "He's still eating in the bed?" she mumbled. *Ugh! We are going to get roaches. Yuck!* She took the remote out of his hand and moved the plate. Samad shifted and gripped the pillow tighter. She laughed at him sleeping with her pillow wrapped in his arms, as if it were her body.

As she stood over him watching him sleep, she recognized the smell of fresh cut flowers. They were neatly arranged on the small table and sitting in a beautiful purple vase. Daisies and red roses were her favorites. She leaned down to smell them. "Mmmm," she said as she inhaled. *Flowers from you always means you're sorry. Keep your fucking flowers!* Heat took her shoes off, then undressed quietly, sliding her jeans down and off. She pulled her shirt up over her head, leaving on her silk Victoria Secret baby doll camisole. After wrapping her hair up in a doobie, she secured it with bobby pins. *I need to hide these bite marks.* She put a little makeup on her neck to cover the marks. She walked to the kitchen and poured herself some fruit punch juice. Before going back to her bedroom, she checked the alarm.

"This boy got every TV in the house turned on," she complained. "It's freezing in here. He got the air conditioner on full blast, turned up."

Heat turned the air conditioner off, and then took a seat on the couch. She reached behind her, pulling a book off the bookshelf. After fluffing the pillows behind her back, she curled her legs underneath her as she got into the book. She glanced at the clock. It was 11:00 p.m. Heat yawned as she felt herself getting tired and eventually fell asleep.

Some time after midnight, Heat yawned and sat

up stretching. "I needed that sleep. It feels good waking up at home." She kept her eyes closed but finally opened them. Samad sat across from her watching her. She smiled because he'd found the robes she'd stolen and was wearing his. "You made sure you found your robe." She knew how much Samad hated her taking the robes, yet he always managed to find his and wear it around the house. Heat's expression changed because Samad wore a frown while looking directly in her eyes. His eyes were filled with hatred, hurt, and anger.

"Why are you looking at me like that?" she asked. Something was definitely wrong.

Samad didn't respond. She blinked to focus because could not believe what he held in his hand. Her heart skipped three beats, dropped to her stomach, then nearly flatlined. He held Moe's letter in his left hand and the cufflink in his right hand. "Ummm," Heat said as her reflexes guided her hands to cover her neck.

"I already saw the marks when I got out the shower while you were sleep. I also found that nigga cufflink, and this letter in the pocket of this robe." He pointed at the robe he was wearing. "You tried to cover that shit with makeup."

"What? What are you talking about?" Heat replied, trying to turn away from his view.

"I already saw the marks on your neck. So I don't know why the fuck you tryna play dumb for." Samad bald his fist tight. She glanced at his knuckles.

"Heat, what the fuck is wrong with you, yo!" he

yelled as he stood. Samad wanted her to be coherent, wanted to make sure she was fully alert.

"What? What are you talking about, Samad?"

"Oh, you gon' play stupid, Heat?"

Samad walked slowly toward her. "What the fuck is this?"

Her world froze. Heat stood and opened her mouth, but she couldn't find her voice. "Ummm."

"Answer me!" Samad yelled.

"Ummmm." She backed away.

"You bitch!" Samad swung his right hand, the same right hand that held the cufflink. With a closed fist he punched her in the face. Heat stumbled from the impact and slammed into the wall.

"No, Samad!" she yelled. "Please don't—"

Samad followed up with his left hand, still holding Moe's letter.

"Stop, Samad!" she screamed.

This time she bumped her head on the bookcase. The impact left two large red knuckle prints on both sides of her face, matching the red bite marks on her neck.

"Stop, Samad!" she screamed. "Please!"

"I can't believe you!" he shouted with venom. "Fuck you! You hear me? Fuck you, bitch!" He smacked her once. "You whore! You piece of shit!" He smacked her again, then lunged for her throat and wrapped his hands tight around her neck. With a firm grip, he began to squeeze. "Grrrrr," Samad grunted.

Terrified, Heat saw the wrath in his eyes. "Bitch!"

Heat gurgled on her words and gasped for air. Her face was turning blue.

Samad snapped out of his trance. He loosened his grasp and stepped back, glaring at her still holding her neck.

"That's why you ran your ass down to Atlanta, huh? So you could be with that nigga? Huh? Huh?"

She tried to regain her composure.

"Answer me, Heat!"

"I . . . feel . . . lightheaded. Dizzy . . ." Heat stumbled.

"You fucked that nigga Moe?" he asked, with his hands still around her neck. Samad applied pressure again and stared at her coldly. "Yo, I cannot believe you!" Samad gritted his teeth.

This nigga is gonna kill me. Heat didn't fight back.

"Oh, now you wanna cry." Tears streamed down Heat's face as she gagged, gasping for air. He let her neck go.

Heat coughed. ". . . I . . . feel weak, Samad."

Samad took a step back and watched her slide down the wall, doubled over in pain, holding her throat.

He extended his arms as if he was going to catch her to break her fall, but he drew back his hands and let her fall to the floor. "Make me understand! How could you fuck that nigga Moe?" he screamed. "Huh? Why Heat?"

Heat tried to talk "I—" She shook her head.

"You probably sucked that nigga dick too!" He dropped the letter, then tossed the cufflink on the couch. "Ugh! I'm disgusted with you." His phone rang. Samad turned away. He walked in the bedroom and slammed the door.

"I can't believe you!" he yelled. She heard him spewing hateful words behind the closed bedroom door.

What a way to wake up! She gazed at the letter and the cufflink and continued crying and coughing and trying to catch her breath. She heard Samad talking loud, yelling at somebody about some murder in Miami. Heat tried to listen to his conversation, until Samad turned the music up in the room drowning out his voice.

Scared to move, she sat balled up in that same spot glancing around the room to locate a weapon to protect herself. Just in case Crazy came back out of the room to pick up where he left off. Her face, neck, and throat were burning and aching.

Samad walked out the room as if Heat wasn't there.

Heat watched him collect money from different spots in the house, and he walked around as if she wasn't there. She heard his every move, and she gingerly rubbed her throat.

He picked up her phone and the keys to her truck. Then he grabbed his car keys and walked out the door. She knew where Samad was going dressed in black from head to toe. *Moe,* she thought.

CHAPTER 33
It's On

Samad drove on the New Jersey Turnpike to the Lincoln tunnel consumed by thoughts of committing a homocide. He was speeding, tailgating behind a black F-150 truck, oblivious to everything around him. *I'm gon' kill this nigga. Bitches gonna be bitches, but this nigga gotta die. He disrespected me. He know Heat is my woman.* Samad turned the radio on and drove to his destination.

After a few minutes, he picked his phone up off the passenger seat, scrolled through the names, and hit the voice activated feature. "Call Mike!" he yelled and turned the radio down.

"Yo!" Mike picked up after the second ring.

"What up? Where you at?" Samad asked.

"Over on the east side. Why? What up?"

"Round up everybody for a quick sitdown, then we need to go handle something. You know. I need to handle this nigga Moe once and for all."

"I heard," Mike replied. "I know where his little workers be at! We could snatch one of them and make them take us to him!"

Samad shook his head no, as if Mike could see him. "Nah. I want to do this right. I don't want any mistakes. I need to go drop some money off first to somebody real quick before it go down. I'm about to tie up a few loose ends. I need a minute before I make my move on Moe. This nigga slept with Heat, and speaking of Heat, she knows about the baby."

"Oh word?" asked Mike. "So if Heat slept with this nigga, you think she's going to let him know what's about to go down? So what about her? How do you want to handle that?"

Samad paused, choosing his words carefully. *Hmmm, what about Heat?* He gritted his teeth and tightened his jaw.

Mike interrupted his thoughts. "So what you gon' do about her? What if she put the nigga on to what's about to happen?" he questioned.

"Nah, she not!" Samad responded sharply.

"How do you know, Samad?"

"Because she's not! I know she's not!"

"You sure?" Mike let his words sink into Samad's mental. You didn't think Heat would fuck Moe but she did. Mike snapped.

Samad understood very well what Mike was saying. "Yeah-I'm-sure. I'm positive! Heat's not going to tell Moe nothin'. I know her inside and out!"

"Hmph! Okay. I hear you, Let's not forget when that whole Eli thing went down, if she would have been anywhere around she would have been laying right along with him. Let's not forget the reason you two met in the first place." Mike responded.

Samad looked in the rearview mirror as he drove faster.

"Mike, you got them thangs? I don't want to go

into it right now over the phone but—"

"Yeah, I got 'em."

"Good," Samad replied. "Good. This nigga is old news. He about to find out what the fuck this life is really about, and all his pawns right along with him!" Samad growled. "I'm talkin' 'bout no mercy at all! Line everybody up. I will be there shortly. One."

"All right, Samad. One."

Samad ended his call, then called his other top soldier, Will.

Will answered on the first ring. "Yo, what's the word?"

"What's shakin', Will? The words of the day is *hostile takeover*. Your man Moe's out of pocket like a motherfucker. Mike will fill you in. You ready?"

"Shit. I stay ready. I like dealing with people out of pocket. That's my specialty. Say no more, Samad."

"That's why I fucks with you, Will." Samad smiled.

They understood each other clearly.

"Meet me at the spot. I can't really talk right now. I'm en route to finish something. And yo, bring them thangs, Will!" he growled.

"Them T-H-I-N-G-S, things?" Will spelled it out.

"Nah Will, bring them T-H-A-N-G-S. Thangs!" Samad responded, spelling it out that he meant the big guns.

"No doubt!" Will responded, knowing what was up.

"I'll see you in a minute." Will ended the call.

Samad reached his destination and pulled up by the side of the building. An older man walked out to the driver side of Samad's car. Samad rolled the window down.

"Papi, I gotta go fast today. It's all there."

The man handed Samad a package, and black duffel bag in exchange for the money, then he smiled. "I trust you, my friend. You always keep your word."

They exchanged a quick hand to hand. Samad took the duffel bag out of the man's hand and placed it between the seats in the first hidden compartment.

Samad talked while he looked inside the manilla envelope. "Your sister is doing a great job cleaning our house."

"Good. I'm working on her papers now, so she will be fine."

"No doubt, Papí. She's in good hands."

"I know she is. You be safe out here, okay? You call me if you need me for anything else."

"I will."

He looked inside the manila envelope pulling out a few letters until he stopped at one. He smiled. Then he stuck his hand inside again, pulling out Keisha's lockbox key. Samad looked up beaming with joy.

"My man."

"I told you, my friend; I would get you what you needed. My niece is the manager of that bank."

Samad had finally got his hands on the letter written by Keisha to her brother. She wrote to him telling him she was about to change her living will, Explaining to him about the fights she and Samad had, the abuse, she didn't trust him anymore, and she would be removing Samad and naming her brother Capone as the beneficiary.

"I will be in touch shortly," Samad said.

"Also, I know you would want to know that Keisha's brother won't be gettin' out of jail no time soon. He caught another charge inside.

He knows nothing about this, my friend."

Samad smiled. "Good."

Eli had to die. He was the only one who knew I cut the brakes on Keisha's Benz. The guy who gave me the wire cutters got caught on another charge, he talked about it to one of Eli's boys when he was locked up. Hell yeah I'm responsible for her death. She betrayed me, fucking with that nigga Eli behind my back. Now that I got this letter, them insurance papers, and that lockbox key back, I'm good.

The video footage confirmed my suspicions Eli and his crew was behind that robbery from one of my old spots back in Brooklyn all them years ago. My gut and instincts never lie to me . . . Don't nobody cross me without consequences. I don't give a damn how many years later it is. I don't forget shit! I got a very long memory, Samad thought.

"Later, Papí."

Samad placed the contents back inside the manila envelope, stuffing it in the second stash spot and hit a few buttons on the dashboard. The compartment between the seats flipped, hiding the packages. Samad put his arm on the armrest then drove off.

"Later, my friend," Papí replied.

"I got other business that needs to be handled."Samad pressed on the accelerator with force. *This nigga Moe wanna disrespect me on another level. He knows I play with them thangs heavy. Okay, he wanna play. Okay. Let's play.*

CHAPTER 34
No More

Heat looked at the alarm and waited for it to turn green, letting her know he was past the security gate, and it was closed. Once she heard the alarm beep, she moved quickly and got up.

She winced as she walked to the phone and dialed Ebony's number. Ebony's voice mail came on. When she tried to speak, her voice came out raspy and hoarse. She forced the words out of her mouth even though her throat hurt. Her tears took over the conversation.

"Ebony, come get me! Please hurry up!"

As if an afterthought popped in her head, she put the phone back to her mouth to give Ebony her home address. "1018-03 Easy Lane Drive. The brownstone by the lake. The only one with the black metal gates with the long driveway going up the hill." Heat hung up the phone.

Damn," Heat mumbled, realizing, neither of her friends knew exactly where they lived. *Wow. How stupid of me. My own mother hasn't ever been here.*

After sixty seconds passed, Heat called Ebony once more. "Did you find my house yet or what, girl?" Heat yelled in the phone.

"Heat, girl I'm lost."

"You right in front of my house. I'm looking at the cameras, and I see you. Turn right, near the black gates. This is the house. I hit the alarm already." Heat noticed a car parked on the side of the truck Ebony was in but dismissed it.

"Girl, you got me in the backwoods. Secret squirrel ass! You need Google maps and Mapquest to find this place! I *think* I'm outside your house, Heat." Ebony read the numbers outloud. "Ten-eighteen o-three. Yeah, this it."

"I just told you it was. I'm looking right at you on the cameras."

"Well, these gates opening slow! It's chilly out here. I'm right here at the door. Open up."

Heat opened the door, and without so much as a glance in Heat's direction, Ebony barged in and looked down at the carpet. Instinct made her take her shoes off first. "Wow!" Ebony was amazed at the layout and decor. The aroma from the watermelon candles filled her nostrils as she enjoyed this tranquil, clean, fresh feeling in the air.

"This is nice. Even the air feels different in here. Feels like I stepped into—" She looked at Heat's face.

"Damn! He must have slapped or punched you hard as hell. I can see marks all over. Ya shit black and blue, Heat. Gotdamn!"

Heat couldn't meet Ebony's gaze. "Well, thank you for making me feel worse than I already feel."

"I'm sorry. I didn't mean it like that but damn! I'm feeling some kinda way about Samad's ass."

"He hit me like I was a nigga, E."

"I can see."

Heat tilted her head and twisted her lips.

Ebony shook her head. "Between you and Unique . . ." She didn't finish her comment.

"I've been trying to get in touch with Aaron for the longest. His phone was ringing at first, now it's going right to voice mail. I'm worried."

"You know Aaron can take care of himself. He's a big boy."

"I know, but this is not like him to not return any of my phone calls. I left him messages all day today."

Ebony ignored Heat's concern and continued looking around the house. "Do you got something to drink in this big place?"

"Yes. The kitchen is that way. Get something quick so we can be out!" Heat pointed to the kitchen.

Ebony walked in the kitchen and opened the refrigerator, grabbing a Snapple and a piece of cold chicken out of the Tupperware plastic bowl. She looked on the shelf and spotted a box of Ritz crackers and took a pack out.

"This house is nice as hell, Heat! Let me find out you and Scarface been living like the Trumps. Lifestyles of the rich and famous!" she said, munching on the cold chicken.

Heat walked out the room struggling with two large duffel bags. "Help me with these bags, please!" She dragged the bags by the door.

"Samad hired a housekeeper to clean this big ass

house? She somewhere in here. I don't even like staying here alone. My next move is gonna be somewhere small."

Ebony saw Heat limping. "Damn, did he hurt your foot too?"

"No, remember I told you about Moe's cufflink."

"Oh yeah, right."

"Your foot still hurt?" Ebony asked.

"I think it's getting infected."

Heat plopped down on the suede couch. "I'm ready to leave because I don't know where he went. He could come back at any minute. He didn't say nothin' when he left.

"He took my phone, the keys to my truck, and the keys for the other car. He knew what he was doing when he left. He wants me to stay here, I guess, until he gets back. But I got a surprise for his black ass."

"What did he say when you asked him about Mercedes and the baby?"

"I never got the chance to confront him. As soon as I woke up, this nigga was sitting right there in the chair watching me sleep. I don't even know how long he was watching me. He could have killed me in my sleep. I've never seen him like this. This nigga choked me and hit me in my face with a closed fist, and he slapped me. I gotta get away from here."

Ebony grabbed one of the bags. "Damn girl, what you got in these bags?"

"As much stuff as I could."

Ebony grabbed a duffel bag and Heat grabbed the

other. She looked at her and Samad's picture on the glass table for the last time.. Heat placed the picture face down and walked to the door. She opened the door, letting Ebony walk out first. Heat punched codes in the alarm system, turned and looked around the house, then closed the door.

They both searched around outside to see if Samad had come home.

"Let's hurry up."

Ebony hit the alarm to the truck. They both put the bags in the backseat, moving quickly.

"Ebony, let me use your phone."

"Hold on, let me finish texting my friend. I'm letting him know I'm about to drop you off in Harlem." Ebony finish texting then handed Heat her phone.

"What do you have Moe's number saved under?"

Ebony looked at her sideways. "You funny, girl. You must ain't get enough of Samad," she said as she reached for her phone.

"Fuck Samad. He can go be with that bitch Mercedes and their son for all I care."

"Moe's number is saved under M$."

Heat scrolled through Ebony's phone, stopping on Moe's number. She pressed the talk key. "It's ringing."

"Yo," Moe answered.

"Hey, Moe, where you at?"

"Who is this?"

"This is Heat."

"Heat? What's good, mamí. Damn, I thought you wasn't gonna ever call."

"Where you at, Moe?"

"I'm in Harlem, at Niketown on Fifty-seventh with my dudes! What's good with you, ma? I miss you! When I'ma see you?"

"I'm tryna see you right now."

"You left Atlanta kinda quick. Did you get my letter? Where you at right now?"

"I need to talk to you! He found that letter," Heat said.

"I'm not worried about him. Are you worried about him?"

"That's not the point. That letter started a big fight. I'm on my way to the city. Where you gon' be at in thirty minutes?"

"Hit me when you get to Harlem. You know your way around Harlem?"

"Yes. I'm very familiar with Harlem!"

"Ebony knows where I'm at. Tell her to bring you to the penthouse apartments on Park Ave. See you in a little while. I'll probably get there before you. But if you beat me there, just have them buzz you up. I'm going to call them now and let them know you're coming. Did you eat anything?"

"I got you on speaker phone. She heard you. No, I did not eat anything."

"You hungry? I'm about to pick up something to eat. Or I can order something when you get there. I need to stop somewhere first."

"That's okay, I'll see you soon."

"Later, ma. Seems like everything is falling right into place," Moe said.

"What did you say?" Heat asked.

"Nothing. See ya later."

Heat pulled down the mirror and leaned forward in her seat. She looked at her face, pulled her makeup out of her small bag, and applied a lot of concealer to cover up the bruises. When she finished putting on her red lipstick, she stared at herself for a moment before closing the sunvisor.

"So what's ya plan, Heat?" Ebony asked. "Are you going back home to your mother's?"

"Oh shit! I left my 'mad money' at the house. I put away a lot of money over the years in case Samad was ever on some bullshit, and I can't believe I left my money and my checkbooks."

"Well, we right here in Harlem now. Fuck that money! Moe got enough money for me, you, and everybody in Harlem. That boy is paid! He could give you whatever you need!"

"You don't understand, Ebony. I saved a lot of money over the years. Also, I forgot to get this paperwork to this new spot I was looking at. I was gonna move away from Samad's ass the last time we had a fight."

Heat hit the dashboard. "I can't *believe* I rushed out the house before getting all my shit. I left a lof of personal things of Eli's I held on to after he died."

Ebony looked at Heat when she said Eli's name. They drove in silence for a long while. Ebony knew Heat had a lot of options to consider.

"Let me see your phone again." She decided to call Aaron to seek his advice. She wouldn't tell him the details because he'd go ape shit on Samad.

Ebony handed her the phone just as she was pulling in front of Moe's penthouse. She put the truck in park. "Well, we're here now."

Heat shook her head. Ebony smiled as the doorman walked to the truck, ready to help.

As Heat was about to step out of the SUV on a Manhattan street, Ebony grabbed her arm. "I love you, Heat."

Heat hugged Ebony and got out of the truck before a tear dropped. She forced a smile.

"Is that everything?" the doorman asked.

She nodded yes, walked toward the entrance, and turned to watch Ebony as she drove off. Heat turned back and followed the tall, light-skinned, middle aged man inside the building. She smiled at the other pudgy doorman and stopped at the front desk.

"Can you ring the penthouse for me, please?" Heat nearly whispered.

"Yes, ma'am!" The receptionist picked up the house phone to alert Moe of his guest. She smiled at Heat.

"Go right up. He's expecting you!" she replied in

a professional tone.

She waited for the elevator.

The doors opened. Moe's friend, AR, stepped off the elevator looking as sexy as ever, stuntin' like the star he is.

Oh boy! His timing could not have been worse. I do not want to see anybody right now. Ugh! she thought.

"Hey, Heat, what's up, ma?"

She faked a smile. "Hey, AR! How you been?"

They hugged. He kissed Heat on the cheek.

"How's the CD doing?" she asked.

"It's doing well!" He stepped back and got a good look at Heat. She folded her arms across her chest defensively. *Come on now.*

"It's been on the charts for a good two weeks so far. Almost platinum! I got the number one video in the country! The number one single in the country! The most requested song on all the radio stations. I got the number one ringtone spot, so I'm good right now. Ready to get back in the studio and work on my next project."

He smiled. "You looking good!" He pinched her cheeks.

Heat blushed and flashed a fake smile, knowing her face hurt from Samad's punches, and now his pinch to her cheek added to her pain.

The attendant held the elevator while they talked.

"How's ya girl Ebony doing?"

"She just dropped me off." Her voice cracked as she spoke. It was raspy and hoarse. He ended the conversation when he saw his security walking toward him. He glanced at his watch.

"Well, it's been nice seeing you again!"

"It was nice seeing you again too. Congrats on your success, AR."

"Thanks."

The attendant stepped aside, making room for Heat to get into the elevator.

Heat stepped in the elevator and smiled. "Thank you."

They rode to the top floor in silence.

Ding!

The doors opened on the top penthouse floor. Moe stood waiting for Heat dressed in a white wife beater revealing his muscular arms. Heat checked him out. *Handsome.*

His infectious smile forced Heat to smile. Moe opened his arms, ready to embrace her. Heat could not hold her smile anymore. Her smile turned into a frown, and tears formed in her eyes. His smile faded when he saw water slide down her sad face.

She relaxed when she saw his welcoming arms opened wide, ready to embrace her. Heat rushed into his arms burying her face in his chest. She let out loud sobs. Moe hugged her tight. "Don't worry, Heat. It's going to be all right."

I needed this, she thought.

He smiled inside as Heat bawled in his arms.

She didn't want to think about what was about to

go down. She buried her head in Moe's chest, closed her eyes, and cried louder. *I'm not ready to jump into a new relationship without exiting another one.*

"If I were a chess player, I'd tell Samad what a fool he is for neglecting someone so beautiful, intelligent, and sweet as you," Moe said, kissing her forehead. "Then I'd beg him to make his next dumb, bitch-ass move. He placed you right where I've always wanted you." Heat cried in his arms.

"Checkmate," Moe whispered. Heat was much too distraught to hear Moe's words.

CHAPTER 35
Somebody Gotta Die

"Is everybody here! How long does it take for you niggas to come in and sit down, so we can get down to business! Niggas is slow-rollin' in here. Hurry up! Come in and take a seat!" Samad snapped.

He focused on his men entering the Harlem barbershop's back room. Will walked in last and closed the door.

"First things first!" Samad said as he stood up. "We good? Are we good? Everybody got their paper?" he asked, looking around the room with a blank stare. Everyone shook their head in agreement. The men were a little nervous because nobody knew what was going on. The only thing Will told them was it had something to do with their boss's enemy, Moe. They sat around the table quietly pulling out their money and lying it on the table.

Will and Mike walked around the room collecting the money.

Everyone's attention was on Samad. His eyes darted from Will to Mike, and back to Will.

They continued collecting all the money made from the kilos of cocaine sold and putting it in duffel bags. Once Will and Mike finished the collection, they both looked at Samad.

Pezo opened the door to let all the new, younger soldiers into the room. Will slowly walked into the vault room to secure the money. Then he quickly returned, locking the door behind him and taking his place next to Samad. He handed Samad the only copy of the key.

Samad turned his attention toward everybody in the room. His silent demeanor threw them off balance.

Face's mind was playing tricks on him because he did not know why Samad called this meeting. He knew Bizz was one of Moe's workers, and he didn't know how Samad really felt about him. He spoke out randomly since Bizz was no where around.

"I'm saying, Bizz cool with me. He getting money right beside me on the block, and even though that's one of Moe's boys, he watch my back, and I watch his out there. I-ain't-got-no-problem-with-son!"

"Hmph." Samad laughed under his breath as he just looked at the young boy, Face. Then he looked across the room. He figured since Moe's name came up, he might as well entertain this Moe character and feel everybody out. He wanted to check their temperature to see where their heads were at.

Samad wanted to see what the mentality of his soldiers was like since he'd been locked up. He wondered if they were still on the same level, psychologically. *I'm not worried about this nigga Moe's money. Moe signed his own death sentence when he slept with Heat.*

"Yo! Regarding that little incident you had, what happened with that?" Samad asked his seasoned worker, Wiz, placing both palms on the table and leaning forward.

"Oh, I'm good, baby!" Wiz replied. "This is chess, not checkers. I planted the seed already! I say we cripple his finances. Which is gon' force him to make a move.

"Because if his money stops flowing, which by the way"—Wiz paused and smiled—"it's already in motion . . . He's gonna wanna know why! You gotta get into that man's mind and fuck with the nigga's money, and fuck with him mentally. Hit 'im where it hurts! Hit 'im in his pockets!" Wiz said, sitting back confidently in his chair and taking a long pull from the cigar. He smiled at Samad while blowing out circles of smoke. "You heard me. Hit 'im in his pockets!"

Samad laughed a little, knowing Wiz was cut from the same cloth. Same school of hard knocks, and he abided by the same rules. Wiz knew the Hustler's Prayer backwards.

"Same rules apply, baby." He stared at Wiz and smiled. "Same rules apply!" Samad replied, shaking his head up and down.

He turned his attention to Jab. "What happened with Moe's boys around ya way in Queens, J?"

"He opened two after-hours spots, one in Queens, and one in the Bronx! This nigga getting' money all night! He ain't lettin' nobody get money around them spots if it's not comin' from him directly!"

"Letting?" Samad interjected, blowing air out of his nostrils. "Hmph!"

Jab continued. "I'm ready to straight run up in all of his spots! Lay everybody down. I don't give a fuck who's there! His mother, his father, his grandfather, kids, dogs. It's about to be a bloodbath! . . . I gives a fuck! That nigga don't know who he fuckin' with!" Jab growled as he started a semi-riot in the room, making everybody let off a loud roar in agreement.

"Word!" a voice from the crowd of men in the back yelled out. "That's what the fuck I'm talking about. Lay these motherfuckers down for real!"

"Simmer down. Simmer down, calm down!" Samad said, pumping his hand up and down, as if dribbling a basketball. "Simmer down! Simmer down! Calm down!"

Samad turned his attention back to Face. "Gentlemen, it seems we have a conflict of interest." He pointed to Face. "Ya man right here thinks it's okay to let Bizz come over here on our side and hustle. Who by the way, is one of Moe's shooters. Cutting in on our profits without paying, mind you. He's not even from around here! Yet Face can't even break bread over on their side, or can't even cop Grade-A weight from Bizz without coming back with garbage that's been stepped on about three times. For twice the money!

"But, in the words of Face he ain't got-no-problem-with-son!" Samad mocked Face's earlier words.

"People might think that, that garbage is our shit, and that's bad for business! I don't deal with garbage. Never have never will! On top of that, this nigga is

271

taking food out of your daughter's mouth, standing right beside you, ski-masking you!

"Every stack he makes, he's taking a stack out ya pocket! You hustlin' backwards, baby! How the hell you out there on your grind, busting your ass, standing next-to-the-man-next-to-the man, Moe? Helping him out! Because that's Moe's man. Make me understand that Face! Maybe I'm missin' something! Whose side are you on? You wanna go work for Moe?" Samad pointed to the door.

Face dropped his gaze.

"Please make me understand that type of mentality?" he asked Face a rhetorical question not really waiting for a response. "What the fuck? Is that a Gucci skirt you got on? Or jeans?"

Some laughed at Face.

One soldier standing against the wall in the back yelled out to Face, "Bitch ass nigga!" Crushing Face's ego even more.

"Yo, I—" Face was about to answer, but Samad cut him off and waved his hand in his direction.

"Fuck that nigga Bizz! I gives a fuck about him or his boss. I'm from the old school. I follow a different set of rules! Fuck them both! As a matter of fact, you can excuse yourself right now, homie! Nice doing business witchu'. But I no longer need your services."

Everybody looked at Face, then turned toward Samad, as he went in his pocket and pulled out a roll of money and tossed it to Face.

Face's nerves and quick reflexes, equivalent to a wide receiver, forced him to catch the money, meeting Samad's deadly stare for a split second. The room knew Face was cut off from that moment.

"Occupational hazards!" mumbled Samad. He did not say another word, making sure everyone fully understood the seriousness of the situation with Moe.

"Anybody else wanna join Face?" he asked, looking around the room.

"Moe got that whole spot in the trap across town on lock," one of the other soldiers from the back spoke out.

"Moe also told Face he couldn't move weight around there anymore ever since you got locked up. He sent a message to Face little cousin to tell everybody he was the man they needed to see, and get approval from him before anything moved from those blocks down there. He knows Face is under you, Samad. So he knows exactly what he's doing."

"Hmph. Oh really? And none of you thought that was information I needed to know when I was locked up?" *See this is that bullshit I be talkin' 'bout.* Samad looked around the room like he knew something they didn't know. "Oh really? Okay . . ."

"But it's only one guy that I know of off hand that cop weight from him. It's only one guy, so it really shouldn't matter!" Hak said, shrugging.

Samad twisted his lips, as if biting the meat on the inside of his right jaw. He stood up.

273

Before Samad could speak, Mike said, "First of all, *we* run the tri-state area. This is home base. New York, New Jersey—"

Will interrupted, "And Connecticut!"

Mike continued. "It shouldn't matter if it's one or one hundred people copping weight from him! Nobody should be movin' *his* product over here. It's the principle!"

Will interrupted Mike. "I never knew the nigga said that. They either come to us, or we don't fuck with them at all. Let them find protection somewhere else. Ya heard! And if they ain't fuckin' with us, it's gon' be a problem!

"I thought Samad made that clear? The tri-state area is ours!" he yelled as he opened his arms to the world.

Samad leaned back in his chair making himself comfortable. His two top soldiers just spoke the exact words in his head. "See, this is the reason I fuck with Mike and Will like I do. They understand principle."

The letter he found in Heat's robe flashed in his mind, as well as the bite marks on her neck. *Bitch ass nigga, Moe.* "If Moe wants a war, then a war it is!"

LB, the newest member in the crew handpicked by Jab, interrupted Samad. "So what do you suggest we do, boss?"

Everybody shifted in their chairs. Samad dropped his head and let out a quick half laugh. He blew air through his nostrils, and shook his head in disgust with his lips slightly twisted.

Samad looked over at Jab, who at this point stared at the ground. *Where Jab find this new dude from?* He gazed at LB with this crazed look.

"You want my suggestions on how to handle him? It's too late in the game for you to have to ask *me* your next move!" Samad yelled. "You do whatever the fuck you need to do! Bust ya muthafuckin' guns! Clunk them niggas in the head with your guns! Kidnap muthafuckas! Send body parts to their family! Shoot their pitbulls at his dog kennel, and send the dead dogs to one of his stores during rush hour! Tie cement bricks to their ankles then toss 'em in the Hudson River! Dump 'em in Central Park! I don't give a fuck what you do, but let it be known it's on!" he yelled at the top of his lungs and looked around the room. "Anybody you see affiliated with Moe's camp, I want bodily harm done to them. I don't give a fuck if it's his mother, father, sister, brother, kids! The fucking mailman—if he or she is there delivering mail. They could get it too! The less people alive, the less people talking! I don't give a damn who it is. Do what you gotta do!"

Samad's phone rang once, easing the tension in the room and disturbing the meeting. He put one finger up. "Hold up. I need to take this. Yo. What up? Papi?"

"I hate to be the bearer of bad news. But!" The voice faded. The words that followed stung Samad. "What! When! Where! How long ago? Say word! A'ight, one!"

His private phone started ringing back to back. He glanced at it, and sent the call to voice mail. It rang again. He sent the call to voice mail again.

For a moment quiet consumed Samad like he needed to digest whatever it was that had his face bloodshot red. Silence filled the room quick. Thick tension smothered the air. He looked over at Mike and Will, then at everybody else in the room. He ended his call. "Let the games begin, Moe!"

CHAPTER 36
Home Invasion

"Samad! Samad! Are you still there?" Papi said.

"Yeah. I'm still here."

"You good, boss?" Mike asked Samad, who wore a confused look.

"Somebody broke in my house . . . " Who did it? replayed over and over in Samad's head.

Samad's first thought . . . "Oh shit! Heat!" *Damn, I left her there at the house.* "I'll be right there in a minute. I heard you." Samad ended the call. "I just found out from a trusted source that Moe had one of our guys murdered. So we about to return the favor. Eye for an eye." He stood, grabbed his car keys, and put his fitted cap on.

"This nigga Moe found out where one of my houses at. He went to where I live or sent somebody. He already made his move. This nigga think I'm playin' with him. He really wanna die. Let's go. I need to go back to my house ASAP! Because I left Heat there." Mike looked at Samad sideways when he said Heat's name.

They exited the building. Samad got in the passenger seat of the black Hummer. He reclined the seat all the way back, letting out a loud sigh.

"Also, boss man, it's been one full day now. Nobody's heard anything from Aaron."

Samad had a gut wrenching feeling in his stomach. He took a deep breath. *Come on, Aaron. Call me, my nigga. I know by now you should be on your way back. Something ain't right. Something happened. Either way this is not good.* He rested his head on the headrest, closed his eyes, tired from this hectic street life.

Mike got in the backseat behind Samad. Will got in behind the driver. Jada Kiss' music filled the vehicle as they drove to his house, nine cars in tow, bumper to bumper.

They pulled up to his property forty-five minutes later, driving right up on a chaotic scene. Samad immediately recognized one of the cops who used to work with Mercedes as a correctional officer. He was in full uniform standing by his gates blocking the entrance. *Fucking toy cop ass,* Samad thought.

The driver put the Hummer in park, allowing Samad to exit.

The cops' car doors flew open, and other officers anxiously jumped out and met the crowd of guys headed in their direction.

One of the cops walked to Samad.

"No one is allowed on the grounds until the owner comes!" he stated, assuming he wasn't looking at the owner Samad himself. "Are you the owner?"

"Yes, I am the owner," Samad stated. "My alarm is going off. Is it all right with you if I shut the alarm off?" Samad asked sarcastically.

"Sure," the cop replied.

Samad pointed his key chain in the direction of the alarm, shutting the sound off. He pressed a few buttons on the panel.

The black gates began to open.

"This is an active crime scene!" the cop stated.

"A crime scene?" Samad asked, looking puzzled.

"Yeah, we got a disturbance call from one of your neighbors."

"Okay, you got a call and?"

"Your neighbors got a little worried and thought someone was trying to break in. Your alarm has been going off for over an hour. The security company has been calling you for the longest; the calls kept going right to voice mail.

"Do you want to file a police report?"

"No. I don't need to file no report." Samad walked up the long driveway with the cop in tow to the front door.

As Samad placed the key in the lock, he looked at the rookie cop. "Have you been inside my house yet?"

"No! Do you want to file a police report?" he asked again.

The other two cops drove to the top of the driveway and stepped out the car.

Samad cut his eyes at the cops walking toward him; then he turned his attention back to the cop.

"How do you know that a crime was committed, or what to put on the report, if you have not been inside my home? All I know is my alarm went off. How do we know it's not a false alarm? I won't be filing any report. Once I get inside, if I notice anything out of the ordinary, then I will take the necessary steps moving forward. So if you will excuse me. You boys can go about your business."

The cop cut his eyes at Samad, offended at his tone.

"This *is* our business. We responded to a silent alarm."

"I know all four of you don't wanna spend your day with me worrying yourself over a little false alarm. I just came home not too long ago, and I want to celebrate by having a pool party with my friends. The ladies will be here shortly. You guys can stay, if you want something to eat." Samad smiled. He knew the cops didn't like him, and he couldn't stand them either. "But I do thank you for your time though! 'Preciate it!" he said again, arrogance and sarcasm oozing through his smile.

"Well, make sure you get that alarm checked out. Every time a false alarm goes off, those are moments taken away from a real emergency we could have attended to."

"Yeah, well, that's what y'all get paid for, right?"

"What! You being a smart ass?"

Samad held his peace.

The cops turned and walked to their squad cars. The other police officer walked down the driveway.

Samad's goons got out of their cars and walked inside his house.

"Take them to the game room," Samad instructed Will.

Mike's phone rang. "Let me take this call in the other room. This my B-More people. I need to find out what's going on with Aaron." Mike walked out the room.

Will walked back into the bedroom with Samad.

"The housekeeper said she found something in my room on the bed when she was cleaning the house," Samad said.

"Housekeeper?" Will said.

"Yeah. My man Papí's sister is living here. She don't have all her paperwork yet. She's afraid of being deported if she go out and find a job, so he asked me to do him a favor and hire her since she needed work. He's good peoples with me, so I told him I would give her a job. But anyway, she found this yellow envelope on the bed."

Samad handed Will the envelope. Will recognized Moe and Heat fucking in the shower. "What the fuck! Yo, this nigga gotta die!" Will said.

"He's a dead man walking!" Will shook his head as he looked through the pictures. Then handed the envelope back to Samad.

Mike walked back in the room joining Samad and Will. "Yo. Last night somebody broke into AR's house. They stole two guns, his music masters, jewelry, and a yellow envelope with some pictures! He said you know what pictures he's talking about," Mike said.

Samad held up the envelope letting Mike know he got the pictures. "I know. Whoever broke into AR's house made sure to personally deliver these pictures here. The same culprit who tripped up my alarm system."

"Also, I just got word too. Aaron was murdered during that Baltimore transaction!" Mike said.

Samad closed his eyes. "Awwww naaaaw, man. Damn!" The news about Aaron stung Samad. He shook his head, hurt.

"I know that nigga Moe's behind this," Will said.

Mike walked over to Samad and put his hand on Samad's shoulder. "I know you and Aaron were close. My man was locked up with him on the island. That's all he used to talk about was how loyal Aaron was to you. Everybody know Aaron is like a big brother to you personally, aside from this shit, so trust and believe me when I tell you, we will make the person pay— whoever's behind this."

Samad nodded. "This last transaction wasn't even necessary." Samad's voice was low and filled with pain.

"He didn't have to go. He wanted to go. Aaron didn't really trust the girl who set up the Baltimore meeting. I told him he should send one of them little niggas. But he wanted to go himself. Dammit!" Samad banged his hand on the wall.

Will read an incoming text. "Yo. Pezo just hit me saying Heat pulling up in the driveway!"

"I need a word with her alone. Take them and go," Samad ordered.

Will and Mike embraced Samad, giving him dap, ready to make their exit.

Samad tossed the envelope on the bed and looked out the large bedroom window. He could see Heat from their room, holding the phone to her ear while she sat in the car in the rain.

He watched her park and wondered where the rental car came from since he took her keys earlier. Yo, *who the fuck is she talking to?*

CHAPTER 37
Heat's Next Move

"So where are you right now?" Ebony asked Heat.

"I left Moe's place. I'm sitting in my driveway. I just left the car rental place in the city." Heat turned the windshield wipers on as it started to rain. The raindrops dripped inside the driver's window on Heat. She hit the automatic button closing all the windows completely as she talked on the phone.

"I told you this nigga took the keys to my truck. He wanted to make sure I wouldn't leave that house. Ebony, I'll call you back. I need to get my money, and a few things, some personal paperwork."

"Wait a minute . . . What! You left Moe's penthouse? That was a waste of my time coming to pick you up and drop you off at his place, only for you to turn right back around and go back to your house. Girl, bye!"

"Ebony, I couldn't stay at Moe's. Once you dropped me off, I stayed for about fifteen minutes, then it dawned on me. This was wrong. Even though Samad is dead ass wrong—me being there with Moe—well . . ." Heat hesitated. "Two wrongs don't make it right. I couldn't stay there. I damn sure didn't want to come back here. I cleared my head in the city by myself, then I thought about it—Samad is not running me out of my own house until I'm ready to leave. Which is right after I get my money I stashed.

"I don't even need to confront Samad about that fucking baby or Mercedes."

"I hear you," Ebony replied with sarcasm.

"I just need to close this chapter of my life with him before I can move forward."

"Well, you better than me. I would not be back at that house after that nigga put his hands on me. You stupid."

"Stupid? Look, Ebony, I'm not stupid! I need to handle this *my* way. I just wanna fuck him up sooo bad, but I'm gon' wait until Aaron comes back, then I'm a let him know Samad put his hands on me, and all the other foul shit he's been doin'! I know I can't beat no man."

"Unique did." Ebony smirked. "Why don't you do what she did to her baby dad-"

Heat cut Ebony off before she could finish her comment.

"You sound crazy Ebony."

"I'm playing Heat. But anyway speaking of him. They will never find his body. Not after we cleaned up, and removed it taking it to the dump piece, by piece day, by day in small plastic bags."

"Ebony, I don't know what you talking about. Whatever it is, you shouldn't be talking reckless like that over the phone anyway." Heat snapped clearing her throat trying to give her a hint. "I know soo many people that got locked up based on things they said over the phone. You know they record calls, I don't trust phones like that. So I don't know what you talking about." Heat repeated herself making it clear.

Ebony caught the hint.

"I hear you." Ebony replied.

"I'll call you later after I charge my phone. It's at one percent."

"You and Unique got issues with these types of niggas! Bye Heat."

Heat ended the call. *Damn, Aaron, where are you?* She held her phone tight in her hand, then grabbed her bag. Heat straightened the wheel, then parked her rental car alongside her truck in the driveway. The thought of Samad taking her keys earlier forced her to shake her head in pity. *Petty ass,* she thought as she got out and walked to the door.

Heat checked to see if the alarm was on. It wasn't. She unlocked the front door and slowly walked in and looked around. Samad was talking loud on the phone in their bedroom about somebody named Born.

She pushed their bedroom door, causing it to fling open, knocking the lamp off the dresser. Samad had lot of one hundred dollar bills in his hand and on the bed.

He turned swiftly when the lamp crashed against the wall before hitting the floor. He stared at Heat, noticing the ton of makeup hiding the bruises on her face.

Heat picked up his Timberland boot and threw it, hitting him on the side of his shoulder. "What the fuck yo!" Samad stopped counting money and stood up. "Let me call you back!" he yelled into the phone. He glared at her, but caught himself from hitting her again.

"That's for my face, and for that bitch Mercedes! How dare you, Samad!" she snapped. "A fucking baby with that bitch!"

"Not right now Heat, there's a lot goin' on!" Samad snapped back at her. He walked to the window and gazed out of it with his back to her. He finished counting the money and stuffed it in his pocket.

"How could you, Samad?" Heat asked with tears in her eyes. "How the fuck could you go to sleep with me every night, knowing you have a child out here somewhere? Feeding me lies every night, day in and day out? Making me look like a fucking fool.

"Here I was defending your black ass! This bitch calls *my* house, *my* phone, tellin' me you the father of her son. Don't try to lie because I saw the boy for myself! The bitch was tellin' me how you had her all up in our home! In *my motherfuckin'* house! In *our motherfuckin' house,* Samad!"

"Shut the fuck up!" Samad stated calmly.

"You shut the fuck up! How disrespectful are you? Then you told her about *my* miscarriage? About me losing our baby! The baby that I lost—worried and stressed out over your black ass! Fighting that bitch. You told this bitch our business, Samad!"

He grinded his teeth, keeping his back to her as he checked his other pockets and pulled out stacks of money.

Heat kept going. "If it was just a fuck, or she just sucked your dick like you lied and told me, then why the fuck are you laying there having pillow talk with that bum bitch? How the fuck do you think that makes me feel? You called me a piece of shit. You the real piece of shit!" Heat pushed him in his back, making him lose balance. Samad stumbled forward, then turned to face her.

"How the fuck you think that makes me feel? You slept with this nigga Moe, you fuckin' 'ho! You talk all this shit like you so innocent." Samad turned from Heat and reached for the envelope of pictures.

"Open it, Miss Holier Than Thou."

Heat snatched the large envelope out of Samad's hand. When she pulled out the pictures, her heart skipped a beat then pounded against her chest double time. "Oh shit!" she whispered.

Samad watched her reaction. "Mmm hmm," he uttered. Then he brushed passed her, bumping her shoulder. He grabbed the rest of the money off the bed, then walked out the room.

Heat remembered being in Atlanta in the bathroom and seeing a red beam like a laser. *Did Moe have these pictures taken? How the hell did Samad get them? Who took these pictures?* She felt her phone vibrating and looked down at the screen. It was Moe. *Oh, hell no! I can't!*

She rejected the call, sending it to voice mail. She noticed her phone battery was very low... She placed the pictures down, she walked to the outlet and connected her phone to the charger on her side of the bed then turned her phone off. She placed her phone on the nightstand. Heat opened a floorboard on the side of her bed. She pulled the black small leather money pouch out of the secret compartment in the floor, and the paperwork she had stashed over the years with her 'mad money,'—paperwork that Eli had asked her to hold before he died.

Heat looked at the small set of keys before stuffing all the contents in her overnight bag. She closed the bag really tight, then placed it on the floor near the nightstand on her side of the bed. *Once I get away from Samad's black ass, I will finally be away from all this street shit. I can finally breath easy. That is when I will go through all of Eli's things he left with me. All I remember is him saying he made a copy of some important paperwork and put it in a lockbox at the bank, and I am the only other person with the originals.* She looked at the lockbox keys again before stuffing Eli's personal items in her overnight bag with her money.

"I wish you were still alive Eli" Heat whispered.

She grabbed a few more things and stuffed it in her other overnight bag. She walked out the bedroom.

Leaving the pictures in the room, she walked down the hall looking for Samad.

"Heat!" Samad yelled. "Come here. I'm in the living room."

She paused briefly before walking into the livingroom. "Yo, I must really love yo ass," Samad said. "Look. I need you to stay out the way because it's —" Heat cut him off.

"Hmph! You don't know what love is. If you love me then why'd you punch me like I was some nigga on the street? Look at my fuckin' face! Is this how you define love, Samad? Yeah, whatever!"

Samad sipped from a glass of juice.

"When is the last time you spoke to my brother? I can't get in touch with him, and I'm getting worried."

"I'm trying to find out what's going on with Aaron too. My men are handlin' that right now. Don't worry about that right now. Street business is none of your concern."

"What the fuck you mean that's none of my concern? Aaron is my brother, and I—"

"Look, my peoples are all on high alert state to state. They all are aware that Aaron is the main concern right now. We'll make sure we find out what's goin' on. Like I said, don't concern yourself with grown man business."

He shot Heat a deadly stare.

"Whatever!" Heat replied.

"But we need to talk about a few other things."

Heat plopped down on the couch and reached for the remote.

Samad stood in front of the TV blocking her view. "On some real shit, I need to find out some things between you and ol' boy."

"Here we go!" she mumbled.

"I just want to ask you one thing. Be honest too. We've been through so much shit together. We better than this," Samad said as he reached for the button on the TV, switching it off.

Heat tossed the remote on the carpet. Samad walked to their bedroom disappearing for a minute. He returned with the envelope of pictures in his hand and filled Heat in about the break-in at their home and the intruder leaving those pictures on their bed.

"I hired AR to take these pictures when you went to Atlanta with your girls."

Heat's face turned pale.

Samad stared at her reaction. He saw her trying not to flinch, but her face gave it away. Heat broke eye contact, dropping her gaze.

"Hmph! Yeah, AR been on my payroll since before I met you. That's my street family for real. Moe don't know that though. The funny thing is, AR never got a chance to personally give me the pictures he took. Somebody stole some of his things along with *these* pictures. Obviously, it's somebody affiliated with Moe's camp, or been around them long enough to get that close to get in AR's things. Think about it. Who else

291

would benefit from me—your man—seeing these pictures of you fucking my enemy?"

Heat listened intently.

"But what I'm more concerned with, is who left these pictures in our house? Did Moe leave these pictures behind? Did you have that nigga in this house when you were fucking him?" Samad asked, trying to control his anger.

"Hell no, nigga. I'm not triflin' like you! Even though both of us are wrong." Heat stared at him with her mouth twisted and her head tilted. She thought about Mercedes saying she fucked Samad in their bed.

"You fucked that bitch in our house. In our fucking bed though? You bastard! You had that bitch in our house, Samad! Oh, excuse me. Your baby mama!"

He rubbed his waves with both hands on his head, let out a loud sigh, and sat down. "Look Heat, on some real shit. You can be mad at me all you want about Mercedes and that baby. We can fight afterwards. You could fuck me up all you want. But just listen to me . . . real talk.

"Who the fuck did you have in this house? Because if you didn't leave these pictures, and ol' boy didn't leave these pictures, somebody must have followed you here! They waited until you left, then made their move or something!"

Heat listened intently.

"Think, Heat! You're smarter than this. Think!" he yelled as he stood back up. "I ran our home security footage back to see who was here, and I saw a Black Rover truck and a Grand Prix parked outside before the tape ran out."

She looked up, letting his words sink in.

After two minutes, she slowly whispered, "Ebony was here. I had Ebony over." She scowled at Samad. "She picked me up after you choked me! Remember that?"

"Ebony?" Samad questioned with a tight face.

"Yeah, Ebony. But she wouldn't do no shit like that. You know it and I know it Where is your phone!"

He looked around the room for her phone, he spotted it plugged up to the charger.

He glanced down at her packed bag one on the bed, and one on the floor near the nightstand on her side.

"Oh, so you leaving me…Again? Hmmmp."

Heat looked at her bag near the nightstand and prayed he didn't open it to see the money she had been saving, along with Eli's personal items she kept safe all of these years. She stared at Samad.

"Call Ebony right now. Get her on the phone. Tell her to meet you in the city somewhere."

Heat stood. She didn't like what he was insinuating. "Ebony's not like that, Samad! You dead wrong for thinking what you're thinking!"

"I didn't say anything, Heat."

"But I know what you're thinking."

"Just call Ebony."

"She would never do that! Not to me! Not to you! Not to us! That's Ebony! Regardless of how she gets down with niggas, that's Ebony!" Heat stated firmly.

"You don't know what she's capable of. I told you to stop thinking you know everything about your little friends. Since you know everything, did you know Ebony's name came up about a murder in Miami?"

Heat paused. *Ebony did say she was in Miami with somebody that day she was arguing on the phone—the day she came to the hospital and brought me my mail.*

"Did you know my people in Miami got connections inside Miami police. They stole information from a homicide file. Cops found Ebony's fingerprints all over the hotel room. Do you know they're putting together a case as we speak, and soon will be coming after Ebony?

"My so-called homie Born went down there with her, and she was supposed to plug him in to this connect. He called himself crossing me. This the second time his name came up under foul circumstances." Samad's mind wandered back to when Eli was dying in the warehouse and Born's name was in Eli's phone. *Burn in hell right alongside Eli, Born. You bitch ass nigga! Good for you!* Heat saw the crazed look in Samad's eyes.

"The connect in Miami is one of Pezo's peoples. They made the switch, but once they got back to the hotel, I guess Ebony crossed Born. Karma is a bitch!"

"How do you know this information is true, Samad?"

"I told you my money's long. You should know that. You spend enough of it." He cut his eyes at Heat.

She stared him then twisted her lips.

"I had my boys follow him from the time he landed in Miami. Ebony was the last person he was seen with. When she left the hotel, two of my guys followed her. Like I said, the information in that file they gave me is not looking good for home girl. The police are putting together a case. I know how them alphabet boys play. They'll be looking for her soon, if they're not already on her ass.

"It's just a matter of time before they figure out she's the one who killed Born. One of the informants that work both sides said Born's phone was found in the hotel, so they are going through his text messages. They most likely will pick her up when she goes to court next week for her father's trial. That's how them people do, slowly build a case against you gathering their evidence, and witnesses, wiretaps,—let you think it's all good— then they run down on you! They gonna surprise her ass and arrest her, mark my words."

"Well, I need to find out if this is true."

"Oh, you think I'm bullshittin'? Call her then. Go right ahead. Ask her who she was with in Miami. You think she's gon' admit this to you?" Samad shook his head. "Did you also know she's working with one of my enemies?"

"No, I didn't know that. Who? Which one of your enemies... Moe?"

Samad stared at her with a blank expression on his face. "Like I said, just call Ebony. But don't say nothin' about this over the phone. Set up a lunch date with her since you know your friend. Watch her body language and movements." He handed her the phone.

She grabbed her phone out of his hands and switched it back on. They both sat waiting for the phone to skip past the HELLO WELCOME screen.

Samad noticed the red light flashing on Heat's phone indicating she had messages.

"Hmph! Probably your little boyfriend calling you to see if you want to go to Atlanta and fuck him again!" Samad snapped as he turned and walked away.

"It probably is!" she snapped back. "He probably was calling to see what size yo' son Samad Jr. wears! So we can pick him up some clothes from the mall," she yelled. *Get the fuck outta here! Black bastard!*

"Touché," he whispered, laughing and shaking his head in dismay as he walked away.

"Samad, you think shit funny?" She looked down at her phone; the battery wasn't fully charged. "I need to use your phone to call her. Mine is not fully charged yet." She reached for Samad's phone.

He stopped walking, then turned to face Heat. He tilted his head and looked at the phone as if he had an epiphany. "A-yo! When you called Ebony to pick you up, what phone did you use?"

She paused for a minute and thought. "The house phone. Why?"

296

"Did you block the number?" he asked.

"No. I dialed her number straight. I couldn't think after your hands were around my neck! Remember—when you choked me?" she reminded him again. "I couldn't think straight!"

"All right, Heat! I get the point! I'm sorry, ma. I love you. And from the bottom of my heart, I really am so sorry for puttin' hands on you."

Heat didn't respond. *I love him but . . . No!* Heat shook her head. "Hmph!"

"Call her from the same phone you called her from earlier." Samad handed her the cordless house phone. He walked to the window and looked outside.

She dialed ten digits. Ebony's phone rang.

"Heat, what's up? You good now? Is Scarface there buggin' out?"

"Huh? Oh yeah, I'm good over here. He ain't buggin' out," Heat said as she cut her eyes at Samad. "Where you at, Ebony? Where'd you go when you dropped me off?"

"I'm at the Trump Hotel in Manhattan. Why?"

"You at the Trump Hotel?" Heat repeated loud enough for Samad to hear. "Can you meet me on Columbus Ave? I need to get something to eat. It's a nice little spot over there with good food. It's between Seventy-second and Seventy-third."

"Okay. Jason is here with me! He's in the shower."

Samad was ear hustlin', hanging on to Heat's every word, trying to figure out what Ebony was doing.

Heat cleared her throat. "Ebony, hold on for a minute. I got something stuck in my throat!"

"Girl, I had something stuck deep in my throat five minutes ago. His dick!" Ebony laughed.

"Oh, for real?" Heat answered, sounding uninterested. "Hold on." She muted the phone and whispered to Samad, "She said she got some guy name Jason with her."

Samad eyebrows furrowed. "Who's Jason?"

Heat shrugged. "He's gonna be the one driving her to meet me. Probably."

Looking up in the sky, Samad squinted, trying to remember the name Jason. The only other *Jason* he knew was his cousin.

"Un-mute the phone and put her on speaker phone."

Heat coughed again and pretended to clear her throat. She put the call on speaker phone. "Okay, I'm back, Ebony." She picked up Samad's glass of juice from the table.

As she sipped from his glass, he half snarled, eyeing her lips touching his drink. His lips twisted in disgust.

Heat rolled her eyes, knowing exactly what he was thinking. She mouthed the words with no audio. *"No, nigga. I ain't nasty like you."* She narrowed her eyes, but turned her attention back to Ebony.

"Girl, I'm sorry about that. I had to get something to drink. I'm dehydrated," she lied. "Now what were you saying?"

"I said my friend Jason is here with me. He's in the shower!"

"So what! Why don't you ask him to bring you? I don't think I ever met him anyway. If I did, I don't remember him."

"You saw him before. He's picked me up a few times, but he was always in a rush. I never formally introduced you two yet."

"I don't remember. Ask him to drive you. I didn't eat anything all day! But you know how guys are, so don't tell him you want him to meet me. Just bring him along. I'll make sure you get back to the Trump. I got you."

Samad mouthed the words, "Tell her to drive."

Heat already knew what that was about. This way, when they pulled up, this Jason dude would have to get out of the car from the passenger's side and walk around to take his place in the driver's seat. Samad could get a good look at him.

"I'm hungry. But he 'bout to leave anyway. He claims he gotta go take care of some business. We got this room for a week. So I'm a come back here. Why don't you come here with me! When he leaves, we could order room service and hang out, girl. He said he's gonna be tied up for a day or two anyway. So tomorrow

299

I'm gonna have this room to myself after I come back from shopping."

"Oh. Okay. I'll come back there with you. Do you need anything?" Heat asked.

"No, I'm good right now! I got what I needed!" Ebony paused. "And for the record, that nigga got your mind fucked up. I just brought yo' ass to the city, then yo' ass went back home and now you ready to come back to the city. That's crazy to me . . ."

Samad stared at Heat. Heat avoided looking at Samad, knowing she loved this man, but she needed to get away from him. She also knew nothing would ever be the same once the truth came out. She had a funny feeling deep down inside.

Heat heard the awkward silence on the phone and covered her intentions. "I just need some fresh air. You know, to clear my mind."

"Yeah, I hear you, Heat. But whatever. All right, I'm almost dressed. As soon as he gets dressed, I will meet you there."

"Okay, Ebony. Lata." She ended the call.

"Who is this Jason nigga?" Samad asked.

"I don't remember ever meeting a guy named Jason," she said.

"Let me see who this Jason dude is. Seems like a real shady cat," Samad said as he tucked his gun in his waist.

CHAPTER 38
Lies

"What's going on now is much bigger than what you think." Samad placed his hand on Heat's hand and caressed it. She moved her hand, then turned her head and looked out the window, wishing she could zap them to the restaurant with a blink of her eyes.

Within an hour, Heat was already settled in the booth sitting all the way in the back facing the big picture window looking outside toward the street. She enjoyed the live band playing in the restaurant while she waited.

The delicious smells coming from the kitchen gave off a mixture of multicultured food being cooked. Heat took in a deep breath savoring the smell.

"Mmmmmm. I smell all kinds of yummy food in here. Italian Food. Soul Food. Spanish Food. Peruvian food. Jamaican Food. But I don't even have an appetite." She looked up at all the flat screens on the walls showing the live band from different angles in the restaurant. "Very nice."

She spotted Ebony walking in the front door and glanced out the window to get a look at this Jason person. *Oh, that's him.* She immediately recognized Jason as the guy who picked Ebony up from the airport when they got back from Atlanta. *That's the same guy that came to pick her up from the hair salon a few times before. I knew I saw him somewhere before. But he looks different for some reason.*

"Ebony! I'm over here," Heat called out.

Ebony made her way to the back. "Heat, it's crowded in here! Why did you pick this spot? They so bougie here!"

"I don't pay them no mind. The food is good. Besides, when I'm hungry, I'm hungry!"

Ebony sat down in the booth with her back facing the street in front of the big window."

"Where's your friend?" Heat asked.

"He said he can't stay. He gotta go meet up with some big time money boss who owes him a lot of bread! You know I am not one to keep a nigga away from gettin' money! He can get it however he get it, just as long as he brings it back to me!" Ebony sipped on the glass of water already on their table.

Heat watched Jason get out of the passenger seat and sit comfortably in the driver's seat. He talked on his phone without noticing Samad parked right behind him in a black truck. Will and Mike were parked right behind Samad in a different vehicle.

Ebony's voice brought Heat back to the conversation. "So what happened with you and Moe? What he talkin' about, girl? You rockin' with him now? Are you 'gon fuck with him heavy now, and stop playin' with that fine ass man or what? What happened when you confronted Scarface about the baby with Mercedes?"

Ebony asked, assuming that's what this get together was really about.

"Girl, all these million and one damn questions. Is this an interview?" Heat laughed.

She finally gave Ebony her full attention once Jason turned the car on and drove off. Samad and his goons tailed him.

"Oh, I still didn't say nothin' to Samad yet," Heat lied. "I'm really stressed out right now! I didn't even stay over at Moe's penthouse when you dropped me off. I left like fifteen minutes later. I saw AR too. He told me to tell you what's up."

Ebony shook her head "You need to be with Moe, and leave Samad in my opinion."

"I need to be by myself.

I just need to talk about something else. I need to get Moe off my mind!"

"I understand." Ebony picked up the menu. "So, you said AR asked about me?"

"Yeah, when you dropped me off. He was coming out the elevator."

"AR fine ass can get it for real! He single too! Paid the fuck up! He got all that money! His music doing good as hell, too, and he's on the Billboard charts! Oh yeah, he could get it! Ain't he handsome?" Ebony laughed.

"Yes, he is handsome, Ebony." Heat looked through the menu, then placed it down.

"I hope he eat pussy too! I cannot fuck with another nigga who do not eat pussy! It's a must you lick this pussy before you fuck me. That's a pre-requisite."

"Girl, you are a trip."

"You saw the news last night, Sean's family put out a mssing report, they showed his picture on the news, asking the public if they have any information to call that 1 800 number." Heat said.

"Yeah, I saw it. I texted Unique just to let her know that this was the first public move his family made just to keep her on point with what's going on up here."

The waitress walked up to the table ready to take their order.

"What can I get you ladies to drink?"

"A watermelon martini!" Ebony ordered. "A little drink won't hurt if I am preg ..." Ebony didn't finish her comment.

"A bottle of Poland Springs Water for me, please," Heat said.

"Are you ladies ready to order, or do you need a minute?"

Ebony wasted no time ordering several things from the menu.

Heat looked at Ebony. "Girl, you pregnant?"

"I'm hungry!" Ebony said. "Are you ordering?" Ebony replied.

"Yes. May I have a slice of strawberry cheesecake?" Heat asked.

"Will that be all?" the server said.

"Yes," they both said in unison.

"Cheesecake? Girl, I thought you were hungry?" Ebony asked.

"I lost my appetite."

"Because of Moe and Samad. I can understand that."

"Did you speak to Unique yet?"

"Yeah, she's good. She sleeps a lot and wakes up screaming. My people say she sits by the pool and don't say shit. The only time she smiles is when she looks at Lil Sean's pictures, or talks about him. Other than that, she gets in the bed and sleeps. She's depressed."

"I'm going to call her when we leave here. With all my drama going on, I forgot to check on her today."

"I called earlier. The calls keep going to voice mail."

Their food arrived at the table. Ebony sipped the martini fast.

"Can you bring me another martini. Pomegranate this time."

"Sure, I'll be right back."

"Do you have money on you?" Heat asked.

"Now you know that nigga always hit me off with cash when he comes in town. He gave me five stacks this time. Why?"

"I was just askin'. I was gon' pay for the food and give you money to catch a cab back to the hotel. I had to take a cab here myself," she lied

"Ebony, let me ask you something. When you came to pick me up, who came with you? Who knew you were coming to my house?"

Ebony paused to gather her thoughts. "Why? Did something happen?"

"Kinda."

"Well, Jason followed me because he didn't believe I was going to your house. As much as I tell him how secretive and strict Samad is about allowing anybody near the honeycomb hideout-slash batcave, he thought I was lying. When I asked him to let me borrow the truck to come get you, he said only if I prove to him that I wasn't lying, and that's where I was going—to your house!"

Stupid. Jason manipulated her into showing him where we live, Heat thought. *And she had the nerve to call me stupid. There's definitely something to this dude.*

"Since I knew I wasn't lying about really picking you up from your house and helping you with your stuff, I knew I needed the truck once you said you packing and you leaving. I agreed that he could follow me. I had nothing to lie to him about.

"I drove the rental, a Grand Prixe. He followed me in his Rover. Then we switched vehicles when I got to your gate."

Heat's mind flashed back to when Ebony was outside her house, and she noticed a car parked on the side of Ebony's truck from the security monitors.

306

"When I dropped you off at Moe's penthouse, he waited for me until I got you situated there too."

"Hmph," Heat said.

"Hmph what?" Ebony asked.

"Nothing. Just thinking out loud. Somebody broke in our house."

"What! When? So hold up, you think I had something to do with this, Heat?"

"No. I know you would never do anything like that."

"So, that's why you really called me here." Ebony folded her arms and placed them on the table.

"Samad wanted me to double check a few things. That's why I asked you who knew you were coming to my house. But after talking to you, I know you didn't intentionally mean no harm."

"Wait, what is that supposed to mean?"

"No, not like that, Ebony. You know how men are. Samad's paranoid ass don't trust nobody knowing where we live. Samad always likes to be careful. Don't mention this to Jason though. I don't want him feelin' like we don't trust him or nothin'." *I really don't trust that nigga. I don't know him.*

"I know how Scarface gets. Paranoid ass don't trust nobody."

"I know exactly what happened. Jason manipulated you by making you think he didn't believe you. Reverse psychology worked on you, girl. Samad does that to me all the time." She laughed it off, downplaying it to make Ebony think everything was all good. "But it's all good. Don't worry 'bout it, Jason's good. I won't mention that part to Samad," she lied.

"Well, thank God. Because I'm tryna have Jason in my life for real. I can't have him on Samad's bad side."

"I just don't remember him, E."

"That's my baby." Ebony blushed and smiled. "I'm in love . . ."

"Girl, I can't keep track of you and your men!" Heat laughed.

"Let me show you a picture of him," Ebony said, reaching in her bag and pulling out her phone. She scrolled through her iPhone searching for pictures.

"Did you go to Miami when I was recuperating in the hospital after losing the baby?"

The expression on Ebony's face told it all. "No . . . W-why you ask that?" Ebony stumbled over her words.

Heat knew Ebony was lying. "Girl, I thought I saw some pictures online of you on the beach in Miami during the time I was in the hospital." Heat flashed a fake smile.

"Nah. Wasn't me." Ebony kept scrolling through her pictures. "I would love to go to Disney World in Orlando though." Ebony glanced at Heat and then focused on the phone. "Maybe when all this drama calms down, Unique, you, and I can take Sean Jr to Walt Disney World."

"So let me see this Jason guy you so in love with."

Ebony showed her several pictures of Jason.

"He looks different in every picture, Ebony."

She handed Heat the phone. "He had braids before. Look."

Heat enlarged the picture to get a better look. She didn't even look at his hair. She zoomed right in on his face.

"He cut 'em all off when he went to his cousin's wedding. These are the pictures we took in the summer when he was driving that black Benz. These are from last winter when we went on that ski trip. These are from Monday. Everytime he come visit me, you know I need pictures of my baby when he leaves, so I can post it all over my social media so them bitches can see me and my baby. Speaking of baby."

Ebony rubbed her stomach. "I missed my period."

Heat wasn't paying attention to anything Ebony said. She was looking at the pictures and thinking about the lie Ebony just told her about not being in Miami.

"I don't have any updated pictures of you. These cute! Can I have some of y'all? They're real cute."

"Yeah, let me text them to your phone right now." Ebony sent the pictures to Heat's phone.

"Excuse me! Excuse me!" Heat called out to the waitress. "Can you please bring the check?"

"Heat, you didn't even eat nothin'."

"I'm stressed out. Got a lot on my mind. I thought by getting out and coming here that I would clear my mind some more," she lied. "I'm about to go home. I'm tired and just overwhelmed by a lot of shit." Heat yawned.

"Why the fuck you goin' back to that nigga after he beat the shit out of you, Heat? Look at your face?" Ebony said, louder than she meant to.

"I can handle myself, Ebony. Damn! Lower your voice." Heat was embarrassed when the couple at the next table looked at her, then began whispering.

She switched the subject.

Heat gathered her things up, ready to leave. She paid for the food and left a tip on the table.

"Girl, I said I got it. Dude in town. You should know me by now. When he's here, I'm good!" She flashed a handful of money.

"Don't worry about it. My treat, Ebony. Save your money.

I know your dad might need you to help pay for his lawyer."

"Yeah, speaking of my dad . . ." Ebony's voice trailed off. "I gotta go to court next week. I hate going to court. They should have a decision soon. We'll finally find out if they gon' find that nigga guilty or not. I can't wait to see the bitch nigga that killed my mother and uncle Breeze, and the other one that snitched on my father. They need to put them niggas under the jail."

"I know how that is, going back and forth to court. I know that feeling. Well, hopefully justice will be served, and your mother and uncle Breeze can rest in peace. I know you're going to be happy when you see your father in court."

"Yeah. Thanks, Heat."

Heat placed the money in the black billfold with the receipt, then left a tip on the table under the glass.

"Let's get out of here." Heat stood up and put her jacket on.

Ebony left a tip on the table alongside Heat's. They headed toward the door. Ebony opened the door, and the wind blew the door back as she stepped outside.

"Dang it's breezy out here."

"Yes it is real chilly out here." Heat closed her jacket.

Ebony continued the conversation.

"I know if they don't find that nigga guilty, it's going to be a motherfuckin' problem. I'm goin' off right in the courtroom. Watch what I tell you."

"Just don't do nothin' stupid, Ebony. They got the evidence on that nigga. Just go and be there for your father. I'll keep you and your family in my prayers."

Heat and Ebony hugged.

"Thanks."

They stood outside and the wind blew hard as they waited by the cab stand. The yellow cab stopped in front of them. Ebony climbed inside.

"I'll call you later."

"Bye Heat."

Heat waved good-bye, feeling different about Ebony. She waited patiently for Ebony's cab to turn the corner out of sight. This Jason guy was either working for an enemy of Samad's or maybe Jason himself was the enemy.

Samad's sister pulled up in a sporty BMW Coupe and stopped curbside in front of Heat. She rolled down the window and smiled.

"What's up, Heat? Get in," Iyana yelled as she turned the music down. "Samad told me to wait for you." Heat hesitated.

"You were right there all that time?"

"Sure was. You ready?"

"Yeah," Heat replied. "I guess."

Iyana popped the locks. Heat got in and sank down in the plush seats. She put her seatbelt on and reclined the seat back.

"What's up, girl? Samad told me to take you to one of his safe houses away from the bullshit."

Heat let out a loud sigh. "Why am I not surprised?" she replied.

"You know that man loves you. And even though you two go through your drama, he'll kill somebody if anything happened to you. He told me what's going on."

Heat felt too overwhelmed to respond. *I'm tired of this street shit. I need to leave everybody alone.*

Iyana turned the music off. "Look, Heat, I know we've had our differences, but you're with my brother, and I know he really loves you. I'm willing to put the drama aside for my brother's sake. How 'bout we let

312

bygones be bygones. Truce?" Iyana held her hand out, waiting for Heat to shake it.

Heat looked Iyana in the eyes, then looked down at her hand. "Truce." The ladies shook on it.

"If you had taken any longer, I was about to curse you out. You're the one that had ya girls jump on me. Don't forget how we got off on the wrong foot in the first place. But we good now." Iyana smiled.

"You're right. I'm sorry about that. It was immature," Heat said.

"That's what's up then. And for the record, I love my nephew. He is a smart, handsome, good little boy. So I see him as much as I can. I'm also still cool with his mama."

"I understand. That's your nephew. Can't speak on the mama though. So it's whatever about her."

"Do you know Samad doesn't see Samad Jr. because of you?"

"Me?" Heat said, knowing she'd have to take this conversation up with Samad later.

"Yeah, you. Samad just do some wack shit. He make sure my nephew has what he needs, but he don't put in no time. He don't love Mercedes either. Never did. Kinda feel sorry for her. He just be using that poor girl. She's finally moving on though."

"I need to do the same thing," Heat said.

Iyana glanced at Heat and turned the music up. Her foot eased down on the accelerator and they cruised toward their destination.

313

"What a day!" Heat mouthed softly and pulled up pictures on her phone and showed Iyana. "See this shady dude right here? This is Jason. My friend Ebony is dating him. I don't care how sexy he is; something isn't right with him."

Iyana stopped at the red light. She took the phone out of Heat's hand and looked at the pictures. She gasped. "Oh *hell* naw! I know this nigga! I *know* this ain't the nigga my brother and them lookin' for. This nigga's the one that killed my friend Cynthia. She got a baby by Pezo. Ain't this some shit! His name is Bono, not Jason."

"But my girl said his name is Jason. She's been seeing him for a while."

"Oh shit! This is about to get real interesting. Ya better warn ya girl about him. She datin' a murderer. And she might be next."

CHAPTER 39
Kidnapped

"I know these niggas schedules like clockwork. He normally comes this way when he's done. They rotate in shifts in this house. Five hours each on duty . . ." At 8:00 p.m. three men sat in a black truck outside a trap house.

"Jackpot! There he go right there, boss!" The driver pointed at Bono.

"Follow him. Don't lose him. But don't get too close either. Keep your distance so he won't spot us," Samad ordered his driver.

The driver stayed two spaces back as he drove and followed Bono to this run-down hotel in Spanish Harlem. Samad pulled his fitted hat all the way down, securing it tightly on his head. He pulled his hoody up over the back of his hat, only revealing the brim. You could barely see his face. A pair of black leather gloves covered his hands. He pulled the nine millimeter out of the hidden compartment in the truck. The driver shut the ignition and lights off.

Will and Mike pulled beside Samad, then parked in the dark area by a tall, thick tree, also shutting the car and lights off. Samad pointed to Bono as he was parking.

"Let him go inside first. I need him alive though. Everybody else—casualties."

"I got you," Will said.

"Not a problem. Let's go," Mike said.

They watched Bono park on the side. He looked over his shoulder, then strolled into the hotel. Will and Mike walked in the hotel five minutes behind Bono. They nodded in Samad's direction. Will pointed to the other door, then pointed to the driver, telling him to block the door.

Samad checked the rearview mirror. He glanced over his left and right shoulder, careful that nobody else was outside. *This is a long way from the Trump Tower, Bono!* He got out and walked to the back of the truck.

An elderly woman struggled with her bags, dragging her things toward the entrance. Samad walked toward the lady. "Let me give you a hand with that," he said, scaring the elderly woman.

Quickly, she turned to see who was offering to help her.

Samad flashed a warm smile, revealing beautiful white teeth.

"Thank you. There's not too many gentlemen left around these parts. I thought chivalry was dead for sure!" she said, revealing a toothless grin and black gums. Samad didn't respond. He was observing his surroundings.

She slid her arm through Samad's arm for support. They walked in the hotel as if they were together.

As soon as they stepped inside, he immediately smelled a strong stench. *Ugh it stinks in here! Smells like pee.*

He walked her to the elevator and gave a friendly wave as the elevator doors closed.

Quietly, Samad moved through the hallway and focused on the clerk sitting behind the desk, who never once turned around. He sat with his back toward Samad.

"Come on, girl. I said I'm sorry. She was just a friend."

Samad saw the guard asleep near the big, red, fire exit door. He glanced at the surveillance camera, noticing wires hanging. *Good. No video tape, no evidence, no witnesses.* He walked up the flight of steps headed to the second floor.

Mike and Will stood outside the room with their guns drawn. A TV show was blasting from inside the room. Mike pointed to the door and kept his gun pointed in that direction. Will raised his Desert Eagle and cocked it, aiming it at the door also.

Samad nodded, giving them the signal.

Like military soldiers, Will and Mike stormed in the room. The guy by the door pointed his gun at Will, who retaliated by shooting him in the head with no hesitation. The impact from the bullet pushed his body back. The other guy pointed his gun at Samad. Mike shot him twice in the head before he could let off a single shot. He was dead before his body hit the floor.

Samad honed in on the girl standing by the window holding a Tech 9. She aimed at Samad and pulled the trigger. Samad smiled when her gun jammed, and he blew her brains out the back of her head. Will and Mike searched for Bono in the other room. He was in the other room stuffing money, and coke in the case, frantically trying to escape when they heard shots fired...

When the room doors flung open, the white guy yelled. "Don't shoot!" He held his hands up, simultaneously dropping the money and the duffel bag on the floor.

"Well, well, well," Mike said, eyeing all the stacks of money spilling out of the bag.

"Jackpot! Looks like we interrupted something huge," Will chimed in.

Bono appeared surprised by the ambush, but was even more surprised to see Samad. He stopped pulling the bricks out of his bag and reached for the gun on the table.

"I wouldn't do that if I were you," Samad said, pointing the gun at Bono.

"So, we meet again, Mr. Samad," Bono said with a smile.

"Get the money, Mike. Get the coke, Will," Samad ordered.

"I have nothing to do with whatever you two got going on. Please don't kill me," the white guy pleaded for his life. "You can have the money. Please let me go." Bono cut his eyes at the white guy.

Will opened the briefcase on the table and smiled when he saw stacks of hundreds neatly lined up.

"Check him," Samad ordered. Mike went through his pockets and pulled out his wallet.

"Please don't kill me. I have a family. I have a wife and three kids."

Mike pointed the gun to the man's forehead, pressing the barrel to his temple.

"Please don't kill me!"

Mike pulled the trigger, emptying the clip in his head.

Samad walked over to Bono and spoke in a calm voice, "We could make this real simple." Just tell me who killed Aaron. And where is Moe's other stash house located?"

Bono looked at Samad with a devilish smirk.

"Okay. So I guess you not gonna tell me who made a special delivery to my house either, huh, Bono?"

Bono laughed. "I don't know what you talking about. Wrong enemy," Bono said.

Samad turned to Mike and Will. "Gather all of his things. Let's go," he said.

Will picked the money up off the floor and stuffed it back inside the duffel bag. Then he picked up all the bricks off the table and stuffed it inside the other briefcase.

Mike picked up Bono's phone and slid it in his own pocket. He switched the television off.

Samad pointed the gun at Bono's head.

"You're not going to kill me. If you were going to kill me, you would have killed me already," Bono said.

Samad hit him across the head with the gun. "Stand up. Get him up. Tie his hands." They grabbed Bono and forced him to stand up.

Mike yanked the phone cord out of the phone. Will grabbed Bono's hands. Mike tied them behind his back, and then put his jacket on over Bono's hands.

Samad opened the door, ready to make an exit. He looked out the door and no one was in the hallway.

Will and Mike placed their guns inside their pockets, aimed at Bono through their jackets. They walked out the side door where the driver was parked and threw Bono in the back of the truck. Will sat on the left side, and Mike sat on the right side. Both men had their guns pressed into Bono's rib cage. Samad sat in the front seat. He turned and smiled at Bono.

"Enjoy the ride, Jason. Oops, I mean, Bono."

CHAPTER 40
Forced Hand

"Pull around back," Samad ordered his driver.

Will and Mike grabbed Bono out of the truck, forcing him to stand up. "Move!" Mike ordered Bono.

Samad stepped out the front seat of the truck with his back turned to Bono, Will, and Mike. Bono looked at Samad's back as if he wanted to rush him and tackle him. Will pointed the gun at his head. "Don't even think about doing nothing stupid."

Mike pushed Bono, causing him to stumble forward and walk.

Trying to get a sense of their location, Bono glanced around. He wasn't familiar with his surroundings. "Where the fuck we at? A dog kennel?" Bono asked when he saw what looked like a breeding ground for dog fights.

As he walked through the dog kennel, he counted out loud. "Thirteen pitbulls. Ten rockweilers. "So business getting that bad for y'all that you grooming pets now? Ha!"

Will hit Bono over the back of the head. "You might want to save your last few breaths to say your prayers," he said.

"Where the fuck is we walking to?" Bono asked, tired from walking through the dog kennel, up two flights of stairs, and then down a long hallway. They finally reached the room.

"Move!" Will stuck the gun in Bono's back, pushing him toward the chair that was waiting for him. He and Mike stood behind Bono while Samad stood behind the chair at the other end of the table.

Once Bono sat in the chair, Will tied his hands behind the back of the chair with a black telephone wire, pulling it tight and cutting off the circulation in his wrists. Then he tied his feet to the chair with rope and duct tape.

Samad pulled a chair out and placed his foot on the chair, resting his elbow on his knee, and scratching his chin. "Do you feel better knowing you're about to die because you made it over my gates and into my home? Or, for killing Aaron?" Bono looked up at Samad and flashed a satanic smile.

"Because I know you did it! Who else is stupid enough to touch one of my men on that side of town but you? A clown. Wannabe thug!" The wad of spit Bono spewed on the floor answered for him.

Samad continued. "But you got heart! I gotta give you props! You know what?" He walked around the table. "I admire your heart. You got balls."

Bono looked him dead in the eyes and smirked.

"You know, for a smart ass nigga like yourself, Bono, you dumb as hell making stupid moves like killing Aaron. Violating my home, not to mention a bunch of other dumb shit. You think Moe can protect you from me?"

Bono's phone rang. Mike pulled it out of his pocket and looked at the screen. It displayed the name Face. One of Samad's old workers he cut off.

"Samad. Face's calling this nigga." Mike showed the name to Samad.

Samad laughed. "I should've known. Now it all makes sense. You, Face, and Bizz. So you thought you was going to make a move on me without any consequences? I'll deal with Face and Bizz bitch asses later. He must have told you about Aaron's little trip out of town. Because nobody knew about that but us."

"You know, for a smart ass nigga like yourself, Samad, you dumb as hell!" He laughed, then flashed that same smirk.

Mike punched him in the face, and Will followed up on the left side and pointed the gun to his temple, ready to end Bono's life.

"Don't kill' em yet!" Samad ordered. "He's more valuable to us alive! Let's see how much your boss really values your life."

Mike punched Bono again, drawing blood.

"Just be patient. A few of my goons going to umm, let's say, pick up your boss. He will be joining us soon. Then you and him can die together."

Samad's phone rang. He looked down. "This is the call I was waiting for. It looks like he'll be joining us sooner. Than later." Samad turned his back on Bono. "Yo," Samad answered.

"We got a problem, boss. You need to come as soon as possible," the voice said on the other end.

"Y'all can't handle that situation?" Samad yelled.

"Now that's some funny shit! Listen to you, yo." Bono chuckled at Samad yelling at his workers. "Seems as though you have a problem on your hands."

Will clicked the gun to safety, then wacked Bono across the head with it. "Bitch ass nigga!" he mumbled. "I can't wait to kill this motherfucker!"

Samad ended his call. "You two come with me." He pointed at Will and Mike.

"Stay with him. Watch him," he ordered Pezo, who had just entered the room. " Samad smiled, knowing this is exactly what Pezo wanted.

"Word on the street is that Cynthia was last seen with Bono," Samad said, gazing at a smiling Pezo.

Samad hit Bono in the head with the gun, splitting his head open. Bono lowered his head. Blood spilled from his head and mouth.

Samad headed toward the door with Mike and Will in tow. Bono looked up at them walking out of the room. He glanced around.

"Keep him company!" Samad laughed, tossing the keys to Pezo. "Do you need help watching him? Or you good?"

Pezo stared at Bono, never taking his eyes off him. "No, I'm good! I wish he would try to make a move!"

Bono stared at Pezo and grinned. "I can still picture Cynthia sucking my dick right before I killed her." He laughed maniacally. "I remember hearing how the cops found Cynthia's naked body in the dumpster where I left her."

Even though the judge dismissed the case on account of a lack of evidence, Pezo heard it word of mouth on the streets there were a few people at the club who'd witnessed Bono leaving with Cynthia.

Pezo stared at Bono when he laughed.

Samad looked at Pezo. "Yo, you good, P?"

"I'm good, Samad. I got this," Pezo repeated, staring Bono in his eyes. "At some point in this evening, or maybe he'll get to see tomorrow, but he's gon' die either way it goes. I can be patient and wait shit out. But, oh yeah, I owe him."

"Good! I'll hit you later to check on things. Come on! We out!"

Samad, Mike, and Will walked out the room leaving Pezo and Bono alone.

CHAPTER 41
Nobody's Safe

Thirty minutes later . . .

Samad looked over at Mike, he glanced down at the Desert Eagle laying on his lap.

Will placed black leather gloves on and adjusted his guns in his waist.

Samad called Pezo to check on him.

"What's good, baby?" Pezo answered.

"Just checking on things. You a'ight? You good, my nigga?" Samad asked, already knowing Pezo would kill Bono, but not until they got the information about Aaron, and a few other killings in his crew.

"I'm good, boss man. No need to check on me. I just sent a text to my daughter saying that her mother Cynthia can rest now. .."

"Come on now P, be easy. Don't do nothing stupid. We should be back shortly."

"I hear you." Pezo replied

"Alright one."

Samad ended his call. "I Need to hurry up and get back there before Pezo ..."

Samad didn't finish his comment. He exhaled loud.

Samad scrolled through his phone and called Iyana's number.

She picked up after the first ring.

"Hey, Samad?"

"Y'all good? Heat good? Where you at?"

"Yeah, we good. She's safe with me. She's sleep. I'm still driving her to the new house.""

"Okay. Hit me when you get there safe. Make sure you take a different route there like I taught you. I'll be up there when I handle this."

"I am taking a different route. I'll see you when you get there." They ended the call.

Samad's phone rang. His eyes knitted when he saw Pezo's name on his display. "What's up, P?"

"Yeah, your little fake killer failed, Samad," Bono said.

laughing. "Get some better killers." Bono said

"Fuck!" Samad cursed then went silent.

He called Iyana back.

"You making me nervous, bro. What's up?" Iyana answered.

"That nigga Bono got away, and he just killed Pezo. Moe is no where to be found. I need to tell Heat that her brother got killed. I didn't want to tell her until you got her away safe. There's a lot going on right now, that's why I need y'all out the way."

"Damn. Pezo and Aaron? . . . Shit!" Iyana hit the steering wheel angrily. "Now Cynthia's baby girl don't have parents. And Aaron was a cool guy. Y'all gotta stop this motherfucker."

"You let me worry about that."

"Okay I need to get off this phone. Heat's wakin' up."

"Okay, don't say nothing about Aaron. I'll break the news when I get up there. Thanks, Iyana. I appreciate your help. I can always count on you."

"You know I got you. Later." Iyana ended the call

Chapter 42
Upstate

"Hey, sleepy head," Heat heard Iyana say as she was waking.

Heat blinked once and looked out the window. "How long was I sleep?"

"For thirty minutes. You must've been tired. You snore too."

"Yeah, I was tired. I been up all day. It's been a crazy day." Heat pushed her seat forward out of the recline position.

"Where you driving to? Where is Samad?"

"Samad told me to drive you to somewhere safe. It's not safe in the city right now. A lot going on," Iyana said. Heat detected sadness in her voice, as if she knew something.

She yawned and stretched and looked around at the highway signs. She had no idea where she was. "Where we going?" she asked.

"Upstate," she responded. "You was knocked out. You was snoring and slobbin'." She laughed.

"Girl, I wasn't slobbin'! Stop playing," she replied. Heat cracked the window to let fresh air in. She pulled down the sun visor and looked at her reflection in the small mirror. She put a dab of makeup on her cheeks.

"You got everything in that bag. Give me some gum or some candy. I know you got gum or candy in there."

"Yup, I sure do." Heat handed Iyana the last piece of gum, then popped a peppermint in her mouth. She fixed her hair, and then closed the sun visor. *Maybe Iyana's not so bad after all. I could get used to her friendlier side.*

"Your phone was ringing crazy back to back."

She looked at her phone. A dozen missed calls and several text messages showed on the display. She dialed her passcode to unlock her phone so she could check her voice mails.

Iyana pulled over at the rest stop to get gas and made a quick run in the store. "You need anything out of the store, Heat?"

"Bring me back some more gum and a bottle of water."

She watched Iyana pay the gas attendant, then walk into the store. Instinctively, she checked her mirrors for her surroundings in front and behind. Iyana walked out the store and stood by the ashtray talking on her phone while smoking a black and mild. When she made eye contact with Heat, she turned her back.

What! Did she think I could read her lips or some shit? Heat watched Iyana's back as she waited for her messages to start. Iyana was acting a little too funny. Something wasn't right.

The first message was from Aaron. "Heat, Neeka driving me to B-More. Tell Samad to hit my phone. I called his phone like five times. It kept going straight to voice mail and it's full. I can't leave a message. Tell him to hit my phone ASAP! I'm tryna get at him on some real shit. I really need to talk to him. Tell him it's very important. I should be back before the sun comes up. Hold on, lil sis!"

"Yooo! What up, I'm good. What's up with you, fam'? Where you get that Rover from? That was you earlier that drove by?" The phone went silent. Heat continued listening, waiting for the rest of Aaron's message. She couldn't hear the other person answering Aaron back.

"What the fuck is Ebony doing riding with ths nigga?"

Aaron suddenly asked.

Heat rested her head on the seat and realized she'd picked up Aaron's conversation....

Damn, Aaron, why are you not calling me back? Where are you? I need to talk to you. I need some brotherly advice. Heat exhaled.

"Yo Heat, let me get off this jack! Look in my old room by the speakers. Hold that for me. Tell Mommy to put me a plate up! I'll be back at her house before the sun rise. I haven't seen Mommy since she got back in town. Yo, you need to talk to your friend Ebony. Tell her to watch the company she keeps. I love you, Heat." She didn't save the message or delete it. A red flag went off in her head, she had a funny feeling in her gut, it had been a few days since Aaron went out of town. She skipped to the next message.

"What's up, Heat? This Unique. I been trying to get in touch with you for the longest. It keeps going to the voice mail! I'm on my way back up there. I checked my bank account this morning. My shit was zero! I called Gwen and the bitch's nowhere to be found with my damn son! I haven't spoken to my son since I called him from the hotel in Atlanta. I'll be up there tomorrow night. So I'll hit you when I get settled.

"All I got is the money I left with! Do me a favor. Send me some money by Western Union. I'll give it back to you when I get there. I got some stashed at my mom's house. You know what name I'm using. Send it under the name and address on my New York ID, same zipcode. I don't believe this shit is happening!" Heat didn't save the message or delete it. She skipped to the next message.

"This Mercedes. Heat, when you get this message tell Samad his son needs to speak to his father, bitch!" She did the same with that message as she had with the others.

Skip.

Beep!

"Heather, this is your mother. When you get this message give me a call at home. It's urgent!"

Heat skipped to the next message.

Beep!

"What's good, mamí? This Moe. Where you at? Why you keep running from me? Answer your phone. I need to know if you okay. What's really going on? I'm tryna see you for real, mami! I'm here for you, but you keep bobbin' and weavin'—runnin' from me. Holla at ya boy!"

Iyana walked over to the car interrupting Heat. "Here you go." She handed her the gum and water. Heat stopped checking her messages and placed her phone on the seat.

"By the way, that was Samad on the phone. He'll be meeting us up here soon."

"Up here where, Iyana?" Heat asked, realizing she was out of her element and didn't know where she was. If Iyana wasn't Samad's sister, she would have never been with her this long without knowing her next move or her whereabouts.

"Well, you know my brother. He just told me to make sure I keep you safe, and he gave me instructions on where to drive you. He's meeting us there. He said he will be here in thirty minutes. Do you need anything else while we're out, before we go to the house? We still got a little drive ahead of us. Do you need to use the bathroom?"

Heat pointed to Applebees. "Pull up to that Applebees so I can use the ladies room."

Iyana pulled inside an empty parking space.

"I'll be right back." Heat walked into the restaurant and asked for the ladies room. *Damn, I left my phone in the car. I need to call my brother again. He's been on my mind all day today for some reason.* Heat used the ladies room quickly. She looked in her bag and slid something up her sleeve, then headed back outside. Once she reached the car, she saw Iyana on the phone again. She hung up when Heat walked to her.

Hmmmm. She keeps acting strange.

"You ready? You good now, so we can get back on the road?"

"Yeah, I had to freshen up real quick. I'm good now. Thank you." *Why is she acting secretive with her phone calls?* Heat felt nervous. This funny feeling rumbled in her stomach. She'd never felt this way before whenever she was around one of Samad's trusted people. *Where is Samad? Why didn't he tell me where I was going?*

Iyana's phone rang again. She looked at it. "This is Samad."

She felt calmer when Iyana handed her the phone. *Even though I'm still mad at his black ass about that damn baby, I need to find out where the hell he got his sister driving me.*

"What's up?" Heat asked with no emotion in her voice.

"Heat. You okay?" he asked.

"No, I'm not. Because I don't know where your sister's driving me to."

"I'll talk to you a little later to let you know what's going on. You hungry?"

"No, I don't have an appetite." She forced herself to have a conversation with Samad just to pass the time.

"I'm not far away. I will see y'all in a little while."

"Mmm hmm." She breathed a sigh of relief.

Iyana noticed Heat looked more relaxed after speaking to Samad, but she could still sense some tension in the air between them.

An hour later, Iyana pulled up to a dirt road leading to a private community. She parked the car in back, a few feet away from the pool. Heat stepped out looking around. The houses were spaced so far apart, no neighbors in sight. *If something ever happened to me up here, no one would hear my screams for miles.* Her mind started playing tricks on her. Paranoia kicked in.

She followed Iyana's lead up the steps, gripping whatever she had up her sleeve. Iyana looked under a fake plant, pulling out a set of keys. She opened the door, allowing Heat to step inside the beautiful home. It was gorgeous. She stepped in the hallway, then walked to the kitchen. Heat turned to watch Iyana as she stepped inside.

Iyana's phone rang. "This Samad again. He's right at the gas station we just left. He told me to ask you are you sure you don't need anything?"

Heat shook her head no.

"Wait, yeah tell him to bring me some pads or tampons. I'm crampin'."

Iyana repeated Heat's request. "I'm about to leave. I'll call you later. My flight leaves in two hours, so I will be out of your hair and far away from here for a while. I'll hit you as soon as I get there." Iyana walked to Heat to give her a hug. "Take care, Heat."

"You too, Iyana." Heat was concealing whatever was up her sleeve but gave Iyana a fake half hug. She kept her right arm down, ready to attack if she tried anything.

Iyana walked to the front door. "Lock this door behind me," she said as if she were her mother.

"Okay, I will." Heat locked the door, then watched her out the window as she drove off. In unfamiliar territory, Heat stood frozen in the kitchen. She reached for her phone, then realized she left it in Iyana's car. Sliding the small gun out of her sleeve, she put it in her bag. She picked up her other phones, but they were all dead. After placing her bag on the hook on the wall, she scanned the room trying to locate a phone. Being in this place made her uncomfortable. Heat walked through the house looking around at everything, including pictures of herself and Samad. *These are pictures we took on several vacation spots. What are they doing here?*

She looked in the closets and saw some of Samad's clothes. She saw her own Gucci and Louis Vuitton luggage in the corner. *Why are our personal things here?*

Outside, a car engine hummed as it approached the house. She walked to the window and saw Samad and his driver pulling up. Samad stepped out of the car. The driver made a U-turn, leaving him alone. Samad made a phone call coming inside the house.

Heat stood in the hallway in plain sight and patiently waited for him to walk through the door.

"What the fuck is going on, Samad!" she asked as soon as he entered the house. "You damn-near have me dragged away by your sister, driving me to this secluded place! Iyana won't give me no straight answers! She was acting funny as hell, all secretive and shit! I need to call my mother. Her message sounded urgent! I have this funny feeling in my stomach! I left my phone in Iyana's car! There's no phone as far as I can see in this—this . . . Where the fuck am I, Samad? Why are some of my personal things here?"

Samad walked over to Heat and gently grabbed her hand and let out a loud sigh. He led her to the suede couch in the living room to make her comfortable. Heat was puzzled. Samad walked to the wet bar, quietly pulling out a bottle of Hennessy. Heat lowered her brows. He poured a drink and gulped it down with one sip and repeated the action three times more. She had not seen him drink this much since back in the day.

He sat down on the couch next to her. Her heartbeat sped up. She knew whatever was going on was serious.

He cleared his throat. "Ahem. . . . I uh . . ." He swallowed before he spoke again. "Your brother Aaron was murdered."

Heat furrowed her brows and tilted her head in his direction. "Come again. What you say, Samad?" Heat wanted to make sure she heard him right. "What?" she asked.

Again Samad cleared his throat. "Aaron was killed. Your brother is dead." He lowered his gaze to the floor. "He was set up when he drove to Baltimore."

The words escaped his mouth, fell into her eardrums, touching her heart and piercing it! Her heart dropped into oblivion. Heat flashed back to the last moment she saw her brother alive when he popped up at the house to see her and Samad.

"What!" Heat screamed. "No. No." She shook her head. She slapped Samad in his face making his head turn. Samad remained in that position looking away from her. "You lying! I just saw my brother the other day." Heat's voice was shaky. "I just listened to his voice mail on my phone. There's been a mistake."

"Heat, your brother is dead. Aaron is dead. It was confirmed."

Heat jumped up clutching her chest. She couldn't breathe and began hyperventilating. "Noooo!"

"How do you know this is true? I don't believe you. Who told you this If it's true, who did this to my brother Who killed my brother?"

"A few of my connections confirmed it was Aaron that was killed in B'more. They are in the process of finding out who was behind this."

Samad held her tight as she let out a loud cry. She pounded on his chest, swinging and flailing her arms wildly.

"Let me go, Samad!" she screamed and yelled, trying to fight her way out of his tight grip. He embraced her, and she fought with all her might to get out of his arms, but she could not overpower Samad's tight grip. "Aaron!" she yelled, crying so hard it echoed in her chest. Every time she coughed and cried, a hollow echo escaped her mouth.

"I need you to stay up here out the way. You'll be safe here. I know who did it. Ebony's boy who dropped her off at our house was behind it. I know it was Bono. Moe's not stupid enough!"

Heat cried softly, but listened to Samad. Whenever he told her about his business, it was always serious.

"How do you know Ebony's friend killed Aaron? Does Jason work for Moe?"

Samad took a deep breath and exhaled loudly. "First of all, his name is Bernardo, not Jason. I don't know where he came up with the name Jason. Some alias he made up just for Ebony. For all I know, Ebony could have set the whole thing up. She was the one that brought him to our house. You can trust that bitch all you want!"

Aaron spoke to somebody named Bono during his phone call to me.

Samad looked over at the bar. "I need another drink." He walked behind the bar and poured himself another drink.

"I'm not in that frame of mind to discuss the loyalty of my friends. You said my brother was murdered. I want to get to the bottom of it."

"Bono is the one behind all the killings going down lately. The business Aaron handles for me out of town, with those out of town connects cut into a lot of people's profits. The product we have is pure uncut, better quality for cheaper prices.

"That's the reason some of their connects stopped dealing with everybody else and came to me. We locked down key markets in this drug game, so of course niggas is feeling some type of way.

"So I knew they would be trying to take my men out, so they can own my spots. I knew they would be coming after my people. I just didn't know what route they were gonna take, or who they would go after first." Samad punched his fist in his other hand.

"I called your mother, and I told her you were with me safe and she don't need to worry about you. That's why I told Iyana to drive you straight up here, to get you away from everything and everybody in the city."

"Oh my God! My mother . . . Aaron . . ." Heat cried. It was all making sense now. *That's why Iyana was acting secretive on the drive up here. That explains the sadness I heard in my mother's voice when she left a message. Oh my God!* Tears welled up in Heat's eyes.

"Aaron . . . I had enough of this crazy life. I want out."

Samad gulped his drink in one sip, then slammed the glass down on the bar. It shattered into tiny, sharp jagged pieces. Blood dripped from Samad's fingers.

THE END
To Be Continued . . .

WAHIDA CLARK PRESENTS BEST SELLERS

DAVID WEAVER PRESENTS

THUGGZ VALENTINE

A NOVEL BY

Wahida Clark

NEW YORK TIMES BEST SELLING AUTHOR

WAHIDA CLARK PRESENTS

TEA

MECCA GLOBAL

NWNDI PUBLICATIONS

KNOWLEDGE OF THE GODS

A.M. MUHAMMAD

WAHIDA CLARK PRESENTS

VINDICATED

A NOVEL BY

TASHA MACKLIN

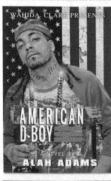

WAHIDA CLARK PRESENTS

AMERICAN D-BOY

A NOVEL BY

ALAH ADAMS

WAHIDA CLARK PRESENTS

SWIPE

A NOVEL BY

KAYENNE

WAHIDA CLARK PRESENTS

Butterfly

WAHIDA CLARK PRESENTS

GAME OF GWOP

A NOVEL BY

TRAE MACKLIN

WAHIDA CLARK PRESENTS

THE ULTIMATE SACRIFICE IV

A NOVEL BY

ANTHONY FIELDS

WAHIDA CLARK PRESENTS

DEEPLY ROOTED

A Novel by

ICE MIKE

WAHIDA CLARK PRESENTS

VENOM IN MY VEINZ

A NOVEL BY

RUMONT TEKAY

WAHIDA CLARK PRESENTS

ENEMY BLOODLINE

A NOVEL BY

UMAR QUADEE

WWW.WCLARKPUBLISHING.COM

WAHIDA CLARK PRESENTS PUBLISHING
60 EVERGREEN PLACE SUITE 904 EAST ORANGE NJ 0701

CPSIA information can be obtained
at www.ICGtesting.com
Printed in the USA
LVHW04s1428250918
591324LV00010B/522/P